BEAUTY REBORN

A Summer Solstice Chronicle

Book 3 of the Solstice Chronicles

ASHLEY BEACH

Copyright © 2022 Ashley Beach.

All rights reserved. No part of this book may be used or reproduced by any means, graphic, electronic, or mechanical, including photocopying, recording, taping or by any information storage retrieval system without the written permission of the author except in the case of brief quotations embodied in critical articles and reviews.

This is a work of fiction. All of the characters, names, incidents, organizations, and dialogue in this novel are either the products of the author's imagination or are used fictitiously.

LifeRich Publishing is a registered trademark of
The Reader's Digest Association, Inc.

LifeRich Publishing books may be ordered through booksellers or by contacting:

LifeRich Publishing
1663 Liberty Drive
Bloomington, IN 47403
www.liferichpublishing.com
844-686-9607

Because of the dynamic nature of the Internet, any web addresses or links contained in this book may have changed since publication and may no longer be valid. The views expressed in this work are solely those of the author and do not necessarily reflect the views of the publisher, and the publisher hereby disclaims any responsibility for them.

Any people depicted in stock imagery provided by Getty Images are models, and such images are being used for illustrative purposes only. Certain stock imagery © Getty Images.

ISBN: 978-1-4897-4538-5 (sc)
ISBN: 978-1-4897-4536-1 (hc)
ISBN: 978-1-4897-4537-8 (e)

Library of Congress Control Number: 2022922240

Print information available on the last page.

LifeRich Publishing rev. date: 11/30/2022

Phyllis
May you find the beauty of rebirth in the purifying fire of God's love
Ashley Beach

DEDICATION

To my dear friend Rachel, who has been an immense encouragement in this writing journey, and to her sweet girls, whose delight and excitement in these stories makes it a pure joy to write. And to all my dear "little" readers who have shown so much enthusiasm for these fairy tales, thank you. The third book is *finally* here.

CONTENTS

Chapter 1 1
Chapter 2 7
Chapter 3 13
Chapter 4 17
Chapter 5 24
Chapter 6 31
Chapter 7 40
Chapter 8 51
Chapter 9 56
Chapter 10 63
Chapter 11 73
Chapter 12 80
Chapter 13 86
Chapter 14 94
Chapter 15 102
Chapter 16 111
Chapter 17 119
Chapter 18 130
Chapter 19 138
Chapter 20 145
Chapter 21 149
Chapter 22 158
Chapter 23 166
Chapter 24 170

Chapter 25 183
Chapter 26 188
Chapter 27 194
Chapter 28 201
Chapter 29 205
Chapter 30 212
Chapter 31 217
Chapter 32 222
Chapter 33 227
Chapter 34 237
Chapter 35 249
Chapter 36 258

"Praise be the God and Father of our Lord Jesus Christ! In his great mercy he has given us new birth into a living hope through the resurrection of Jesus Christ from the dead." 1 Peter 1:3 NIV

"He will give a crown of beauty for ashes, a joyous blessing instead of mourning, festive praise instead of despair." Isaiah 61:3 NLT

Chapter 1

"King Godric, the Sun King, and Queen
Osanna, Lady of the Rose,
cordially invite you to witness the union of their son,
Prince Gabriel, the Golden Prince
to Queen Erianna, the newly crowned Snow Queen
To take place the eve following the Summer solstice
At the four corners where our realms are joined as one."

King Azar crumpled the gilded invitation and threw it across the room.

"Curse that cousin of mine." He gestured for one of the page boys that stood waiting off to the side of the throne. The page boy stepped forward. "Bring Lord Amir to the throne room. Tell him I have an urgent matter to discuss with him."

The page boy bowed and left the room.

The king stood and stepped down from the platform where his black marble throne sat. He walked over to the windows overlooking the eastern valley that lay below his palace.

Lord Amir entered a few moments later. "Your Majesty. You sent for me?" he asked as he bowed and waited to be welcomed into the throne room.

King Azar turned slightly. "Yes, Lord Amir. I have just received an invitation from my cousin in the Spring realm for his son's wedding to the Snow Queen."

"I see," Lord Amir responded, unsure of how the king was expecting him to react to this news.

"It is to be held the eve after the Summer solstice," King Azar said with a wearisome sigh. He stared out the windows with his hands clasped behind his back and shook his head. "Planning his son's wedding for the eve following the Summer solstice. Is it not enough that he received the sun magic that was meant for this land? Does he have to take away from our sole Summer celebration as well?" The king gave a dejected sigh and continued to stare languidly out the windows. "Not to mention that a union of this kind between the Winter and Spring realms leaves our realm in a precarious situation."

Comprehension dawned in Amir's face as to why the king was upset by the news from his cousin. "I understand why you would feel slighted by this announcement, Your Majesty. Your cousin has always tried to take what belonged to you and usurp your authority over this realm. It is most inconsiderate of him to plan such an event so close to our own solstice celebration. And I agree. This union will leave our realm wide open for attack if they ever decide they need to take over more than just your magic and our solstice. I suggest we make contact with the Fall realm and create an alliance of our own," Amir said as he stood close behind the king.

"The Fallen realm?" King Azar thought for a few moments. "Their realm is still reeling from the brutal takeover by that rebel soldier who thinks of himself as king. He is not royal. The council will never allow his kingship to be official, even if he married the queen of the king he murdered to get there. I'm not so sure an alliance with them would be in our best interest. It could bring us more trouble than we care to deal with."

"I understand your hesitations, Your Majesty. It is true that the self-declared ruler of that land seems a bit abrasive in his approach to ruling, but his rebel forces were able to overthrow the throne, which means they have power and strength in soldiers that may come in handy if the realms were ever to go to war. I believe it would be a profitable alliance if we can make it work," Lord Amir replied in a sickeningly soothing voice, trying to win the king over to his way of thinking.

"And how do you propose we create this alliance?" the king asked, still not convinced of the idea but unsure of what else could be done to stand up to his cousin and make sure the Summer realm remained under his rule.

"Why, the same way the Spring and Winter realms are aligning themselves. Through marriage, Your Majesty."

The king looked askance at Amir out of the corner of his eye and quirked up his eyebrow. "Marriage? You can't be serious, Lord Amir. Who is to marry whom?"

"I believe the rebel ruler has a son born by the late queen of the Fall realm. He should be about the same age as Princess Amber. If we strike up an alliance of that kind, that will create a bond between our realms that will ensure their alliance in war. And, if the rebel ruler's own son is joined to our realm by marriage, it may keep him in check and prevent him from striking out against us in future. Or taking matters into his own hands as he did with the Fallen realm," Amir responded.

"No," King Azar said as he turned and walked back to his throne. He stepped up onto the platform and sank into his throne.

Amir followed him over to the throne. "Your Majesty. Please consider it. It would be our best option. The rebel ruler may think it unnecessary to join with us on his own because of his prideful independence. But, if the realms were joined by marriage, it would secure that alliance should we ever need it."

King Azar sighed and rested his head on his hand that was propped up on the arm of his throne. "I hear what you are saying, Lord Amir, and I appreciate your words of wisdom. I'm just not sure the rebel ruler would be inclined to join his son to a princess in Amber's state."

Amir thought for a moment before responding. "What if the rebel ruler didn't know about Princess Amber's malady?" he asked as he looked at the king with a malicious glint in his eyes.

King Azar moved his hand away from his face and looked at his vizier. "And how do you propose to pull that off, Lord Amir?"

Amir smiled. "We use a stand-in for Princess Amber. We can use that girl who sits with her and reads to her and such."

The king raised an eyebrow as he listened to Amir's suggestion. "Her companion? Have you lost your mind? We can't wed a companion to a prince."

"She wouldn't actually wed the prince from the Fall realm. We would just use her in place of Princess Amber for the time-being until they agree to the marriage. We can cover her face so the prince won't know the difference, and when the time comes for the wedding, have Princess Amber wed him. The union will be binding, and he won't be able to back out once they are wed."

King Azar stroked his salt and pepper beard as he thought about it. "I'm not sure, Amir. Do you think a scheme like that would actually work?"

"I believe it will, Your Majesty. We need this alliance with the Fall realm."

King Azar sighed. "I suppose we have no other choice. Send a message to the Fall realm and invite their prince to visit our kingdom, and we can introduce him to Amber– or her companion, rather– and see what happens from there."

Amir smiled. "Of course, Your Majesty. I will send word to the Fall realm right away." He bowed and exited the throne room.

King Azar sighed again and rubbed his wrinkled forehead. "I hope they don't find out about Amber too soon," he said to himself.

"What are the plans, Father?" Sir Erick asked Lord Ragnar.

"I have received information that indicates the other half of the gem is indeed in the Summer realm's palace. We need to figure out a way to get you into the Summer palace and find the other half of the gem. With the two halves of the gems united, our kingdom will have endless power and will never Fall to anyone else," Lord Ragnar replied as they bent over the maps of the Summer realm in his study.

"Lord Ragnar," a messenger boy said as he bowed in the doorway.

"Yes," Lord Ragnar said as he looked up at the boy.

"I have a message from the Summer realm," the boy said as he stepped into the room and held out a missive to Lord Ragnar. Lord Ragnar took it and broke the seal. He unfolded the parchment and began to read. A sinister smile filled his angular face.

"Good news?" Erick asked.

"Fortuitous," Lord Ragnar replied. Pulling out a piece of parchment from his desk he bent and scrawled a response on it. He blotted the page to make sure the ink was dry before he folded it. He then grabbed his wax spoon with some residual wax still in it and held it over the candle. Once the wax had formed a coin size puddle on the outside of the page, he set the wax spoon aside and took his ring off to seal it with a crest he had designed for himself when he had taken over the Fall realm. He handed the page to the boy.

"Here is my response to the king of the Summer realm."

The boy bowed and left the room.

Erick stood straight with his muscular arms folded over his chest. "What was the news?" he asked.

"The king of the Summer realm has asked to meet to form an alliance," Lord Ragnar replied.

Erick smiled. "That is fortuitous."

"My Lord," a soldier ran into the study.

"What is it?" Lord Ragnar replied harshly.

"Someone broke into the treasury and stole the Phoenix gem."

"Then why are you standing here instead of chasing after the insolent thief?" Lord Ragnar demanded. He looked at Erick and nodded his head. "Go. Catch that thief and bring them back. I want them to know the pain they have brought on themselves for breaking into our kingdom and thinking they could get away with such a precious treasure."

Chapter 2

A few weeks after they had received the invitation from King Azar, Prince Aiden rode beside his brother and a small entourage of soldiers that were conveying them to the Summer realm.

"It is certainly warmer the closer we get to the Summer realm. The trees are greener too. They actually have leaves on them," Aiden said, trying to break the silent tension that had been the constant companion of their trip.

Erick stared straight ahead without acknowledging his brother's remark.

"We have been traveling for three days now, and you have barely said a word to me. You won't tell me why we are going to Ashteria or anything about this trip. Could you be human for once in your life and actually communicate with me?" Aiden asked.

Erick stopped his horse short and moved it in front of Aiden's, forcing Aiden to stop. Erick nodded for the soldiers surrounding them to continue ahead.

"I haven't told you anything because it is not your concern. We are going to Ashteria to arrange an alliance between our kingdoms that will protect and strengthen our realms. If Father had wanted you to know, he would have told you. It is my job to get you there.

Isn't it enough to just accept a command and do as you're told?" Erick asked with a cold hard stare.

"Look, if you are still upset about not catching the thief that stole the Phoenix gem, you don't need to take that out on me," Aiden replied defensively. "I was simply asking why we were journeying to the Summer realm. Not trying to start a fight."

Erick raised up slightly in his saddle. He was big anyway for a man, tall and broad through the shoulders with dark short hair and a scar that ran down his face beside his right eye and down his cheek, giving him a frightening appearance. He was also gruff and often came across as uncaring, which only added his already intimidating size. He was the epitome of their father in flesh and blood, and Aiden was the exact opposite. Aiden had always been smaller than Erick and their father always seemed to view him as the weaker son. He had also been drawn to things like music and art, which had never helped improve his father's view of him.

Erick had been born to their father before their father took over as ruler of the Fall realm, so he had no legal right to the throne. Aiden had been born to the Fall queen, which gave him royal blood and made him the heir to the throne. Erick had often been Aiden's protector growing up, but Aiden always wondered if not being heir to the throne bothered Erick. He had certainly become more distanced from Aiden and stand-offish to him over the years and now treated Aiden more and more like an enemy than a brother. Aiden rarely did anything to rouse Erick's anger because he knew Erick could crush him like wheat beneath a millstone if he ever became angry enough, but he had been growing tired of the cold silence and couldn't stand it anymore. When Erick raised up in his saddle, Aiden knew he had stoked Erick's ire. He turned his horse's head slightly and backed up.

Erick knew he had struck the right chord of intimidation into his little brother when Aiden pulled his horse away. He smirked. "Just do what you are told, and we will both be fine," Erick said in a haughty manner.

Aiden glared at his brother. "Fine," he said shortly as he moved his horse around Erick's and carried on.

Aiden rode the rest of the way in silence behind Erick. They entered the iron gate of the Summer palace around dusk and were greeted by a servant boy who asked who they were. When Erick told him, he ran into the gray stone palace to fetch someone to welcome them. Aiden sat with his shoulders slumped on his horse, exhausted from the long three day journey—and still put out by his brother's patronizing remarks earlier. His eyes roved across a section of outer wall that appeared to be set up as stalls for horses with small sections walled off to separate the horses and piles of hay everywhere. A clanking sound landed on his ear, causing him to turn and see the blacksmith shop not too far from the horse stalls, the smithy hard at work hammering out a fiery orange horse shoe. He turned the other way and saw a stone well near the gate and a few smaller stone structures with colorful cloths draped between them that bled into the vast wall that surrounded the palace. Must be some kind of marketplace, he thought.

He continued to take in the graystone palace that stood out like a fortress against the dimming light of the setting sun. A bright red flash caught his eye and drew his attention to a small tower above them. His breath caught in his throat as he saw a beautiful young woman standing in the window wearing a crimson dress with bell sleeves that was trimmed with gold embroidery. The woman had red hair that burned like flames in the fading sunlight. Aiden stared at her, taken in by her fiery beauty as strands of her hair blew in the wind and whipped around her head like dancing fire. A soft, sweet sound reached his ears as he watched her. Curious, Aiden leaned forward in his saddle to see if he could figure out what the sound was above the din of the courtyard noises. He smiled when he realized what it was. His smile widened as he looked back up at the woman. She was humming, and from what he could hear of it, she had a beautiful voice.

A sudden jolt to his arm stirred him from his daydream.

"Wake up, baby brother. We don't want you all blurry-eyed when we meet the king."

Aiden was about to respond to his brother when the servant boy came back with someone who appeared to be the king's vizier. The man was dressed in a red robe covered in black embroidery. He bowed. "Welcome to our humble kingdom. I am Lord Amir, advisor to the king and overseer of the palace. Please, follow me, and I will get you settled in before you meet the king."

Erick dismounted, followed by the other soldiers who had traveled with them. Aiden glanced up at the tower window to see if he could catch a glimpse of the young maiden again before he dismounted. No one was at the window. Aiden let out a small sigh of disappointment. Erick nudged his leg, prompting him to get off his horse. Aiden dismounted and let one of the servant boys take the reins. Erick grabbed his shoulder before they walked into the palace.

"You better keep your head out of the clouds and focus on why we're here. If either of us mess this up, Father will have our heads."

Aiden chafed under Erick's tight grip. "How can I be focused on why we're here if I don't know why we're here," Aiden replied through clenched teeth.

Erick squeezed Aiden's shoulder tighter, causing him to grimace. "You'll find out soon enough why we're here. Just do as you're told, little brother, and everything will be fine."

The vizier turned back to see if they were coming. Erick gave Aiden's shoulder another warning squeeze and pushed him forward to follow the vizier into the palace.

Erick stopped by Aiden's room before they went to dinner. "Come on. We have been asked to meet the king in the throne room."

"I don't need an escort everywhere I go. I could have found the throne room on my own," Aiden balked at the idea of Erick always feeling like he had to herd him like a lost sheep or something.

"From what I remember, you were always getting lost in our own palace because your head was always who knows where. It became easier to just keep eyes on you instead of always having to seek you out," Erick said in a wry tone. "Now, come on. We don't want to keep the king waiting."

Aiden glared at his brother. He finished buttoning the brown and gold doublet with golden leaves embroidered into it that his father had insisted on him bringing to make a good impression on the court of the Summer realm and followed his brother out of the room.

As they walked down the hall, Aiden heard a soft, sweet sound drift through the halls. He stopped to listen.

Erick stopped and turned an agitated glare on his brother. "See, this is exactly what I was talking about. Had I gone on without you, I would have been standing awkwardly by myself in the throne room for who knows how long waiting for you to finally make your appearance."

Aiden took a few steps and looked around, trying to see where the music might be coming from. "Don't you hear that?" he asked as he took a few steps back towards his room.

Erick stared at him blankly. "Hear what?"

Aiden stopped and looked at him with surprise. "The music," he replied.

Erick's stare hardened. "What music?" he asked, growing increasingly annoyed at always having to be the one to keep his brother in check.

Aiden studied Erick for a moment to see if he was simply ignoring the music so they could get going, or if Erick truly didn't hear it. After a few moments, the music stopped. "Well, the music stopped anyway so I guess we can go."

Erick looked like a stone statue the way he glowered at Aiden. "You had better stop all this foolishness, and soon. There is far too much riding on this meeting to have it thrown to the wind by a daydreamer." Erick turned and stalked down the dim stone hallway.

Aiden glared at his brother's back as Erick walked away from him. His ears perked up when he heard a small snidbit of the sweet melody again. He smiled. "This trip could be worth it after all," he said to himself as he let the melody soothe his irritated spirit before following his brother to the throne room.

CHAPTER 3

"His Royal Highness, Prince Aiden of the Kingdom of Havilah, and the champion warrior of the Fall Realm, Sir Erick the Fearless," a servant announced as they entered the throne room.

Erick stepped aside to allow Aiden to enter the room first. They stepped to the thrones and bowed.

King Azar acknowledged them and threw out his arms in a welcoming gesture. "Welcome to Ashteria. I hope your journey was not too arduous between our realms."

Erick straightened and acknowledged the king. "Our journey was most enjoyable, Your Majesty. We appreciate your generosity in extending such an invitation to meet with you here in your beautiful realm."

Aiden eyed his brother. He never used such refined and elegant language at home. In fact, Aiden had no idea his roughrider brother could be so diplomatic. Erick cleared his throat quietly and nudged Aiden, prompting him to follow suit.

"Ah, yes. Thank you, Your Majesty, for allowing us the opportunity to meet with you. It is an honor and a privilege to join our realms in such a noble endeavor," Aiden said as he took a step forward and bowed his head towards the king.

The king smiled. "Join indeed," he replied with a surreptitious glint in his voice.

King Azar gestured to the servant who had announced the visitors. The servant bowed and stepped out of the room.

"We have many things to discuss in the hopeful joining of our kingdoms," the king continued.

Aiden quickly lost interest in the conversation as Erick continued in generic small talk with the king. He stood with his hands behind his back as his eyes drifted up to the wooden beams that lined the ceiling and then to the windows that looked towards the east. It was too dark to see anything outside, but he imagined they must showcase some sort of incredible view to be included in the throne room. He looked down at the black and gray tiles. The gray design in the black marble tile almost gave the appearance of wispy smoke blowing across the floor beneath their feet. The smoky tile matched the black marbled throne the king sat in that was covered in bright red velvet and bled into the red drapes that lined the wall behind the king. Aiden noted the identical–though slightly smaller–empty throne beside the king's and wondered if the king's wife would be joining them. His eyes continued around the perimeter of the room and landed on a small area off to the side that housed a golden harp along with a few other instruments. Instruments weren't normally on display in a throne room unless someone in the royal family played them. Aiden smiled as he thought again of the fiery woman he had seen in the tower window earlier and the sweet melody she had been humming. He hoped the sight of the instruments meant that she was the princess.

The king stood and gestured behind them. "Ah, my sweet azalea."

Aiden and Erick looked back as a woman entered the room. She looked pretty in a red, gold, and orange gown similar to the one Aiden had seen earlier, but it wasn't quite the same. The woman wore a thick, shimmering veil over her face and hair. She was escorted to the front of the throne room by a guard, who helped her up the two velvet steps that led to the thrones.

Aiden watched curiously as the guard took a stance close to the woman.

"Prince Aiden. Sir Erick. May I present my beautiful daughter, and the shining sun of our realm, Princess Amber."

Erick bowed and nudged Aiden to do the same. Aiden bowed but didn't take his eyes off the veiled woman. Though he couldn't see her face clearly or see the full color of her hair, he was pretty sure this woman was not the same woman he had seen in the tower earlier. Strange. He had been almost certain that the woman in the tower must be the princess when he saw the instruments on display in the throne room. Why else would they be kept in such a prominent place? The king certainly didn't give the appearance of being an accomplished musician.

Erick straightened, as did Aiden, and stepped forward with a small mahogany box that housed one of the unique onyx stones from the Fall realm on the top. Erick presented the box to the princess and said, "Your Highness. It would be an honor if you would accept this gift from the Fall realm as a sign of the hopeful union between our two realms."

Erick opened the box, revealing a beautiful yellow-orange garnet necklace.

Aiden's eyebrows shot up as he watched, surprised their father would have parted with such a beautiful piece of jewelry. The young woman hesitated as Erick held the box out to her. She seemed uncertain about taking the offered gift. Her head tilted slightly towards the king, who gave her a warning look in return. Aiden watched as the princess's hand trembled slightly as she reached out to take the necklace. She put it around her neck and clasped it, her hands still shaking slightly, and nodded her head in acceptance of the gift.

The king beamed. "Now, shall we adjourn to the dining hall so we may celebrate this blessed union?"

Erick stepped back and bowed his head towards the king. "Of course, Your Majesty."

Erick looked at Aiden and gestured with his eyes towards the princess. Aiden got the hint. He stepped towards the princess and bowed.

"Your Highness. Might I escort you to the dining hall?" he asked.

The guard who had been standing beside her stepped closer. The king grunted and gave an unspoken command to back off, causing the guard to step away.

The princess hesitated for a moment before taking the offered hand of the prince. Aiden helped her off the small platform. The lowered voices of the king and his brother reached his ears as the princess put her shaking hand on his arm to be escorted from the room.

"This marriage will surely form an unshakeable alliance and bring much prosperity to our realms," the king said.

Aiden faltered slightly as his foot scuffed the tile floor at the remark. The princess glanced at him. "You didn't know about the marriage did you?" she whispered.

Aiden carried on as if nothing had happened as he responded.

"No. I had no idea."

CHAPTER 4

After dinner, Aiden and Erick returned to their rooms. Once they were behind the closed door of Aiden's room, Aiden turned to his brother.

"Marriage?" he asked incredulously, repulsed at his father's and brother's secret schemes. "I was brought here to marry the princess of this realm? Don't you think that is a discussion I should have been included in?" he asked as he began to furiously unbutton his doublet.

Erick leaned apathetically against the stone wall beside the door frame as he watched his little brother struggle with his doublet.

"Father didn't think you would have agreed to come on this trip if you had known," Erick replied with a smug smile. He enjoyed watching his brother squirm with the news of why he had been brought here, and for once he was glad he wasn't the blood heir to the throne. "Besides, with the prince from the Spring realm wedding the queen from the North, we needed a stronger alliance between our two kingdoms for our protection. This was the best solution for both realms," he said coolly as he casually picked at something under his fingernails.

"You two have been planning out my life since I was a child. I have never been able to make my own decisions or choose what life I want to live. What if I don't want to marry the princess of this realm?"

Erick pushed himself away from the wall. "We've always had to make the decisions that best suited the kingdom, *little* brother," he emphasized the word to remind Aiden of how much smaller and younger he was compared to his brother. "Besides, you marrying the princess isn't the only reason why we're here."

Aiden looked at him. "What do you mean?" he asked as he tugged at the last button in his doublet, which seemed to be stuck in the buttonhole.

Erick stepped closer to Aiden and lowered his voice. "We found out that there is a second half to the Phoenix gem that has been hidden away in this kingdom. It is said that if the two halves are united, it will create boundless power. We've fought long and hard to take over the fallen realm, and we need to ensure our rule is secure. We get the other half of the Phoenix gem, and our family will be on the throne for a very long time."

Aiden stopped tugging at the button, suddenly intrigued by this mystical piece of news.

"But what about our half of the gem? You haven't been able to find the thief anywhere. Besides, what if the thief knows about the two halves? They could have stolen ours first since its location was known and be headed here to steal the second half and use the gems' power for themselves."

Erick towered over him menacingly. "Then I suppose we need to find the other half first, don't we?"

Aiden glowered up at his brother. He hated it when he did that. Aiden knew Erick was much larger than he was, and a far better warrior. He didn't need the constant reminder.

A thought crossed his mind as he stood under his brother's threatening gaze. Maybe he was somehow intimidated by Aiden and his position in the kingdom and that's why he always asserted himself as the bigger and better brother. A small smile cracked his lips.

"What are you grinning at?" Erick demanded.

Aiden let his smile widen even further to set Erick off edge. "Oh, nothing. Just a wayward thought that brought me some minor amusement," he quipped as he finally loosened the button from the hole and took off his doublet. "So, what is to be my part in this?" he asked as he laid his doublet on the end of the bed.

Erick eyed him speculatively. "That depends on how well you can keep your flitty head out of the clouds and on the tasks at hand," his brother replied.

"I'm in this scheme whether I like it or not, so tell me what to do."

"How about you try to get whatever information you can out of the princess about the gem?" his brother asked as he continued to study him. "Since you are now her betrothed, she may be freer with certain information with you. I can keep a lookout throughout the palace while you're romancing the poor girl."

"Poor girl? I'm not that bad of a catch," Aiden responded dejectedly.

"Just find the gem and seal the marriage deal. Father is counting on both of us to make this work," Erick said as he shoved a pointed finger into Aiden's chest before he turned to leave.

Aiden folded his arms in front of him and glared after his brother. "Oh, don't worry. I'll do what I need to get what Father wants," he said loud enough to make sure Erick heard him as he left the room.

"And I won't need your help doing it."

Aiden woke up a few hours later to the sound of sweet music drifting down the stone hallway. As much as he enjoyed music, he was tired from the long journey to the Summer realm and wanted to ignore it and go back to sleep. It stopped, allowing him to drift off again. A few moments later, the music worked its way into his dreams and woke him up again. This time, it sounded like it was passing outside his door. He sat up as it grew louder. He wouldn't be going back to sleep now.

Aiden got up and shuffled his bare feet across the stone floor towards the door. The stones weren't as cold as he would have expected them to be beneath his feet. The warmer temperatures in the Summer realm must keep everything warmer in general. If he were back home, he would have been met with a certain chill if he got out of bed in the middle of the night. And he definitely would not be traipsing across the room in his bare feet.

He quietly opened the door and glanced into the hall. Nothing was visible down the left side of the hall. As he looked the other direction, a flash of red caught his eye before it disappeared around the corner. Thinking it might be the girl he saw in the tower when they arrived, he stepped out into the hallway and closed his door behind him, eager to meet the mysterious red flame at last.

He ran quietly to the end of the hall where he had seen the blaze of red and peered around the corner. Another flash of red vanished around the next corner. He followed it until he saw a glimpse of it going into a room with large double doors. He snuck up to the doors and opened one slightly. The room was dark, making it impossible to see much of anything. The hallways at least had dim candles burning on the walls, but this room was pitch black. Stepping quietly into the room, he shut the door behind him. He stood by the door for a few moments, waiting for his eyes to adjust to the dark room. A dim light on the other side of the room registered with his eyes. He wondered if the light was coming from a covered window where moonlight was being blocked out by heavy drapes. Aiden cautiously took a few steps into the room. Strange that whoever was in the room didn't have a candle lit or light a fire in the fireplace. His shin hit something hard.

"Ouch!" he cried out as he steadied himself and held out his hand to find whatever object he had bumped into.

"Who's there?" a sweet voice asked from the darkness.

Aiden stood still, surprised to hear the feminine voice. He rubbed his shin and gently put his foot down.

"I could ask you the same question," Aiden replied as his eyes searched the dark room, trying to figure out where the voice had originated.

"It is my castle, so I believe I deserve your answer first," the girl replied. Aiden could hear a slight smile in her voice.

"Your castle?" he asked as he took another cautious step into the room, hoping he wouldn't bump into anything else.

"I am *the* Princess Amber of the Summer realm, so yes, it is my castle. Well, my father's anyway," she replied, a mock piety now lacing her voice.

Aiden looked in the direction of the voice. That was strange. This woman didn't sound anything like the woman he had dined with tonight. Of course, the princess he had dined with had a heavy veil over her face, so maybe the material covered some of the tones of her voice. But there was something musical about this woman's voice that he was sure he would have noticed, veil or no veil. He decided to play along to see what information he could get from her.

"Ah, *the* Princess Amber. My apologies, Your Highness. I did not recognize you in the dark."

He heard a breath like she was about to answer, but it fell away before she said anything.

"Did I offend you by something I said?" Aiden asked the darkness.

"No. You did not offend me. It's just," she paused. "Well, nevermind," she finished, faltering on the last statement.

Aiden stood there awkwardly for a few minutes, trying to think of how to continue the conversation.

"Do you normally sit in dark rooms by yourself at night?" he asked teasingly, trying to lighten the awkward mood in the room.

The woman hesitated again before she replied.

"Yes, actually, I do. I am so used to it I guess I didn't notice it was so dark."

Her response caught Aiden off guard. Strange that she was used to sitting in dark rooms by herself. And, for her not to notice how dark it was? Stranger still.

"Might I light a candle?" he asked as he took a wary step towards the voice, still afraid of bumping into something else.

"No!" she responded a little quicker and sharper than she had intended to.

Silence filled the void between them once again. She continued after a few moments. "I'm sorry, I didn't mean to respond so defensively. I just–prefer the darkness. Too much light affects my eyes and gives me headaches."

Now it was Aiden's turn to hesitate..

"I'm sorry to hear that," he said at last. "I didn't realize. I shouldn't have commented on it."

"You couldn't have known," she replied apologetically. "It is not a usual problem for most people, I would imagine."

She carried a certain sweetness and innocence in her voice that made Aiden think of a baby animal who was curious to explore but also timid and shy and yet untouched by the world.

"You are the first that I've met," Aiden responded with a slight smile.

"You have a nice smile," the princess said.

Aiden's brows furrowed at her statement. "How can you tell that? We're in a dark room?" he asked.

"I can just tell," she replied in her lilting voice.

"It must be some sort of magic you possess. I can barely tell where you are at," he replied with a slight laugh on his breath.

The woman's voice fell. "It is no magic, I can assure you. I've just learned to rely on other senses outside of just sight and can sense certain things or moods."

"Most interesting skill to have developed," Aiden said.

"Yes," she replied, the diminished chord of her voice lingering somberly in the air without resolving.

The dark room was cast into awkward silence once more, causing Aiden to feel like he had ungallantly intruded on this woman's privacy.

"Well, I don't want to keep you from your time to yourself, so I will leave you to enjoy the solitude of the room," Aiden said as he took a step backwards towards the door.

"Wait," the girl piped up. "I very rarely have the pleasure of carrying on a full conversation with anyone. Must you go so soon?" she asked.

"Admittedly, I have very much enjoyed speaking with you as well, but I have had a long journey and my body is telling me it is time to go to bed, regardless of what my mind is wanting to do."

"Long journey. Where did you come from?" she asked.

Aiden looked curiously towards the voice. This phantom of the night had completely piqued his interest. Surely if he had dined with the princess tonight, she would know where he had come from and what they were doing here.

"I come from the Fall realm," he replied, not sure if he should remind her of their conversation at dinner or if he should stay silent and try to figure out what was really going on in this castle.

She sighed. "Sounds fascinating. I would like to hear more about it sometime," she replied dreamily.

"And I would like to tell you about it sometime," Aiden replied with a wistful smile.

"But, not tonight. You must obey your body's call of tiredness and return to your room for some much needed rest. Would you meet me here tomorrow night so we can continue this conversation?" she asked hopefully.

Aiden's smile widened. "I would be honored, *Princess*."

She smiled in return. "Wonderful. Until tomorrow night."

"Until tomorrow night." Aiden enacted a slight bow even though he knew she probably couldn't see him, but he did it anyway out of respect. He turned to go and carefully shuffled his way out of the room to avoid hitting anything on his way out.

CHAPTER 5

Aiden spent the next day with the veiled princess. They had been escorted to an area near the palace for a picnic so they could get to know one another better. The guard who had accompanied her the night before remained close by during the entire picnic. Aiden could understand why the princess would escape to a room by herself at night if she was this heavily guarded all the time. When she had also mentioned her eyes being affected by light, that made sense as to why she would be wearing such heavy veils on her face. Aiden wished he could remove the veils from this woman's face so he could look at her, just to confirm whether this princess was the woman he had seen in the tower. With the guard keeping such a watchful eye on them—and tight grip on his sword—Aiden figured it probably wouldn't go over well between them if he tried to remove her veils, or ask her to take them off.

Regardless of the heavy veils, which muffled much of the princesses' voice, Aiden could hear a distinct difference between the woman he had spoken with last night and the one he spoke with now. The voice he heard now did not carry the same lilting, musical tones as the voice he had relished listening to the night before. In fact, this woman's voice was almost monotonous compared to the other princess. Not to mention, the generic conversation he had been having with the veiled princess lagged quite a bit compared the night before. And, he did not feel the same connection he had felt with the phantom woman. Perhaps she was just more subdued in the company of the over-attentive guard.

Aiden graciously kept up a conversation with the veiled princess, but was relieved when the guard announced that it was time to head back to the palace.

Later that night, after another long and dull dinner, Aiden stepped into his room, hoping he would hear the enchanting music that would lead him to the mystery woman again. He was anxious to find out if the woman he had met last night was the same woman he had spent the day with or if there were indeed two Princess Amber's.

His brother followed him into his room before he could close the door. Aiden gave Erick an annoyed look. "Do you trust me so little that you can't leave me alone for more than two seconds?" Aiden asked as he crossed to the trunk at the end of his bed and sat to take off his boots.

Erick made sure no one else was in the hall and shut the door. "No rest for the lazy, brother. We have a gem to look for."

"I thought that was your job," Aiden replied with a vexed tone as he pulled his boot back on to help in the search. He was already put out by his brother's presence in his room and now he was irritated by the fact that he might miss hearing the music if he were in parts unknown in the palace helping Erick search for an elusive gem he didn't care about.

"I was in counsel with the king most of the day discussing the alliances between our kingdoms as well as strategies should the other realms ever attack, so I haven't had time to look for the gem," Erick grunted as he stood impatiently at the door with his arms crossed.

"Well, I've been on princess duty all day, so you can't expect me to make headway on finding it during the day."

"Maybe not, but you can ask her questions and see if she knows anything about the gem's whereabouts," Erick replied.

"Have you tried to talk with her?" Aiden asked. "She has so many veils over her face that I can barely hear what she says."

"Then I guess you will have to be creative in how you obtain the needed information," Erick replied as he stepped towards his brother in his usual menacing air.

Aiden rolled his eyes inwardly. His brother's constant need to intimidate him was growing old. "Don't you think it is odd that the princess's face is so heavily covered?"

"Maybe she has a malformed face and the king doesn't want anyone to know that he has an ugly daughter," Erick scoffed.

"And I'm just supposed to marry her with no questions asked? What if there is something wrong with her?" Aiden asked.

"Then you might want to keep the candles dim and the fire low on your wedding night," Erick teased as he pushed a pillow into Aiden's chest.

Aiden shoved the pillow back into his brother's chest. "Your manners are ghastly. I guess that's why Father chose me to marry the princess instead of you," Aiden jabbed as he walked past his brother towards the door.

Erick stiffened at Aiden's remark. "Father only chose you because you're the only one who has royal blood running through his veins. But, then again, you're only half royal," he said with a re-assertive triumph in his voice. "We need to find the gem."

Erick shoved Aiden as he walked out the door, causing Aiden to stumble forward and almost lose his footing. "One of these days you won't be able to rely on your brute strength to save you. Then where will you be?" Aiden muttered angrily under his breath.

He stopped short as he steadied himself in the dimly lit stone hallway. The bewitching music he had heard the night before was drifting down the hallway once again. Erick had started walking the opposite direction of where the music was coming from, obviously oblivious to it like he had been the night before. Aiden listened to the enchanting melody for a moment, the beautiful notes calling to him and beckoning him to follow it.

"I'll check the rooms down here," he whispered to his brother. "I think there is a library that might have some information."

Erick turned around and glared at his brother. "You better not duck back into your room after I leave. I'm not looking for the blasted thing by myself all night."

"I swear, I will do my part. You can trust me, Erick."

Erick studied Aiden for a long moment. "I want a full report in the morning," he replied stiffly as he turned and walked down the other side of the hall.

Aiden made his way down the hall toward the room he had seen the fiery-haired woman slip into the night before. He stopped at the large double doors and took a breath before entering, hoping she would be inside. He pressed down on the handle. The door clicked, and he slipped quietly into the room. It was dark, just as it had been the night before. Aiden carefully shuffled his feet across the floor with his arms stretched out in front of him to try to avoid running into anything.

"Oof," he grunted as the toe of his boot bumped into something hard.

"Who's there?" the lilting feminine voice asked through the darkness.

Aiden paused before answering. "I, uh, I spoke with you last night."

He put his hands out and they brushed a hard surface. He must have bumped into a table of some kind.

"Oh," the voice replied. "Hello again."

"Hello," Aiden replied.

He looked around and tried to see if his eyes had adjusted enough to see anything in the dark. There was the same dim light outlining what he still supposed to be a curtain on the other side of the room, but no other light.

"Do you mind if I light a candle or open the curtains or something?" Aiden asked.

No answer.

"I know you mentioned last night that the light affects your eyes, but unfortunately, I am not as familiar with this room as you are to navigate it in the dark."

After a few moments, the voice responded. "I understand. You can light a candle if that will help you."

"Thank you," Aiden replied.

He moved to the right, hoping he was stepping in front of whatever table he had run into, but banged his shin hard against it.

"Ouch!" he exclaimed.

"Oh no. I'm sorry. It probably is very dark in here. Stand still for a moment and say something."

Aiden reached down to rub his shin. "What would you like me to say?" he asked.

"That's just fine. Take a step back."

Aiden did.

"Now, step to the left a few paces, and take a few steps towards my voice."

Aiden's brows knit together. This was highly unusual, but he did as she said. A few paces to the left and a few steps towards her voice.

"That's good. Now, reach out your hand."

Aiden lifted his hand out in front of him. He felt something soft and warm brush his fingers.

"There you are," she said as she took his hand in hers. "There should be a candle on this table beside me and a matchstick for the fire beside it."

She guided his hand until he felt cold metal and continued to direct it to the base of what must be the candlestick. His fingers found the match and he felt around the table until found the edge where he struck the match. An orange flame flickered to life and he carefully moved it up to the candle, holding it there until the wick caught the flame. He blew out the flame at the end of the match and set the stick by the candle.

The candle emitted a small but warm circle of light, illuminating the small table it sat on that was nestled between two armchairs. In one armchair, he could see the shadowed figure of a woman. He looked around the small vicinity that was now encompassed in the candlelight and saw a fireplace behind him and what appeared to be the faint outline of a bookshelf.

"Would you mind if I got the fire going to give us more light?" Aiden asked as he took a step towards the fireplace.

"Oh no." The woman reached out and grabbed his arm. "Please don't."

Aiden's brows knit together as he studied the woman in the shadowed light of the candle. He knew the light affected her eyes, but the urgency with which she kept him from lighting the fire made him wonder if there was another reason why she didn't want it lit.

She quickly removed her hand from his arm. "I'm sorry. I didn't mean to be so abrupt. I just, my eyes- I-, I have trouble with a lot of light," she faltered.

"You mentioned that last night. Is this light too much for you? I can move the candle so it is not so close to you if that would help," Aiden replied, trying to figure out how to make it so he could see, but not bring discomfort to the strange woman.

"Perhaps if you moved it to the mantle on the fireplace," she responded.

Aiden reached down and grabbed the ornate black candlestick. As he moved it, he saw more of the large bookshelf beside the fireplace. He stepped closer so he could look at some of the titles.

"I don't mean to be rude, but I can't help but wonder what someone would be doing in a dark library at night by herself," Aiden said as he held the candle close to some of the books.

"I'm not by myself," she responded with a smile in her voice.

Aiden smiled and looked back at her. "Touché." He continued to look at the various books on the shelves "But, it is curious."

The girl hesitated before answering, "I used to come here all the time when I was little. I loved seeing the shelves of endless books and always dreamed of reading every single book in this library. I would run my fingers along the spines and learn the different engraved scrawlings that made up some of my favorite titles. I can't read them myself anymore, but I still love to come down here and run my fingers along the spines and find my familiar old friends. I sometimes pull them out and open them as if I'm reading them again and play out the story in my mind." She paused.

Interesting she couldn't read them to herself anymore, Aiden thought to himself. He wondered why, but didn't want to ask.

"Would you mind reading this one to me?" she asked shyly as she held up a book she had tucked under her folded hands on her lap. "It's one of my favorites."

"I'll have to move the candle closer so I can read," Aiden replied, as he took a step towards the intriguing woman. He tried to take in some of her features in the shadowed light of the candle as he stood in front of her. He could see the fiery red of her hair that was the same color he had seen dancing in the sunlight when he had arrived. He couldn't see much of her face, but he was convinced this was the woman he had seen in the tower and she was much too beautiful to be kept covered up and shrouded in darkness all the time. A soft smile played across his lips as he stared at her.

"I think if you sit in the chair on the other side of this table, that should be fine," she replied as she held the book out to him.

Aiden took the book from her and looked at the gilded title. *Phoenix Rising.* His smile widened as he read the title. Not the book he expected a princess to read, but then again, nothing was ordinary about this princess. He placed the candle on the small table and moved it closer to the other chair. Sitting down, he opened the book and began to read.

CHAPTER 6

The sun started to peek through the thick drapes that covered the window on the other side of the room. Aiden looked up as he finished the second book they had been reading.

"It looks like the sun is coming up. I didn't realize we had been reading all night." Aiden stood and walked over to the floor-to-ceiling bookshelf and put the book back on the shelf.

"Thank you for reading to me. It was nice to actually hear those stories again instead of trying to just remember them in my mind."

Aiden turned to face her. "Can I ask why you are unable to read them for yourself anymore?"

She sat silently in the chair, trying to think of how to respond.

"You don't have to answer if you don't want to," Aiden quickly added, realizing he may have asked a question that was too personal.

Amber finally responded. "I don't mind answering. I've just never had to answer that question before."

Aiden crossed his arms in front of him as he leaned against the fireplace, "You've never had to answer that question before?"

"No. My father keeps me pretty well hidden away from the world. Actually, besides my companion, you are one of the few people I've had the privilege of speaking with. She has been ill or something this past week, so I haven't even had her to talk to."

Aiden thought about this for a moment before responding. The veiled princess hadn't said much in the two days he had been with her, but she did make general responses to the king and even to his brother, so he hadn't been the only person she had been talking to since they had arrived. But this girl just admitted that she hadn't talked with anyone except him. He was becoming more convinced that the two women he had been interacting with were not the same person. Aiden was about to ask her about this when she continued speaking.

"Anyway, you asked about why I can't read the stories to myself anymore. There was a fire many years ago. I was very little, I think about five years old, and I was sound asleep in my bed. I didn't smell the smoke or anything. I remember my nursemaid waking me up and trying to get me out of bed. My entire room was pretty much engulfed in flames. She pulled me from my bed and we tried to make it to the door. I had dropped my favorite doll and I went back to save her from the growing flames. As I did, the glass in my window exploded beside me because of the intense heat from the fire. It threw me back and knocked me unconscious. Someone must have gotten me out, but I don't know who or how. I woke up a few days later, but even though I was awake, I couldn't see anything."

"That must have been terrifying, especially at such a young age," Aiden replied sympathetically.

"It was. I can't describe what it feels like to be able to see your entire life and then one day have everything go dark. My sight came back slowly, and I was able to see for a few years, but it started to fade again the older I got. By the time I was twelve, my sight had pretty much faded to black again. When it started to fade again, I made a point to read and see as much as I could so I could commit as much to memory as possible."

"So, you can't see anything anymore?"

"I can see occasional light and shadows, but it's almost too much for my eyes to try to see anything rather than just letting them exist in darkness. That's why I was in here with no light the other night when you found me," she said with a self-conscious tone in her voice as though apologizing or embarrassed that she had been weirdly sitting in a dark library by herself. "There are two sets of large windows on the wall over there that let in exuberant amounts of light during the day and it can be wearing on my eyes, so that's why I usually come down at night when it's dark. And, most of the servants have gone to bed at that point so no one will bother me."

"Is that why you wear such heavy veils over your face during the day?" Aiden asked curiously as he stepped towards her.

Now it was Amber's turn to be confused.

"Veils? No, I don't wear veils over my face. I usually stay in my room during the day. My father put me up in the south tower so I wouldn't have to face too much sun during the day but I can still enjoy its glow as it rises and sets without it pouring directly into my room. Why did you ask about me wearing veils?" she asked.

Aiden looked at her dimly shadowed face. "You haven't been the one who has been visiting with us since we arrived, are you?"

Amber gave a soft laugh. "No. I haven't been visiting with anyone. Like I said, my father keeps me in my room pretty much all the time. He doesn't want me to get hurt because I can't see anymore, so he would rather keep me contained in one familiar room than risk me bumping into things or falling or something. My companion usually comes to my room and spends the day with me, and the servants bring me all my meals. I only sneak down to this library at night so my father won't find out that I leave my room on occasions."

Aiden was beginning to put the pieces together.

"You said you haven't seen your companion for about a week now?" he asked.

"No. I assume she must be sick or maybe had to visit her family or something because she hasn't been coming to visit me, but no one has said anything to me about her."

"Did your father ever mention my visit to your realm or why he brought me here?" Aiden asked.

"No. I didn't even know we were going to have visitors. Clearly I'm in the dark in more ways than one," she replied with a rueful smile.

Aiden liked that she kept her sense of humor intact despite her circumstances. "My father and your father have been discussing an alliance between our kingdoms since word reached them that the prince from the Spring realm and the queen from the Winter realm are to be wed, aligning their kingdoms with the bonds of marriage. I believe our fathers wanted to form a similar alliance in case anything ever happened between us and the other realms."

"A similar alliance? If the Spring prince and the Winter queen are to be married, then you're saying my father is wanting me to marry –?" She broke off suddenly and lifted her face towards him.

"Me," Aiden replied, gauging her reaction.

She sat motionless in the chair for a moment, processing this information. "If my father wants me to marry you, that must mean that you are a prince."

"I am. My father is ruler of the Fall realm; although, he is not the lawful Harvest King. He overthrew the throne before I was born and married the queen, so I'm only half a prince, but I guess our fathers see it as a better alliance than just joining armies and weapons."

Amber grinned. "A half-prince. Well, that does seem like a pretty low standard, but at least you are half-a-somebody and aren't completely a nobody. My father thinks that high enough standing to marry me off to, I guess."

He could hear the joking tone in her voice. "Yes, I'm at least half-a-somebody, I suppose." He replied with a slight chuckle.

"Marriage. I didn't even know my father had been thinking about marrying me off. And now, apparently you are here to do just that. It's strange that he hasn't mentioned it. How soon are we supposed to be married?" she asked.

"I have no idea. I wasn't told about it either until we arrived and your father and my brother struck the deal."

"You didn't know either? I wonder why the two people who are supposed to be marrying each other are the last to know."

"I can guess why I wasn't told. My brother Erick was born to my father before he took the throne, so he has never truly been considered royal. I think he has held a grudge against me for being born and taking any chance he may have had at being heir to the throne. He likes to have the upper hand and feel like he still has control over my life even though he can't ever be king. My father sent us to present a gift to the king of Ashteria as a sign of good faith between our realms. I had no idea I was the gift."

Amber laughed. "Well, that is quite the unexpected gift."

Aiden laughed too. "Indeed. It feels almost like I'm being offered as a golden sacrifice on some peace altar."

"I feel that way too now that I am aware of the *arrangement*," she said with a joking emphasis on the last word. "But, you said you've been interacting with someone who has been wearing heavy veils over her face? If you've been introduced to someone that you are supposed to wed but it wasn't me, I don't understand who or why."

"You said you haven't seen your companion for about a week and no one has said or mentioned anything to you about her. I think your father is using her as a stand-in, though, I can't imagine why."

"My father has never really known what to do with me since I lost my sight. I think he views it as degrading to the throne or as a weakness. Perhaps he didn't want your father to know that I was blind to prevent our kingdom from being taken over or invaded because of the incapable princess." Her light tone darkened with a shadow of sadness covering the happy sound she had previously had in her voice.

"Do you really believe that's what your father thinks of you?" Aiden asked.

"He's never said it, but I can tell when he visits me that he feels awkward and doesn't really know what to say or do with me. That's probably another reason he has kept me in the tower room since I lost my sight. If no one sees me and sees that I am blind, they will never know that the Summer princess has an infirmity."

"I'm sorry," Aiden replied. "I can't begin to imagine what it would be like to live life without my sight. You mentioned your father doesn't seem to know what to do with you. I think my father feels the same about me. My brother has always been the active, get-it-done, soldier and protector of the kingdom. He's the captain of our army and has always been bigger than me and followed in our father's more aggressive, hard-nosed nature. I've always been viewed as the weaker brother, and I have never had the same desires and ambitions that they have had. And I've always loved music and poetry and creating beautiful things, but of course, that is greatly looked down upon and is not seen as qualities that instill fear in others as a mighty warrior king."

"You like music?" Amber asked, her voice raising slightly with excitement.

Aiden's voice softened as a whimsical smile spread across his face. "I do. I love it. I've always felt there is something magical and inexplicably beautiful about music that reaches past the natural bounds of this world. It communicates things people can't normally say with just words. It illuminates people's emotions and reaches into their souls in ways nothing else can."

"Quite eloquent for a supposed-to-be warrior prince," Amber replied with a slightly mocking tone. Her joking smile filled with warmth as she thought about her own connection to music. "I love music too. It is all the things you said and so much more. I used to play quite a few instruments, but I haven't been able to play since I lost my sight the second time. I miss it," she sighed longingly.

"Were you singing at your tower window the other day as the sun was setting?" Aiden asked.

Amber blushed. "I was. I didn't realize anyone could hear me," she replied as she tilted her head down in embarrassment.

Aiden knelt beside her. "It was the most beautiful sound I have ever heard," he said as he looked up at her shadowed face.

"No one is supposed to hear me sing. My father doesn't want me drawing attention to myself. I just can't help it sometimes. And I had no idea we were expecting visitors. I probably shouldn't have been singing at my open window." Amber twisted her hands nervously together in her lap.

Aiden placed his hand over hers. She stilled them suddenly, not expecting him to touch her. "It was beautiful. You should never be ashamed of it or try to hide it. Besides, I don't think anyone else was paying enough attention to notice, so your secret is safe with me." He gave her hands a reassuring squeeze.

She looked over his head, not quite sure where his face was. "Thank you," she replied quietly.

Aiden smiled as he looked up at her. The room was still too dim to see any of her features clearly with the thick drapes blocking out most of the sun, but he could tell she was beautiful, both inside and out.

"Well, we should probably get you back to your room before your father finds out that you're out and about. The last thing I would want is for you to get in trouble, and I've probably kept you here longer than you usually stay."

Aiden stood up and pulled her hands to help her out of the chair.

"Aiden." Amber pulled back on his hands. He turned back to face her. "Thank you."

"For what?" he asked as he looked down at her.

"For sitting with me last night and talking with me. And reading to me," she added with a sweet smile.

Aiden smiled. "You are more than welcome," he replied as he squeezed her hands in his. "Can I walk you back to your room?" he asked.

"Yes, thank you," Amber replied as she put her hand into the crook of his arm and let him lead her from the library.

"You'll have to tell me which direction. I've only followed you from my room down the hall," Aiden said with a playful smile.

Amber laughed. "I'll let you know when to turn."

They went down a few hallways and finally came to a wooden door that led, he supposed, to her tower.

"I bid thee a good day, my lady. May you have the sweetest thoughts and most fond remembrances of things once seen."

Aiden brought her hand to his lips and placed a gentle kiss on the back of her knuckles.

She blushed and her smile widened at the feel of his lips on her hand. "Quite the gentleman. That's a good quality in a potential husband, I suppose."

She pulled back suddenly on Aiden's grip.

"What is it?" he asked.

"Aiden, I–." Amber hesitated. "I don't know what to do about this whole marriage thing. I didn't even know about it until you mentioned it to me, and if my father is having my companion stand in for me, I'm not even sure what the rest of his plans or intentions are. Maybe he was going to have you marry her or spring me on you at the last moment. I joked about the marriage, but honestly, I hadn't even really thought about it until you mentioned it. I've always thought I would probably just be on my own for the rest of my life in my tower room. I don't–" she paused again, unsure of how to continue.

Aiden put a gentle finger to her mouth to stop her from talking. "We can figure that out," he said gently. "Let's get you back to your room and then we can meet up tonight in the library and talk things out. Does that sound all right to you?" he asked.

"Yes," she said in a breathless whisper.

Amber felt a strange tingle in her lips at the feel of his finger touching them. He moved his finger away.

"All right. Until tonight, Princess."

"Until tonight," Amber whispered.

Aiden's hand slipped from hers and she heard his footsteps as he walked away from her. She touched her lips where his finger had been and then touched the back of her hand where he had brushed her knuckles with a kiss. She felt her cheeks heat as she recalled the lingering sensations but couldn't stop the broad smile that crossed her face. She turned with a dreamy glow on her face and pushed open the door, her fingers subconsciously feeling along the wall until she reached the stairs that led to her tower. She would certainly have good dreams now.

Chapter 7

Aiden returned to his room after delivering the princess to her tower door. He hadn't been keen on the idea of being presented as a bargaining chip in an alliance between the Fall and Summer realms, but after talking to the real princess the night before, he was coming around to the idea of marriage. Especially if he would be marrying Amber.

He wondered if he and Amber could make a real relationship work. He genuinely wanted to get to know her better and see if they had anything there, but he was also afraid that any feelings between them would feel forced or clouded out by the pressures of an arranged marriage. Unfortunately, he knew his father would not allow a delay in the marriage just for the sake of getting to know one another better, and time was not on their side. His father was desperate for this alliance and the gem, and the king of the Summer realm seemed just as desperate.

Besides the pressures of his father to marry the princess, it was concerning that her father was using a stand-in for her, and Aiden wondered if he really would have ended up marrying Amber, or if he would have married the imposter. And, if the king of the Summer realm was so concerned about his daughter's blindness being found out, why had he sent the initial invitation to his father to create the alliance? Perhaps Lord Ragnar had been the one to initiate the alliance and King Azar felt backed into a corner, so he was trying to cover up the truth about Amber until the deal was sealed.

Aiden shook his head. This whole setup was beginning to feel like some of the mazes they used to set up in the corn fields when he was younger. Many different paths and routes, but who knew which one led to the truth.

Aiden opened his door and closed it behind him.

"Where have you been?"

Aiden jumped at his brother's gruff voice behind him. "What are you doing in my room at such an early hour?"

"I asked you a question first. Where have you been all night?"

Aiden hated that his brother discounted the fact that he was in *his* room, invading *his* privacy and personal space, and yet he still expected his question to be answered first. Instead of starting an argument with his brother, he decided to just answer. Maybe the sooner he answered, the sooner Erick would leave, and he could get a few hours of sleep.

"I was in the library trying to find out needed information," Aiden replied shortly. It wasn't a lie. He had gathered some pretty interesting information about the princess—the *real* princess—even if he hadn't learned anything about the Phoenix gem.

"Did you find anything?" his brother asked as he swung his feet off the table that sat by the wall near the fireplace and stood up.

"Nothing about the gem, but there are hundreds of books in there. I'm sure there has to be something in there about it," Aiden replied coolly.

Erick's lip curled up in a sneer. "We are not here so you can spend your time dilly dallying through the hundreds of books in the Summer king's library. We need to find that gem and fast."

"I have a really strong sense that there is valuable information in that library about the gem. I'll spend tonight looking through some more books. If I don't find anything, I'll move on and start searching elsewhere," Aiden replied, trying to stave off the growing annoyance at his brother's condescension.

Erick took a few steps toward Aiden and stopped in front of him. He looked down on him with a menacing glare. Aiden stiffened his back, trying not to look intimidated by his brother's looming stature over him, and held his gaze.

Erick studied Aiden for a few moments before he said anything. "Maybe there is some information in that library. If you don't find anything tonight you move on though, are we clear?"

"I told you I would move on if I didn't find anything tonight," Aiden replied, bristling under his brother's scrutiny.

"Ask the princess some subtle questions as well. She might know more than anyone about the gem's whereabouts."

"I will."

"Good," his brother sneered as he brushed past him. Erick turned back when he reached the door. "Get some sleep. We don't need their highnesses suspecting us of anything."

Aiden kept his staunch gaze on his brother's back as he left the room. He let out a breath he didn't realize he had been holding in.

"At least while I'm sleeping I don't have to deal with him," Aiden sighed.

He pulled off his boots and fell into the feather bed and was sound asleep within a few moments.

At dinner that night, Erick excused himself early, saying he had to go check on something. Shortly after Erick left, the king invited Aiden to join him and the veiled imposter in the library so they could talk easier. Aiden watched as one of the guards stayed close to the veiled princess the entire walk, and then stood fairly close to her while they were in the library. After discovering the truth about the stand-in, it made more sense as to why this veiled princess remained so heavily guarded all the time. The king was probably afraid she might slip up or make a run for it or something.

Aiden took in the magnificent library, now flooded with light from the roaring fire blazing in the fireplace and sconces with candles lit all around the room. Quite the difference from the dark room he had sat in the night before. Dark wood shelves filled the walls from floor to ceiling with a couple of staircases in the corners of the room that led up to the second stack of shelves. The thick drapes that had blocked out the moon the previous nights were wide open, and Aiden could see the immaculate windows that revealed the reflection of a beautiful sunset on the horizon. He pictured how beautiful the sunrise must be out these windows. It was a shame Amber couldn't see any of this.

Aiden wandered over to the bookshelf nearest the fire where he had retrieved the books he had read to the princess the night before. He looked at the *Phoenix Rising* title and smiled. She had said that was one of her favorites. He wondered if he could broach the subject of the Phoenix gem without creating suspicion with the king.

"*Phoenix Rising*. Does this talk about the legend of the Phoenix?" Aiden asked.

The king stepped over to the bookshelf and stood behind Aiden as he looked at the book.

"I'm afraid I wouldn't know. My daughter reads most of the books in this library," King Azar responded.

Aiden noticed the hesitancy in the king's voice.

"I see," he replied. "I just wondered. I have always been fascinated with the legend of the fiery bird that lived for hundreds of years before dying and being reborn. I've also heard stories about an ancient Phoenix gem that possessed the power of the Phoenix. From what I remember, it was broken in half at one point, and the pieces were separated. I wonder where they are now, if the legend were true, of course. Can you imagine having that kind of power in your possession?" Aiden asked as he turned to face the king.

The king narrowed his eyes slightly at Aiden and studied him for a moment before responding. "It is merely a child's story, I am sure. Such a powerful gem could be quite dangerous in the wrong hands."

Aiden returned the king's studious gaze. King Azar's sharp-eyed gaze made Aiden think he was well aware of the gem's whereabouts, but he also sensed the king's wariness at Aiden's questions. He better tread carefully before the king suspected him of anything.

He turned to the veiled princess. "Tell me, Princess Amber. What is your favorite story?"

The princess gave a muffled reply. "There are so many. How could one choose?"

"Indeed. There are a vast number of books in this library. Far more than any one person could read in a lifetime," Aiden replied. He felt his lips twitch in a near smile as he thought about how the true princess would have responded right away with her favorite book, and probably go on to talk about a handful of other books she loved to read. And she couldn't even read them for herself anymore. He wondered how long this charade could truly go on before someone slipped up.

A big commotion in the hall drew their attention. The large library doors were thrust open as a harried servant burst into the room.

"Your Majesty, the west wing is on fire."

The king turned quickly. "Gather as many servants as you can find and start a water brigade. Get everyone out as quickly as possible."

The servant nodded and ran from the room.

The king shook his head and muttered under his breath, "I can't believe this is happening again." He looked at Aiden. "Take the princess outside immediately."

Aiden nodded and took the hand of the princess to lead her outside. Once outside, Aiden made sure the veiled princess was safe on the other side of the courtyard. He scanned the crowd and saw Erick running from one of the side doors. He ran over to him.

"What happened?" Aiden asked as he looked at the traces of dark soot on his brother's arms.

"We need to get out of here, now," Erick replied as he brushed some of the soot from his arms and hair.

Aiden eyed his brother suspiciously. "Why would we need to leave so suddenly?" he asked, skeptical and worried that his brother may have had something to do with the fire.

"Let's just say something went wrong with the search for the gem, and the king of the Summer realm would not be happy if he found out that our kingdom might be the cause of his castle's destruction."

Aiden's eyes widened. "I can't believe this. Did you do this on purpose to try to find the gem?" he asked.

Erick glared back at him. "How dare you accuse me of such a low act. It was an accident."

Aiden shook his head in disbelief. "You better hope no one gets hurt and that they can contain the fire quickly."

Aiden brushed past his brother to join the brigade. His eyes scanned the crowd for the girl with the fiery red hair. She would be easy to spot, even in the dimming light of sunset and the chaos that filled the courtyard. He didn't see her anywhere.

"Aiden, come on. We need to go," Erick called to him from behind.

Aiden turned and shook his head. "I have to get the princess out."

Erick looked around and saw the veiled princess standing on the other side of the courtyard.

"Aiden, she's over here!" Erick shouted.

Ignoring his brother's shouts, Aiden ran into the palace. He hurried down the halls that led to Amber's tower. When he reached it, he saw the king trying to open the door. Aiden ran towards him.

"Your Majesty. You should get out of here. The fire is getting too close," Aiden shouted over the roar of the flames.

"No, I have to get her out."

As the king said this, a beam from overhead cracked and fell in front of the door. Aiden quickly pushed the king out of the way.

The king fell back and started choking from the black smoke that was spilling into the corridor. He pulled Aiden close to him and whispered, "You have to get her out."

Aiden nodded and made sure the king was a safe enough distance from the flames before he stood and stepped to where the beam had fallen. Mustering his strength, he pushed as hard as he could against the beam to move it out of the way. When it finally gave way, Aiden let out a frustrated growl as the door refused to budge. He turned the handle again and heaved his shoulder against it with what remaining strength he had left. It took several tries, but he finally got the door to open. He fell through the door and stumbled towards the smoke-filled stairway. Aiden covered his mouth with his sleeve and ran up the stairs to the tower.

"Amber," he called out once he reached the top of the stairs.

Smoke burned his eyes, causing them to water, and made it difficult to keep them open. He stepped into the cylindrical room and called again.

"Amber!"

Amber coughed from the other side of the room. "Aiden?" she replied.

"Amber, I'm here. Don't worry. I'm going to get you out."

Aiden kept his arm in front of his face to protect it from the heat and smoke surrounding him as he stepped cautiously across the room. He finally caught a glimpse of Amber standing next to the window. He looked around the room for something Amber could use to cover her mouth. His burning eyes landed on the pillow lying on her bed. He snatched the pillow from the bed and ripped the pillowcase off of it. Reaching out, he grabbed Amber's hand and placed the pillowcase in it.

"Keep this over your mouth as much as possible," he shouted.

Amber nodded and held the pillowcase loosely over her mouth. Aiden grabbed her free hand and put his arm over his mouth again. They stepped towards the doorway as a flame jumped across the entryway. Aiden stopped short causing Amber to run into him.

"What's wrong?" she shouted.

Aiden had to get her out of there quickly before the entire room was engulfed in flames. He watched the flames intently, waiting for a safe moment to cross the burning threshold. When the moment came, Aiden squeezed Amber's hand signaling for her to move forward, and pulled her quickly through the doorway. He tried to guide her quickly and carefully down the stairs, but felt her stumble a few times behind him since she didn't have her hands out to feel where she was going. They finally reached the bottom and Amber felt her arm pull to the left as Aiden directed her around the jammed door and into the hallway.

Aiden stopped and turned to Amber. "Stay here for a moment."

Aiden let go of her hand and knelt beside the king. The king was coughing even more now and he was having trouble breathing.

"Your Majesty. If you can stand, I can help get you out of here," Aiden said as he reached for the king's hand to help him up.

King Azar shook his head. "I will only slow you down," he coughed. "Make sure my daughter is safe, and then you can come back for me." The king broke into a fit of coughing, preventing him from saying anything else. He waved his hand at Aiden and pushed him away. "Go."

Aiden stood and took Amber's hand. "Let's go," he said.

Aiden gasped for fresh air once they reached the outside of the palace. The courtyard was a wild mess of people running back and forth from the water brigade with buckets both full and empty. Still holding Amber's hand, he led her away from the chaos to a secluded spot by the well. He turned and put his hands on her shoulders to let her know he was still there.

"Stay here. You should be out of the way and safe here. I need to help them, all right?" he asked as he briefly examined her, making sure she was unharmed.

Amber nodded but started coughing. Aiden looked around and saw a small bucket by the well. He ran to it and sank the dipper into the full bucket. Trying not to spill the water, he ran back to Amber and lifted her hand until her fingers touched it and helped guide it to her lips.

"Drink slowly," he said as he helped tip the ladle back. "Will you be okay for a little while?" he asked as he took the empty ladle from her.

Amber nodded and rasped out, "Yes. I will be fine."

Aiden ran to the middle of the courtyard and surveyed the crowd for his brother. He didn't see him anywhere.

"Coward," Aiden whispered under his breath.

He ran back towards the line of servants and looked for a couple of men. He found a footman and one of the kitchen boys.

"I need your help. The king is still inside. I couldn't get him out on my own," Aiden shouted over the noise.

The two men passed their buckets to the next people in line and ran with Aiden into the palace. Aiden led the way through the smoky hallways to the south tower. By the time they reached the king, he was unconscious. Aiden directed the men to get on either side of him as he grabbed the king's feet. On the count of three, they hoisted the king up in their arms and carried him out as quickly as they could. Once they got out of the palace, they took the king to a less crowded area and laid him down on the ground.

"Do you have a healer within the palace or in the town?" Aiden asked as he tried to catch his breath.

The kitchen boy nodded and replied, "Yes. Magdala is our healer. I will try to find her."

The boy stood up and started searching the frenzied crowd for the healer.

Aiden was anxious to get back to Amber and make sure she was all right. He looked at the footman.

"Can you find a servant girl to stay with the king so you can get back to the brigade?" Aiden asked.

The footman nodded and stood to find a servant girl. Aiden stood on his knees, searching the crowd for Amber. A hand on his arm startled him and caused him to look down. He was surprised to see that the king was somewhat conscious now. The king looked like he was trying to speak. Aiden leaned down so he could hear what the king needed to say.

"Get my daughter away from here and make sure she is safe." King Azar paused as he drew in a shallow breath.

"Keep her away from Am–," the king's words were cut off by a wheezing cough.

Aiden squeezed the king's hand. "I will keep her safe, I promise," he replied.

The king looked like he wanted to say more, but he was having trouble forming the words. He gestured for Aiden to lean closer.

"Phoenix tear," the king said, his words weak and thready, before he slipped back into unconsciousness.

"Phoenix tear? What does that mean?" Aiden asked as he looked down at the king.

The footman returned with a young servant girl at the same moment the kitchen boy returned with the healer. The healer knelt down beside the king and Aiden stood up to get out of her way. Reassured that the king was in good hands, Aiden looked around to make sure Amber was still in the same place. He spotted her across the courtyard where he had left her and ran towards her. As he did, a loud cracking noise sounded in the courtyard. Everyone stood back as one of the towers started to collapse. Aiden watched in horror as the tower fell into itself. He hoped that if Erick had been the cause of the fire that he was still close enough to see the damage he had done to the Summer king's palace. Luckily everyone was out, including the king.

Aiden turned back and made his way to Amber. Once he reached her, he knelt and gently placed his hand on hers. Amber flinched at his touch.

Aiden squeezed her hand to calm her. "It's alright. It's me."

Amber let out a relieved, yet shaky, breath. "What was that sound?" she asked.

Aiden looked back over his shoulder at the remaining splinters of beams that stuck out from where the collapsed tower had just stood as the palace continued to burn.

"One of the towers collapsed in on itself," he said as he turned back to look at her. He could feel her hand trembling beneath his. He took both of her hands in his and gently rubbed his thumbs along the backs of her hands, trying to comfort and calm her.

"Amber, we need to get out of here. Do you trust me to protect you and get you out of here safely?" he asked as he continued to rub her hands, hoping to instill trust in her and calm her nerves.

Amber nodded. Aiden stood and helped her up. He squeezed her hand and led the princess away from the roaring destruction of the fire.

CHAPTER 8

Amber woke up with a start the next morning. Something did not feel right. She started to push herself up to gauge where she was at, but her body was stiff and achy, making it difficult and painful to move.

"Are you alright?" she heard a masculine voice ask.

Amber lifted her head towards the voice. "Where am I?" she asked as she tried to sit up. She felt gentle hands on her shoulder and arm as they helped her sit up.

"We are not too far from the palace," the voice replied. "Do you remember anything from last night?"

Amber's brows creased as she tried to remember. The sense of intense heat came back to her and pricked her skin. Amber rubbed her arms at the sensation.

"Princess Amber, are you hurt?" the voice asked. The gentle hand moved to where she had rubbed her arm. "I couldn't tell if you had suffered any injuries from last night in the dark," the voice continued as the hand gently moved her arm and inspected it.

Injuries? Last night? The voice reignited her memory. She moved her head towards the voice beside her. "Aiden?" she asked as she reached out to feel where he was.

"Yes," he replied as he took her hand in his. "Do you remember what happened last night?" he asked again.

Amber shook her head. "I feel like something dangerous happened, but I'm not sure if what I'm remembering was from last night or from many years ago."

"There was a fire at your palace. Your father asked me to get you away from the fire and to safety, so I led you into the woods."

Amber let out a shuddery breath as she remembered how hot and smoky it had started getting in her room the night before. She hadn't known where the heat was coming from or how she would have gotten out of there on her own. A shiver shot down her spine causing her shoulders to shake slightly.

Aiden placed a warm hand on her shoulder and gave it a reassuring squeeze. "It's alright. You are safe now," he said.

Amber nodded and took in a shaky breath. She could hear Aiden moving beside her as his boots made noise on the leaves on the ground.

"We need to figure out something for food and what our next plan of action is," Aiden said.

"How far are we from the palace?" Amber asked.

"Maybe about a mile. I didn't want to go too far in the dark last night. I'm not familiar with this area and didn't want to get us lost somewhere," Aiden said as he looked around at the surrounding area.

"Which gate did we go out of?" she asked.

Aiden looked back at her. "The western gate, near the well, opposite of the stables."

Amber tried to conjure up a picture in her mind of the courtyard and the area surrounding the palace from her childhood. "If we left through the western gate and you said we are in the woods just outside the palace, then there should be a small creek somewhere nearby. I used to play in it all the time as a child."

Aiden shifted and looked around. He squeezed her hand to let her know he was still there before standing and walking a few feet away. He changed direction and went a few feet the other direction.

"There is a small creek just a little ways away in this direction," he said so she could hear him clearly. She heard him walking back towards her.

Amber nodded. "Okay. I think I have a pretty good idea of where we are. Do you think we should go back to the palace?" she asked.

She heard Aiden let out a small breath before he responded.

"I'm not sure what is left of the palace, to be honest. I don't even know if any of my stuff would be left to grab some money for food or if my horse is still there."

Amber's face fell. "The fire was that bad?" she asked.

"It was pretty bad," Aiden replied grimly.

She lifted her head towards him suddenly. "You said my father got out?"

"Yes, I went back in to get him and made sure he got out. He was trying to get you out, but a beam had fallen and blocked the door to your tower. He wanted me to get you out before I helped him get out."

Amber smiled in relief but then her brows quickly fell into a concerned crease again. "Is he well? What happened after you got him out?"

She felt Aiden shift beside her, and she could tell he was trying to figure out how to tell her something.

"He inhaled a lot of smoke. I sent a couple of men to find the healer to tend to him. He was conscious for a few moments, but then he slipped back into unconsciousness before the healer arrived."

"Did he say anything?"

"He asked me to get you out of there and make sure you are safe." Aiden paused.

"Anything else?" she prompted.

"He started to say something about keeping you away from someone or something, but his words were cut off by his coughing. He also said Phoenix tear," Aiden replied. He watched her reaction as he said it, trying to gauge if that meant anything to her.

"Does that phrase hold any significance for you or guidance on what we should do?" he asked after a brief silence.

Amber sat quietly for a few moments before she shook her head. "No. I don't know what that could mean. And who or what would my father want you to keep me from?" she asked. The lines of worry and confusion that creased her beautiful features were accentuated by the traces of soot on her face.

Aiden studied her for a moment. He wasn't convinced that she didn't know what it meant, but he decided that she didn't want to talk about it at this moment, so he let it go. He reached up and wiped some of the soot from her face. She jumped at first, not expecting him to touch her face.

"Sorry. You had some soot on your face. I was just trying to wipe it off and didn't even think about warning you that I was reaching out."

Amber touched her face where Aiden's hand had been. She cringed inwardly, only imagining how awful she must look after escaping a raging fire and sleeping in the forest all night. "What should we do now?" she asked as she wiped at her cheeks and chin too, hoping to make herself a little more presentable.

"I'm not sure," Aiden replied. "Your father said to get you out of the courtyard and tried to tell me to keep you away from someone or something, but I have no idea who or what or if he wanted us to return to the palace once the fire was put out."

His voice kept changing directions, so Amber guessed he was looking around as he talked to her. She sat there thinking for a moment.

"Do you have anywhere else you can go? A relative's house somewhere?" he asked.

Amber shook her head. "My cousins live in the Spring realm but I would have no idea how to get there. They haven't visited our realm in many years, so I don't even know if I would be welcome there. My father had an older brother, but he and his wife and children died a long time ago, making my father king. I have no idea what to do now." Her hands messed with a piece of grass she had plucked from the ground while she had been talking.

Aiden continued to look around the area as he tried to figure out what they could do. He turned back to her. "Let's go back to your palace since we are close. I can see what is left of it and how things stand. If things seem unsafe, I will take you back to my realm and we will try to figure out what to do from there. Does that sound like an agreeable plan?" he asked.

Amber nodded. "It seems like the only plan right now," she replied somberly.

"All right. Let's go." Aiden grabbed her hands and pulled her up and led her back to the palace gates.

CHAPTER 9

When they arrived back at the palace, Aiden led Amber through the gate near the well. He paused for a moment to make sure no one was in the courtyard. It was eerily quiet compared to the chaos that had filled it the night before. Everyone must still be in bed and trying to rest after the previous night's ordeal. He glanced up at the blackened skeletal beams that had been a stalwart tower just a day before and grimaced at the dismal sight. Some of the horses knickered or gave out soft whinnies from their stalls on the other side of the courtyard. At least the horses were still here.

Aiden squeezed Amber's hand and led her towards the stalls. He opened the door to the stall where his brown regal was stabled and left Amber near the wooden half-door while he quickly saddled his horse.

"Have you ever ridden a horse?" he asked as he finished tightening the strap.

"Not for a very long time," Amber replied as doubts about riding mixed with a sad longing in her face.

Aiden took her hand in his and gently placed it on the horse's nose. "This is Saleem," he said as he guided her hand up and down the horse's face.

Aiden's horse knickered softly and nudged Amber's hand.

"I think he likes me," she said with a smile that brightened her whole demeanor.

Aiden smiled at her reaction to his horse. "Stay here with him. If you hear footsteps, duck down. I'll let you know when it's me."

Amber nodded and kept stroking the horse in front of her as Aiden ducked out of the stall behind her. He stopped short and looked up at the palace in the dawning sun's light. A good portion of the southwest side of the castle had been burned and was now a bare bones blackened silhouette against the morning sky. Aiden's stomach dropped at the sight.

He quietly entered the palace, trying to avoid being seen by anyone who might possibly be up already, and made his way to his room. When he entered his room, he was relieved to see that it was mostly untouched by the fire, just a little singed in parts. Aiden stepped to the armoire and grabbed his saddlebag and the small bag of coins that he had kept hidden behind a wooden box on the floor of the large wardrobe. He grabbed two of his cloaks as well, one for him and one for Princess Amber, and left the room. As he left his room, Aiden thought about the king. If the king was conscious, maybe Aiden could get more information from him on what he wanted them to do.

He crossed over the main hallway that split into two different passageways and made his way down the other hall. He stopped when he heard voices a little further down the hall. Aiden ducked back into an alcove and stood there listening to the hushed voices.

"How is the king this morning, Magdala?" he heard a man whisper.

"He is still unconscious, my lord. I'm afraid he took in a lot of smoke last night. I've tended to the surface burns he had on his arm and leg, but other than caring for those and making sure he is comfortable, there is little else I can do," a woman whispered back.

Aiden peered out from the alcove to see who was speaking. He saw a man in a dark embroidered robe, much like the one the vizier wore. He also saw an older woman who looked like the healer from the night before. Two guards stood just beyond the healer and vizier.

"And there is still no sign of the princess or those two insolent boys from the Fallen realm?" the man asked the guards.

"No, my lord. The princess must have gotten out somehow because we didn't see any signs of her in the room after it stopped burning. Most of her tower is gone. And there have been no traces of the visiting prince or captain from the west since last night. We can only assume they left and returned to their realm."

The vizier returned his attention to the healer. "You may go, Magdala. Thank you for taking care of our king."

The woman curtseyed and walked towards Aiden, causing him to flatten himself against the wall of the alcove. He was relieved when the woman walked past him without even looking up.

The robed man watched the healer walk down the hall and made sure she was well out of earshot before turning back to the guards. He lowered his voice even further than it had been.

"I suspect our visitors had something to do with this. Their disappearance as well as that of our princess and the poor health of the king makes me wonder if they had been planning this all along. Put the kingdom on alert to be on the lookout for two men and a young woman with fiery red hair. Send some scouts to the Fall realm to see if they returned to their home with the princess. They tried to kill our king and kidnapped our princess, and for this, they must pay."

The robed man looked around and leaned in closer to the men. Aiden leaned out as far as he dared to try to hear what else he was going to say.

"And make sure the Phoenix gem is secure. If they have gained possession of that, we will have far bigger troubles to deal with than an ailing king and missing princess."

The guards nodded, bowed, and took off in the other direction down the hall. The robed man turned and walked towards Aiden. He flattened himself against the wall in the alcove and waited for the man to pass him by. Once the man was past him, Aiden left the alcove and headed in the direction of the guards.

He caught up with them not too far down the hall and followed them through a series of hallways that led to a small room covered with a mosaic of a Phoenix bird fighting against the people of the land. Aiden watched as the guards stepped up to the mosaic and ran their hands along the wall. One guard's hand landed on the crystal eye of the Phoenix while the other guard's hand landed on the head of one of the arrows that a king was holding. They nodded to each other and twisted the eye and the arrowhead at the same time. The mosaic started to move backwards and to the side, revealing a secret passageway beyond.

Aiden waited just outside the room until the guards were fully in the dark corridor behind the mosaic, then made a run for it, squeezing into the passageway before the door moved back in front of the entryway. He was met with instant darkness once the door fully closed behind him, causing him to stop suddenly. As Aiden's eyes adjusted, he saw a small orange glow in front of him. He went to take a step towards it and almost lost his footing, not realizing it stepped down. Aiden caught himself and grabbed onto the wall beside him to prevent himself from pitching down the stairs and alerting the guards to his presence.

Aiden carefully stuck his foot out in front of him and felt for the edge of the step. He made his way cautiously down the dimly lit spiral stone staircase. When he was almost at the bottom, he saw the guards opening a secure case. A brilliant gem that looked like it was on fire in the torchlight appeared in the case.

The other half of the Phoenix gem, he thought to himself.

Aiden suddenly realized the predicament he would be in once they re-secured the Phoenix gem. There was only one way in and out of this secret treasury, and Aiden was standing right in the way they would use to exit. He couldn't go back up the stairs because he didn't know how to trigger the door from this side and would be caught for sure if he did that. His only option seemed to be to figure out how to step further into the room without being noticed by them and hide out in there until they were gone. As he thought through his escape, the thought also crossed his mind of how probable it would be to get the other half of the gem. That would serve Erick right if Aiden was the one who ended up finding it and bringing it back to their father.

Aiden quietly fished in his saddlebag for something he could use. His hand landed on a coin. He pulled it out and threw it over the guards' heads. The coin landed with a metal clink on the stone floor, drawing the guards attention. Their hands went immediately to their swords as they stepped towards the alarming sound with their backs towards Aiden. A self-satisfied smile crossed Aiden's lips as he watched them cautiously investigate the sound. He fished out another coin and threw it a little to the right of them. As they moved towards it, Aiden stepped down off the final step and quietly inched towards the golden box that was still partially open.

He reached eagerly for the gem, but the guards turned around right at that moment and saw him. Aiden's hand hovered over the gem, his fingers itching to just grab it and run. The guards didn't give him a chance to grab it as they drew their swords and stepped towards him. One of the guards swung his sword at Aiden's head, forcing him to duck down, the sound of the sword clanking against the golden box reverberating above his head. A sharp pain stitched his side as he suddenly tumbled forward, feeling the impact of one of the guards kicking him away from the box. The blade of another sword struck the stone near his shoulder, almost skimming the fabric of his shirt. Aiden rolled over and desperately grasped at anything he could use to defend himself. His hand landed on a large gold bowl near his head, which he quickly picked up and used as a shield in front of his face as the other guard's sword came towards his face. The sword made contact with the bowl and Aiden was hard-pressed to keep the bowl from crushing his face beneath the weight of the sword. He grimaced and thrust his feet into the guard's stomach, pushing him back against the gold case that housed the gem. Aiden saw the stand the case sat on teeter and was afraid the gem would fall out and shatter. He stood up and swung the bowl forcefully at the head of the other guard, knocking the guard unconscious. He heard the other guard behind him and he turned just as the other guard started to throw himself at Aiden with his sword drawn and ready to strike. Aiden quickly stepped aside, causing the guard to trip over his fellow guard and sent him hurtling forward. The guard landed with a loud thump on the floor followed by the clanking sound of his sword hitting the ground.

Aiden stood still for a moment, catching his breath, and waited to see if either guard would move. When neither moved, he knelt and made sure they were both alive. Assured that they weren't dead, Aiden stood up and opened the golden doors that covered the fiery gem. He was relieved to see that it was still encased in the velvety cushion that lined the box. He quickly grabbed the gem and thrust it into his bag. Stepping over the guards, he made his way to the stairs and ran up the spiraling stone stairs.

At the top of the stairs, he searched frantically for a loose stone or something to release the door from this side. Not finding anything to trigger the door, he descended a few steps to where a torch sat on the wall. Aiden pulled down to grab it and heard the door unlatch. He let out a sigh of relief, but was urged back up the stairs by the sounds of the guards stirring below. He reached the top of the stairs and waited anxiously for the large piece of wall to move back so he could get through.

"Come on, come on, come on," Aiden muttered under his breath as he glanced over his shoulder for any sign of the guards.

The door finally opened enough so he could squeeze through. Aiden bolted from the little room and down the hall, hoping the door would close on the guards before they could get out and keep them from following him.

He made it out of the palace without being seen or followed and made a beeline for his horse. Aiden flung open the stable door, causing Amber to jump.

"It's me, Aiden. We need to get out of here."

Aiden tossed his saddlebag over the saddlehorn and practically threw Amber onto his horse. He pulled himself up behind her and urged Saleem into a quick getaway.

As they passed through the palace gates, he heard the vizier's voice ring out across the courtyard..

"Stop them. He is kidnapping the princess!"

Aiden didn't look back. He just urged his horse faster and faster into the woods.

CHAPTER 10

Aiden rode hard and fast most of the day. They stopped for a rest around noon. He wished he would have grabbed some food before they left, but his unexpected plan prevented him from getting that far. After they had rested a bit and drank their fill from the stream, Aiden put Amber back on the horse, and they kept riding. He knew there wasn't much in the way of water between the border and the Fallen kingdom, so he stopped shortly before they crossed into the Fall realm just as the sun was beginning its descent. He hoped they had ridden far enough away from the Summer palace to be safe in the onsetting darkness for the night. Even if the guards were close, if the sun set quick enough, they would have to stop for the night as well, and Aiden and Amber could get some rest. He pulled a weary Amber off of his horse and set her on the ground. He found a relatively soft spot and helped her sit before leading his horse to the stream to drink.

Amber felt around to see where Aiden had placed her. "Where are we?" she asked as her hand transitioned from soft plants to rough tree bark not far from her.

"We aren't far from the Fall realm. There's a stream where we can get some water."

Amber's stomach growled. She quickly put her hands to her stomach to quiet the embarrassing noise.

Aiden smiled. "Unfortunately, I didn't have time to grab any food before we left."

Amber lifted her head in the direction of his voice. "Yes, we did leave in quite the hurry, didn't we?" she replied. "Are you going to tell me what happened?" she asked.

Aiden studied her, unsure of how much he should share.

"Are you okay to stay here by yourself while I look for something to eat?" he asked instead of answering her question.

Amber nodded and stayed seated where Aiden had placed her. She heard his boots move across the forest floor away from her.

"I suppose that's a no," she said to herself.

Amber sat silently for a few minutes, trying to distinguish the sounds and smells around her. She smelled pine trees and heard the small trickle of water nearby. That must be the stream Aiden had mentioned. Amber was as thirsty as she was hungry. She wondered if she could find her way to the stream and take a drink. It didn't sound too far away. She put out her hand to find the tree her hand had bumped into earlier. She found it and cautiously put both of her hands on it to pull herself up. She hugged the tree and reached out her other hand to try to find another tree near her. She took a step away from the tree and stretched her hand out further until she felt another tree. She smiled. She continued this way until it sounded like the stream was beside her. She held onto the last tree and inched her foot out as far as she could to see if she could tell where the edge of the stream was. Frustrated that she couldn't find it, Amber carefully lowered herself down to the ground and crawled slowly toward the sound of the water.

She reached out in front of her but stopped when she heard Aiden's horse neigh softly beside her. She felt the horse's head nudge her side and bite at her dress. Amber reached back and touched the soft nose of the horse and stood up.

"It's alright, Saleem," Amber cooed. "Was I too close to the water?"

Amber rubbed the face of the gentle horse and inched her foot out slightly until she felt a splash of water hit her slipper.

"Oh!" she exclaimed. "I was pretty close, wasn't I? I might have tipped in head first if you hadn't stopped me." Amber touched her head to the horse's head. "Thank you for protecting me, boy."

Amber felt for the horse's reins, grabbed hold of them with one hand, and dropped straight down to the ground. "Now, if I hold onto your reins and stay back, will I be safe to get a drink?"

Saleem knickered softly and nudged her arm gently.

Amber smiled, "Okay."

She leaned out slowly and reached her other hand down until she felt cold water. She leaned down to take a drink.

"Amber!" Aiden exclaimed as he ran towards her. Aiden's horse whinnied and danced around at the sudden outburst and almost knocked Amber into the stream. Aiden grabbed for her and pulled her back just as she felt herself lurch forward.

Amber pushed back at Aiden. "What are you doing?" she asked as she tried to get away from him.

"You could have Fallen into the water," Aiden replied as he tried to contain her flailing arms.

"I was perfectly fine until you scared Saleem. He was watching over me."

"Hold on. Calm down. You're going to hurt yourself." Aiden grasped for Amber's hands and tried to stop them from flying all over the place.

"I'm fine," Amber shouted as she broke free of Aiden's grip. She stepped to the right and found a tree. She reached out in the direction she thought Aiden had left her earlier and took a step forward, tripping and falling flat on her face.

Aiden helped her up and started to guide her the other direction but Amber pushed his hands away.

"I can do it," she said defiantly. She stood there for a moment, trying to figure out her bearings. "Just put me in the right direction, and I'll be fine."

Aiden led Amber a couple steps to the right and let her feel the tree beside her. "Now, just walk forward a few trees, and you'll be back where I left you," Aiden said, a slight hint of anger and irritation in his voice.

Amber felt her way back to where she had been sitting while Aiden went to pick up the logs he had dropped. Amber sat down on the ground and listened. She heard footsteps walk away and stop, then she heard something rub against leather. After a few moments the footsteps came back towards her.

"Here," Aiden said sharply as he grabbed her hand and put something hard and round in it. "It's a canteen full of water from the stream." He guided her hand to the top where the open mouth piece was.

Amber lifted it to her mouth and put the mouthpiece to her lips and tipped it back carefully. She took a long drink and finally lowered it.

"I'm sorry about my outburst. I'm not used to having someone there to actually help me or guide me. Most of the time I explore on my own and find where things are at or figure out how to get from place to place on my own."

Aiden let out a frustrated breath. She could hear him stacking something and striking two objects together nearby.

"That is in a protected palace. You probably can't do much that will get you hurt in that environment. Here, we are out in the woods. You have no idea where things are at or if there is something dangerous in your path."

"I could hear the stream nearby and thought I could get to it on my own. Saleem pulled me back when I was too close. And I was fine until you came back and scared Saleem. I was holding his reins and leaned over just far enough to feel the water."

Aiden sighed and came to kneel beside her. "I just don't want anything to happen to you. Your father trusted me to protect you. I get that you are comfortable around the palace and have figured out how to do things and get around on your own, but out here, there are things I may not even see—snakes hiding in the grass; wolves waiting in the shadows to pounce. There could be any number of places you could fall into, and I don't want you to end up in dangerous situations. At least, not when I'm not around to save you." He finished the last sentence with a slight smile as he squeezed her hands in his.

Amber gave him a small smile in a response, but felt slightly defeated at being reprimanded by him.

"I found some berries that will have to make due for food for now," Aiden said as he stood up and walked away from her again.

He came back and placed some berries in her hands. Amber felt some warmth coming from in front of her. She turned her face towards it and smiled.

"I love the warmth of a fire," she said as she ate a few of the berries.

"We sometimes have large bonfires to celebrate the harvest," Aiden said as he leaned back against a tree not too far from her. "We would play games and sometimes create a maze with the remaining corn stalks before we finished harvesting it."

Amber's smile widened. "That sounds like fun. Do you still do that?"

"No. We haven't for a long time. Our land has been in a drought for many years. I wish I could figure out a way to end it and bring back the harvest."

"I'm sure you will figure it out."

"I hope so. Do you have any Summer celebrations?"

"I don't know," Amber replied, a little sadness in her voice. "My father is afraid of me getting hurt, just like you are. Since I lost my sight, I've always been kept in my room, so I don't know if we have celebrations or not. I can hear the villagers celebrating sometimes though. Their music filters into my window and I can hear their laughter and imagine the fun they must be having," she said wistfully. "Even if I can't join them, I love to sit at my window and listen to the music."

Aiden sat and thought for a moment. He stood up and walked over to Saleem and pulled his violin from his saddlebag.

"I was able to save one thing," he said as he sat down. He plucked a couple of the strings.

Amber's head perked up. "What was that," she asked with enthused curiosity.

"My violin. My brother always cuts me down for carrying it with me everywhere, but I can't imagine being without it."

"Will you play for me?" she asked as she leaned closer.

Aiden bit his lip.

"I'm sure we are far enough away from anyone who would hear us," Amber said. "Please, even if you play quietly, I would enjoy it immensely."

Aiden shook his head and smiled. "Alright. But if we get caught, I'm blaming you."

He plucked a few strings to see if it was in tune and then started to play. He played a beautiful melody that made Amber think of a beautiful landscape. It almost sounded like the song of a sweet magical bird. Amber began to hum along and sing with Aiden as he played.

As Aiden ended, there was an ethereal silence in the woods around them. Aiden looked over at her and smiled. "I knew the music I had heard at the palace was you. You have such a hauntingly beautiful voice."

Amber smiled. "Thank you. But, when would you have actually heard me singing? You said you only heard me humming the day you arrived, and I never sang while we were in the library together."

"I heard it as you passed my door on the way to the library those two nights."

Amber's brows pinched together in confusion. "What do you mean? I wasn't singing when I went to the library those nights."

Aiden's forehead creased with confusion. "That's strange. Something woke me up the first night, and when I opened my door, I saw you running past it."

"That is strange. Wait. Do you hear it now?" she asked as she sat still, trying to listen.

Aiden sat quietly. "No. But now you hear something?"

"Yes." Amber reached out her hands. "Can you help me up?"

Aiden set down his violin and stood up. He pulled Amber up beside him.

"It's coming from over here," Amber said as she took a step forward.

Aiden stood beside her, making sure she didn't step anywhere she shouldn't. She walked towards the saddlebag that still sat on the horn of the saddle. She reached out and touched it.

"May I open it?" she asked as she looked back in his direction.

"Sure," Aiden replied, curious about what she thought she heard coming from his bag.

Amber lifted the cover and felt inside. Her fingers brushed something smooth and hard. She reached in with both hands and pulled out the interesting object.

"What is this?" she asked as she turned back towards Aiden.

Aiden's eyes widened at what she was holding.

"That's the Phoenix gem. Part of it anyway. Do you know anything about it?" he asked as he watched her handling it.

Amber shook her head. She moved it from hand to hand and ran her fingers along it, trying to figure out its shape. "Describe it to me?"

"It's kind of an odd shape. I believe it is half of the full gem. Legend says it used to glow with the fire of the Phoenix. It was forged by the flame of two lover's hearts, but fate kept them apart, causing the flaming heart to break. The flame dimmed and has never shown as brightly since."

"How tragic," Amber replied. "If it was supposed to contain the Phoenix flame, does it glow like a normal fire?"

"It's red and dull with some orange streaks. It's not as bright as a roaring fire. It looks more like a dying ember that won't go out."

Aiden stepped closer and put his hand around hers as she held it. When he did, the gem began to glow.

"Ouch!" Amber exclaimed as she dropped the gem. "It certainly felt like a real fire and not a dying ember."

"It lit up when I touched your hands. I'm sorry. Did it burn you?" Aiden asked as he looked at her hands.

"No, I think it just shocked me."

Amber knelt down to find the gem. She found it and picked it up. A memory flashed through her mind as she did. She let out a small gasp and dropped it again.

"What happened?" Aiden asked as he knelt beside her.

"I saw something when I touched it," Amber replied as she sat there stunned by what had happened.

Aiden tried to look at her face. "What? Like you saw something with your eyes?"

Amber shook her head. "No. It was more like a memory." She felt for the gem again and cautiously picked it up. She held it in both of her hands and let the memory play out.

"What do you see?" Aiden asked as he watched her face.

"I think it's my mother," she smiled. "She is chasing me around my room before bed. She caught me and is hugging me close. She is carrying me over to my bed and tucking me in. And now, she's singing:

> *The Phoenix takes flight to meet an old friend,*
> *For he knows his journey is nearing an end.*
> *He leaves a precious treasure behind–*
> *A gift that will forever remind.*
>
> *He flies high over painted sands*
> *To a place where his healing tear forever will last.*
> *He cries one last tear and takes to the sky*
> *And watches the world go flying by.*

His journey ends and he builds his nest,
filling it with spices and twigs for a final rest.
He gives himself willingly, and says goodbye to the earth,
And bursts forth again in a fiery rebirth

Amber stopped and let go of the gem. She put her hand to her head. "Are you alright?" Aiden asked.

Amber nodded. "Just lightheaded from the long journey, I believe."

"That was a beautiful song," Aiden said as he thought back over the words. His head cocked to one side as one of the phrases stood out to him. "'To a place where his healing tear forever will last.' Do you think that is talking about the Phoenix tear your father mentioned?" he asked.

Amber shook her head. "I'm not sure. I had forgotten about that memory and the song that my mother used to sing to me all the time. Who knows if it actually means anything. It was probably just a song she sang to me to get me to sleep. She knew I always loved the story about the Phoenix."

Amber yawned and Aiden could tell she was getting sleepy.

"Whatever it is, it's getting late. We should get some sleep. Maybe my father will have more answers when we reach my palace," Aiden said as he stood up.

Amber reached for his hand. She felt it and held the gem out to him.

"Keep this safe for the night."

Aiden nodded, then cringed, realizing she couldn't see him nodding. "Of course," he replied.

He pulled her up and walked her closer to the fire. He helped her sit down and went back to his saddlebag. He carefully placed the gem in the bag and pulled out the cloaks he had grabbed. He walked over to where Amber was laying down and gently placed the cloak over her.

"In case you get cold during the night."

"Thank you," she replied as she pulled it tighter around her shoulders. She heard Aiden shuffling around but she couldn't tell where he was.

"Aiden?" Amber asked as she lifted her head off the ground.

"Yes?"

"I just wanted to know where you were."

"I'm just on the other side of the fire. Don't worry. I'll be here all night to protect you."

Amber nodded and laid her head back down. "Good night, Aiden."

"Good night, Amber."

CHAPTER 11

Aiden woke up the next morning as the sun was starting to rise. He looked over and saw Amber sound asleep. She looked so peaceful, he hated to wake her, but he knew they should get going before the Summer guards found them. He stood up and stepped to where she lay, kneeling down to wake her. The dim morning light reached some of her features. He hadn't really had a chance to look at her since meeting her. Most of their time together had been spent in shadows and on the run. He took in her ivory skin, as of yet, hardly touched by the sun. Her eyelashes lay gently over her cheeks like delicate feathers. He gently brushed a fiery red strand of hair from her face. The movement caused her to stir. He pulled back his hand and gently shook her shoulder.

"Amber. Wake up. We should get going."

Amber's eyelashes fluttered against her skin as she slowly woke up. She moaned. "Five more minutes."

Aiden smiled. "Come on, sleepyhead. No time for lazing around."

He stood and went to check on Saleem. Amber let out a few more moans in protest, but begrudgingly pushed herself up. After stretching her arms above her head and yawning, she reached out her arms on either side of her and turned her head side to side to try to feel where she was at. She couldn't feel anything in the near vicinity, making it hard to know exactly where she was in relation to the dying fire and the trees.

"Can you help me up?" she asked as she reached out her hands. "I'm not always the most cognizant in the mornings, and my bearings are off since I'm not in my familiar room."

Aiden finished tightening the saddle on Saleem and made sure the saddlebag was secure. He went over to her, reached down and pulled her up. As he did, she stumbled forward into him. He looked into her eyes and wondered what they must have been like before she lost her sight. As he took in her features, the sun's rising rays flicked off of something bright red behind her. His eyes grew wide as he saw her fiery red hair now lying on the ground a little past her feet.

Amber could sense Aiden's shift in posture and felt his body tense.

"What's wrong?" she asked as her unseeing eyes lifted in the direction of his face.

His grip tightened slightly on her shoulders.

"Aiden?"

"Uh, I'm not sure how to say this, but your hair seems to have grown overnight."

Amber's nose crinkled up. "Grown? What do you mean?" she asked as she removed her hand from his chest and reached up to touch her hair.

Aiden pulled her down to a kneeling position, took her hands, and guided them to the long tresses behind her. Amber's hands pulled back at the unexpected length of her hair. She tentatively touched it and tried to feel how long it was.

"What on earth?" she asked as her fingers tried to ascertain what had happened.

"Didn't you feel a little spark or something when you were holding the Phoenix gem last night?" Aiden asked as he stared at her long, red hair.

Amber nodded slowly. "Yes. Do you think that is what caused my hair to grow like this?"

"I don't know. I can't imagine hair growth is a part of the Phoenix gem's powers, but I don't know what else it could be. I've never seen anything like it before," he said incredulously.

Amber's stomach growled. She clenched her hand over her stomach, hoping Aiden hadn't heard it.

Aiden smiled. "I should see if I can find some more berries or something to tide us over until we reach my palace. Will you be alright here for a few moments by yourself?" he asked.

Amber nodded. She sensed Aiden stand in front of her and move away from her.

He paused. "Don't try to get your own water again. I don't need you falling into the stream or getting swept away in a current," he said with a mock scolding in his voice.

Amber rolled her eyes and smiled. "As you wish," she replied sardonically.

She reached her hands up to the back of her neck and pulled as much of the long hair over her shoulder as she could feel. She began weaving strands into a braid to hopefully make it easier to travel with. By the time Aiden returned, she had almost finished braiding the long strands together.

"I could only find more berries. Sorry it's such a meager meal," Aiden said as he knelt beside her. He placed the berries in her hand and stood to fill the canteen with water. He brought it over to her and let her drink.

"We should get going," he said after he refilled the canteen and kicked some dirt onto the fire to make sure it was out completely before leaving the area.

Amber popped the remaining berries in her hand into her mouth and stood up. She was slightly off-balance with the new length of her hair and the fullness of the braid on one side of her body. Aiden caught her before she fell and held her up.

"Well, this is going to take some getting used to," she said as she held onto his forearms.

"Do you think you can stay on the horse with your hair that long?" Aiden asked with a slight laugh.

Amber smiled up at him. "I hope so."

"Let's give it a try, shall we?" Aiden led Amber to where Saleem stood by the stream. "Grab your braid so it doesn't catch on anything."

Amber slung the thick braid over the crook of her elbow so she could keep it close as Aiden hoisted her into the saddle. She held onto the saddlehorn as she waited for Aiden to mount behind her.

"Well, I'm on. Hopefully I can stay on," she said.

"Let's hope so," Aiden replied as he pulled himself up behind her. He wrapped his arms around her again, grabbed the reins and took off, crossing into the Fall realm.

Aiden and Amber rode through the Fall realm all morning and arrived in the outskirts of the kingdom of Havilah shortly after noon. Aiden stopped just outside the palace gates near the village. He dismounted and helped Amber down.

"Are we here?" she asked as he pulled her off the horse.

"We are near the palace but not within its gates," Aiden replied as he pulled his saddlebag from the horn of the saddle. "Stay here with Saleem. I'm going to find some food in the village. I'll be back shortly." He pulled one of the cloaks out of his bag and put it on, pulling the hood up over his face to avoid being recognized.

Amber remaine next to Saleem and stroked the horse's nose while she waited for Aiden to return. She soon heard footsteps approaching and her nose perked up at the smell of something baked and fresh. Aiden took her hand and gave her something warm. She bent her head down and smelled it.

"Mmm," she said as she took in the delectable aroma. "This smells amazing."

"The baker had just pulled a batch of breakfast rolls from the oven and I couldn't resist. He usually puts cheese, sausage, and chives in them. I used to sneak out to the village to get one when I was a child," Aiden said as he pulled another roll from his bag for himself.

Amber smiled and took a bite of the savory bread.

"I need to check on some things before I bring you into the palace," Aiden said around a bite of his breakfast roll.

Amber stopped eating for a moment. "You mean your father and brother might not take kindly to finding out you kidnapped the princess of the Summer realm?" she asked with a joking tone.

"You came quite willingly, might I remind you, but yes. My brother and father can be a little high strung, and I'm not sure where things lie with your realm at present. Do you feel safe being on your own out here?" he asked as he finished the pastry.

Amber nodded as she finished her pastry. "I probably won't go exploring or anything, but I'm sure Saleem will keep me safe," she said with a playful smile.

"I'm sure he will," Aiden said with a smile. He untied Saleem from the post and took the reins in one hand while taking her hand in the other. "Come on. I'll get you out of the main thoroughfare and off by yourself."

He took her down a side path that led into a more deserted area of the village just outside the walls of the Fall palace. He tied Saleem to a tree and made sure she knew where the horse was.

"I will be back. Stay here and don't talk to anyone." Aiden looked at her bright red hair that stood out like a field of poppies against the brown landscape of the village. He pulled the other cloak from his bag and placed it around her shoulders, pulling the hood up over her hair to cover it.

"Is my hair that noticeable?" she asked as she readjusted the large hood on her head.

"No. Not at all. I just know our air can get a little crisp at times, so I wanted to make sure you stayed warm."

Amber raised an eyebrow. "Right," she responded with a cynical tone in her voice that told him she didn't believe him for one second.

"You can see right through anything can't you?" he asked with reverent admiration as he finished adjusting the large cloak that engulfed her.

Amber smiled. "I can see what most people can't because I pay attention to more than just what our eyes tell us."

"Well, now I know not to try to hide anything from you," Aiden smiled. He reached into his bag and pulled out a small bundle. "I got a few more pastries and some cheese. Eat what you want," he said as he placed the extra food in her hands.

"Thank you," Amber said as she accepted what Aiden handed her..

Aiden gazed at her for a moment. "Are you sure you will be alright on your own out here?" he asked as he tucked a stray red curl into the hood of the cloak.

Amber's temple tingled at the touch of Aiden's hand brushing the stray hair from her face, causing an unexpected shiver to run through her. Aiden stopped.

"Are you cold? You can have my other cloak as well if you need it," he said as he began to undo his cloak.

Amber reached out a hand to stop him. "No. I'm fine. Really."

Aiden studied her for a moment to make sure she was truly fine. "Alright. I'll be back soon," he said as he tied his cloak again.

Amber nodded. "Be careful," she said as she lifted her head in the direction of his voice.

Aiden smiled at her concern for him. He should be more concerned about her since she couldn't see, and yet, here she was telling him to be careful.

He gripped her hand in his. "You too. I'll be back."

Aiden's hand lingered on hers for a moment before he let go and turned to leave.

Amber felt a slight flutter in her heart as his hand lingered on hers and felt her cheeks heat after he walked away. She was experiencing all kinds of new feelings and emotions since meeting the young prince from the Fall realm and she would be lying to herself if some of her thoughts weren't starting to revolve around their potential marriage. She clenched her hand to her stomach at the thought and wondered if Aiden felt the same.

Chapter 12

Aiden entered his father's palace. He looked up at the familiar flags that hung all around the cylindrical entryway. The black flags bore the crimson crest his father had vainly created for himself when he usurped the throne: a hawk stepping on a serpent. He thought he was invincible. Never mind if the snake is poisonous and could bite the leg of the hawk. Just like his father to pick a crest like that.

Thinking about how volatile his father could be, doubts about bringing Amber here crept into his mind, but he had no idea of where else to go. He was glad he had at least left her outside for now instead of outright springing her on his father. His eyes roved around the tiled entry looking for a servant so he could find out where his father and brother were, but no one seemed to be around.

The steward stepped into the grand hall as Aiden was pulling off his cloak.

"Hamlin. Good to see you. I was beginning to wonder if the servants had been given the day off," Aiden said with a wry tone in his voice.

The faithful steward gave him a satirical glance as he stepped towards him. "That would be a miracle, wouldn't it, Your Highness?" he said with a tone that matched Aiden's.

They exchanged knowing smiles.

"Welcome back, Your Highness. We were worried about you when you didn't return with Sir Erick. He said the Summer palace caught on fire. Are you alright?"

Hamlin reached out to take Aiden's cloak and saddlebag.

Aiden tightened his grip on the bag and put up his hand to stop the steward from taking it. "Thank you, Hamlin. I'll hold onto my bag and cloak for now. Where are my father and Sir Erick?"

"They are in the library, Your Highness. Can I get you anything? I can have the cook prepare a meal for you."

"No, thank you, Hamlin."

"Very good, Your Highness," Hamlin said with a smile and a slight bow before returning to the servant's wing of the palace.

Aiden opened the wooden door that led to their poor excuse for a library, especially after he had seen the one in the Summer palace. Much of the library had been destroyed when his father had sieged the palace and overthrown the king, so there weren't many books left. It was a small, dark room that his father had never seen the need to repair once he had taken control. Aiden's nursemaid had mentioned on more than one occasion how much his mother loved to read, and had saved some of his mother's favorite books before the siege. The beloved nursemaid would read them to Aiden as many times as he would ask her to and had given them to Aiden before she died a few years ago. He cherished those books almost as much as he cherished his violin. He had always loved and appreciated her for stepping in and being as much of a mother to him as she could since his mother had died giving birth to him. Come to think of it, she had been the closest thing to a mother he had ever experienced. How he wished for the comforting embrace of his nursemaid, or better yet, his mother, right now. Either one of them would know what to do in this situation, and he would much rather talk with them about it instead of the ominous Lord Ragnar.

Lord Ragnar and Erick glanced up from what looked like an old map when Aiden entered.

"Ah, the prodigal returns at last. We thought you had sold your loyalties to the crown of the Summer realm when you didn't return right away," Erick said derisively as his brother stepped into the room.

"I had to stay and make sure the king and the princess were safe after your little accident. I'm sure killing the king and princess would not have boded well for our kingdom," Aiden replied tersely.

Lord Ragnar looked at Erick. "You didn't tell me you started the fire," the king said coarsely.

Erick's shoulders slacked, and he looked slightly uncomfortable under their father's menacing gaze. Aiden smirked. At least someone intimidated his brother.

"I didn't start the fire," Erick replied defensively. "I was searching one of the lower rooms for the Phoenix gem, and all of a sudden, the room was filled with flames and smoke. I got out of there as quickly as I could so they wouldn't blame me for starting it. I don't know how or where it started."

Aiden covered his saddlebag with his hand at Erick's mention of the Phoenix gem. He wondered if he should tell them he found it.

Lord Ragnar gave his eldest son a severe look before turning his cold stare on Aiden.

"And what took you so long to return home?" the king asked as he glowered at his youngest son.

Now it was Aiden's turn to shrink under their father's unrelenting disapproval. "I– I told you. I had to make sure the king and princess were alive and well to prevent scandal or anything not above board."

"And are they alive and well?" his father asked coldly.

"Yes. They at least got out of the palace before a good portion of it burned. The king had been trapped in one of the hallways and took in a lot of smoke. He was still unconscious when I left. The princess–" Aiden stopped before he finished divulging the information of her whereabouts. "The princess is safe," he finished abruptly.

Lord Ragnar looked between his two sons. "You both better hope this doesn't start a war between our two realms. I sent you there to make an alliance, and you leave the palace half-burned and the king unconscious. And without the Phoenix gem besides. We can't afford to start a war at this time. Especially not without our half of the gem in our midst."

Ragnar turned his attention back to the maps that lay spread out on the table. Aiden stepped towards the table to look at the maps.

"We may need to set up defenses here and here," Lord Ragnar said as he pointed to two areas on the map of the realms. "If the Winter and Spring realms catch wind of what just happened, they could join forces with the Summer realm and attack."

Aiden leaned over the table to look at the places his father was pointing out. As he did, a strange orange glow lit up the corner of the map nearest him. Aiden pulled back to get a better look, but when he did, the glow disappeared. He leaned close again, and it started to glow. Aiden reached down and touched his bag where the gem was secured. It was slightly warm. He wondered if the gem was causing the map to illuminate somehow. He leaned back again, and the orange glow disappeared. That had to be it.

Erick pointed to an area near the middle of the Summer realm where the gem had just been illuminating part of the map. Aiden stepped back to keep the gem from causing the map to glow.

"I received word this morning that some of my men have tracked the thief that stole our gem to this region," Erick said as he drew a circle with his finger around a desolate, barren part of the Summer realm. "I will dispatch more men to go and help them."

Their father nodded. "Yes. And while they are apprehending the thief, you return to the Summer realm and see if you can find their gem. It might be easier now since some of the palace is burned and the king is out of the way, at least for now. Take a peace offering and tell them we wish to help them rebuild. Offer them the use of the cedar trees at the edge of our realm to help with the supplies."

"Yes, sir," Erick replied.

"My Lord," one of the soldiers burst into the room. "The captain of the Summer realm's guard has requested an audience with you. They believe the young prince kidnapped the princess and brought her here, and they've come to search for her and take her back."

Lord Ragnar shot a piercing look at Aiden. He nodded to the soldier. "Tell the captain to wait in the throne room. We will be there shortly."

The soldier bowed and left the room. Lord Ragnar and Erick both stared at Aiden.

"Did you take the princess with you when you left the Summer realm?" Ragnar asked gruffly, subtle anger lacing his voice.

"No, of course not. Why would I do that? I made sure she was safe and outside the palace, and then I grabbed my horse and made my way home. I didn't know what else to do since Erick had left me there to deal with a burning palace and endangered king," Aiden replied as he shot a defensive glance at his brother.

"I told you to come with me when I was getting ready to leave," Erick said in a low, gruff voice. "Why did you feel you needed to stick around? Surely, if neither of us were there, they couldn't blame us for anything that happened."

Erick widened his arms and planted his fists on the table, making himself look wider than he was and more intimidating. Aiden resisted rolling his eyes at his brother's inflated stance.

"Or they would cast more blame on us for fleeing in the midst of tragedy, which is what they will believe happened," Aiden replied angrily as he leaned across the table, matching Erick's menacing eyes stare for stare. He caught the slight glow of the map out of the corner of his eye and pulled back slightly. Erick smirked, thinking he had intimidated his little brother once again.

"Erick. Come with me. We will tell the captain that we do not know the whereabouts of the princess but will gladly aid in their search. You will go back with them. Use this as the opportunity to search the palace for the other half of the gem."

"And you." Aiden's father stared down at him from across the table. "You've caused enough trouble. You will stay here and help me figure out how to defend our land. It's about time you took your future duties as king seriously and learned the ways of a ruler."

"Yes, Your *Majesty*." Aiden said the word tersely and folded his arms over his chest.

Lord Ragnar's eyes narrowed at the mock title Aiden had used. He turned to Erick. "Come. We must take care of this before it gets even further out of hand."

Erick and Lord Ragnar left the room.

Aiden let out an angry grunt and banged his fists on the table. The corner of the map glowed again as he leaned over it. Making sure his father and brother were completely out of the room, Aiden carefully pulled the Phoenix gem from his bag and held it over the map. It glowed in a line that led from the Fall realm to the Summer realm. Aiden traced the line back to the origin and saw that it landed on their palace. His eyes widened.

"That must be the other half of the gem," he breathed out softly.

Aiden carefully folded the map and it and the gem back in his bag. His eyes shot up from his bag.

"Amber!" he exclaimed to himself as he sprinted from the room.

CHAPTER 13

Amber heard the pound of horses' hooves approaching on what sounded like some sort of stone pavement. She stood up from where she had been sitting against the wall and stepped to where Aiden had left Saleem. She stroked the horse's nose as she leaned in to to hear what all the commotion was on the other side of the wall.

"We wish to speak with Lord Ragnar immediately," a man said.

"Cassias?" she whispered under her breath.

"Who is demanding an appointment with the ruler of the Fall realm?" she heard another voice ask.

"Tell him Captain Cassias of the Summer realm's guard. The princess has gone missing, and we believe the ruler's son may have taken her."

Amber gasped. "Oh no," she whispered to herself. "They think Aiden kidnapped me."

Saleem sensed her nervousness and knickered softly while shifting his feet back and forth.

"Come with me," the other man responded.

She heard footsteps clicking against stone before dying away.

"Psst."

Amber turned at the strange sound behind her.

"Psst."

There it was again. Amber turned her head side to side trying to distinguish where the sound was coming from. She pulled back the hood so she could hear better.

"Psst. Miss. You shouldn't be here."

Amber turned her head towards the sound of a whispered voice.

"Who's there?" she asked.

"Shhh. Quiet. They'll hear you. Come on. You shouldn't be out in the open like this."

"What do you want? What do you mean I shouldn't be out in the open like this?" Amber asked, trying to figure out if the voice belonged to a man or woman. It was so gravelly, she couldn't tell through the whispered tones.

"Come on," the voice said urgently.

Amber felt a strange hand on hers, causing her to draw back.

"Who are you?" she asked, desperation and fear growing within her.

She pulled her hand back, but the person gripped it tighter. The hand felt bony and leathery, and the distance of the person's voice from her made Amber think they must be rather short as well. Perhaps the person was older and maybe hunched over or shrunk.

"Amber."

"Aiden," Amber replied with a sigh of relief.

Aiden saw an old woman holding onto Amber when he rounded the corner of the palace wall.

"Hey! Get away from her," he shouted as the old woman tugged at Amber's arm.

Amber pulled her hand out of the old woman's grasp and held it out to him. He went to her and took her hand, letting her know he was there.

"Have you no brains in your head, boy?" the old woman scolded as she swatted at his leg. "Do you want to alert her guards that she's here? Come. Come. We have to get the two of you out of the open air where everyone can see you."

The old woman turned and started to walk away from them.

Aiden watched the old woman, beyond confused as to why she was so concerned about them being out in the open and why she wanted them to follow her.

He heard some of the Summer soldiers on the other side of the wall. "Cassius said to search the village while he is inside with the Fall realm's ruler. They might have hidden her somewhere outside of the palace."

"Come on," the old woman urged, gesturing with both hands for them to follow her.

Aiden looked at Amber. "Should we follow her?" he asked.

Amber's brows creased. "I'm not sure, but if my father's soldiers are searching the village for me, it might be our best option right now."

Aiden looked over his shoulder and glimpsed one of the red-clad soldiers. "Alright. Come on." Aiden squeezed Amber's hand and led her towards the old woman.

After walking for a few minutes, the old woman led them to a small cottage that was set back from the village amidst the sparsely leafed trees in the forest. The woman opened the door and beckoned for them to follow. Aiden led Amber into the small cottage. It was dimly lit and smelled of strange herbs and spices. Amber's nose crinkled up at the strange smells.

"Where are we?" she asked quietly.

"I'm not sure. It almost looks like an old witch's cottage from one of the fairy tale stories my nursemaid used to read to me," Aiden whispered back.

The old woman turned abruptly to face them and said in a high-pitched, screechy voice, "Well, I'm glad I got you two out of sight of prying eyes before anyone spotted you. I sensed you were coming and knew I had to get to you before anyone saw you."

She turned towards a small kitchen area and busied herself getting tins down off of shelves and opening them to see which tea she wanted to serve. "Please, sit. Sit. Make yourselves at home. You must be tired after your long journey," the woman said as she pulled down a tea pot and some cups. She bustled around and poured some water from a bucket into a large pot and put it over the fire.

Aiden looked around the small, closed-in cottage and spotted some chairs just behind them. "Would you like to sit down?" he asked as he led Amber to one of the chairs.

"I guess we should. Who knows what she would say if we didn't," Amber replied with a sweet chuckle.

Aiden smiled. "It's right behind you," he said as Amber reached down to see where the chair was.

"What is she like?" Amber asked as she sat down.

Aiden sat down beside her and looked over at the old woman, who was now humming and putting together some sort of stew.

"She's shorter, looks slightly hunched over, and old. Her hair is white and gray and curly and sticks out all over, kind of like a hedgehog," Aiden whispered so the old woman wouldn't hear.

Amber smiled at Aiden's description and tried to imagine what the old woman looked like. The picture in her head was quite comical.

"What are the strange smells?" she asked.

Aiden looked around the cabin and saw various roots and herbs hanging from the ceiling. "It looks like a bunch of different plants she's hung everywhere to dry out."

"Interesting," Amber replied, her nose trying to decipher what some of the smells were.

"Well. Now we're all comfy cozy. I'll let the stew cook for a bit and get down to why you're here," the old woman said as she brushed her hands together and then held them up, bare palms out, to show she was done. She brought a tray over with the teapot and cups and sat down in a chair opposite them and started pouring the tea.

"Now, I'd say you are a vanilla rooibos sort of tea," she said as she poured a steaming cup and held it out to Amber. Aiden took it and brought Amber's hand up so she could feel it and placed it in her hands. The woman looked at him, slightly affronted that he had taken the cup from her and then looked back at Amber and gasped.

"Oh! Yes, yes, yes. I nearly forgot. You can't see, can you, my dear? That is why you didn't look at me when I first whispered at you. Oh, silly old me." The woman laughed and shook her head at her forgetfulness. "I'd forget my own head if it weren't attached." She laughed again and poured another cup for Aiden.

"And you. You seemed more like a spicy robust cinnamon tea with a pinch of honey to show your sweetness inside," the old woman cooed as she spooned some honey from a small jar into the cup. "I scraped this honey from one of my hives myself, so I think you'll like it. No one has better tasting honey than this in all the realms, I guarantee it," she said as she winked at Aiden when she handed his cup to him.

"Now, tell me. Why have you come to see old Seraphina?" the old woman asked as she spooned some sugar into her tea and sat back in her well-worn armchair to look at them.

Aiden's eyebrow quirked up, accompanied by a slight wrinkle in his forehead as he lifted the cup to his nose and smelled it before taking a sip. "We didn't come to see you. You led us here," he responded respectfully, despite the woman's obvious forgetfulness.

The woman looked up at him, puzzled for a moment before she crowed and laughed again. "Oh! You're right. I'm so sorry. My mind isn't what it used to be."

Aiden glanced at Amber wondering if they were safe in this strange little house with the peculiar woman.

"Well, you young children have been on quite the journey, haven't you?" Seraphina asked as she stirred some more sugar into her tea.

Aiden hesitated, unsure how much they should share with this woman. Amber held her tea cup in her lap and looked in the direction of the old woman's voice.

"We have had quite the journey," she replied as she lifted the cup to her lips and took a sip.

The old woman stared at them with a big, partially toothy smile. "Yes, yes. Did you say there was a fire? Horrible business fires. They can cause so much destruction. But they can also bring life and renewal. Sometimes it takes the burning heat of a fire to open up some of the hardest seeds." The old woman shook her head as if saddened by the news and took another sip of her tea.

Aiden looked at her with a quizzical brow. "How did you know about the fire?" he asked cautiously. "We haven't said anything about it."

He lifted his cup to his lips but the cinnamon was quite strong and made him not want to drink it. The old woman looked up at him over her teacup.

"Oh! My, my, my. I am getting ahead of myself, aren't I?" She let out a cackling laugh. "It has been so long since I've had visitors, and especially ones that came after one of my visions, I almost forgot how this works. Vision comes to me, visitors come after, they tell me their story, and I confirm the details. Ah!" she exclaimed. "Well. Why don't you tell me your story, and I'll see if I can fill in any details for you, all right?"

The woman settled into her chair and looked at them expectantly, like a small child waiting to hear their favorite story.

"Oh! Hold on a minute now! I have to put more spices in the stew and stir the pot," the woman exclaimed suddenly as she stood up and walked to the kitchen area to gather more things to put in the stew.

Aiden was growing uncomfortable sitting with this crazy old lady in her cabin. He rubbed his palms on his thighs and shifted in his chair. Amber sensed his growing uneasiness. She reached out her hand and touched his hand. Aiden stopped and looked at her.

"It's all right, Aiden. I believe we can trust her. She has a good heart and a good soul, even if she's a little forgetful." Amber smiled her sweet smile at him.

Aiden shook his head. "How can you tell all of that without seeing her?" he asked quietly.

"I don't know. Without my sight, I've learned how to hear different things in people's voices or how they carry themselves and can usually pick up on things others don't because they are focused on the surface outside appearances."

"Incredible," Aiden replied as he squeezed her hand.

"What are you two lovebirds whispering about," Seraphina asked as she turned from stirring the stew.

Aiden's head shot up, and he removed his hand from Amber's immediately.

"What? We're not–" Aiden stumbled over his words and his throat suddenly went dry. He gulped down the remains of the spicy cinnamon tea, but the strong cinnamon made matters even worse. He coughed and started choking on the strong spice that had hit his dry throat.

"Oh dear," Seraphina said as she stepped over to Aiden and started patting him on the back. "You shouldn't drink such a strong tea so quickly."

Aiden kept coughing as the old woman lifted his arms above his head.

"Now, let's see. Is it lift the arms above the head for coughing or for hiccups?" She moved his arms this way and that as Aiden continued coughing. "Ah! that's right."

She let his arms drop suddenly and ran across the room, rummaging through some of her bags and boxes that sat on shelves. She pulled out a heart-shaped amber stone and ran back over to Aiden. She placed the stone over his chest and made motions for him to breathe in and out slowly. Aiden did. As he did, he felt his chest starting to calm, and his coughing eased to nothing.

"There, now. I thought that would do the trick."

"What did you do?" Aiden asked as he held his chest where she had placed the stone.

The old woman looked at him with a twinkle in her eye. "Amber– calms things down when they are agitated."

He glanced at Amber again. Princess Amber certainly seemed to live up to her name, Aiden thought to himself as he continued to rub his chest.

The old woman's face was drawn to the saddlebag Aiden had set beside him on the floor. "Much like something else you have, I gather."

Aiden looked at the bag. Before Aiden could stop her, the old woman reached into the bag and pulled out the Phoenix gem. Her eyes widened at the glowing orange gem.

"Oh my. In all my years, I never thought my eyes would lay sight to this again," she said as she handled the gem carefully and looked at it.

"Again? You've seen the gem before?" Aiden asked as he studied her carefully, making sure she didn't drop it or break it or do anything to damage it.

"Aye. Many years ago when another young couple sat in my cabin. Only the gem was whole then," she replied as she looked up at Aiden over the gem. "A couple very much like you two. Same energy. They were also running from something, but I don't think it was the same thing you are."

The woman's eyes moved from Aiden to Amber, and she studied them both for a long moment. "What is your name, child?" she asked as she moved closer to Amber.

Amber sensed that the woman's question was directed at her. "Amber," she replied.

The woman stepped towards her and took her hand in her bony hand. She turned Amber's hand over and looked at her palm before looking back at Amber's face.

"Interesting," she said as she examined Amber's palms. "The same power runs through you that ran through her." She studied Amber's face. "You look very much like her, you know," the woman said with a soft smile.

Amber's brows drew together. "Like who?" she asked, removing her hand from the woman's bony hand.

"Your mother, of course," the woman replied with her toothy smile.

CHAPTER 14

Amber's body stiffened, and she sat up straighter in the chair at the old woman's words. She folded her hands together in her lap and stared forward with her unseeing eyes. She took in a small breath before answering. "My mother?" she asked cautiously. "Did you know my mother?"

The woman smiled. "Aye. Sweet Zamina. Your mother was one of the sweetest people I have ever met. Her skin was ivory, much like yours, but when she was in the sun for a while, it glowed and darkened to a beautiful bronze color. Her eyes were the prettiest amber color, like warm honey and cinnamon. She had red hair, much like yours, only not so much of it," Seraphina said as she walked around Amber's chair and looked at the long braid that sat beneath Amber's cloak.

Amber touched her hair. "Oh. We were trying to keep it hidden. We didn't want anyone to see it and know it was me."

The woman looked at it in wonder. "Might I touch it?" she asked.

Amber's mouth twitched in a slight smile at the woman's request. "I suppose that's all right," she said as she undid the clasp that held the cloak on. Aiden stood and helped her pull it off and set it on top of his bag.

"Shiminy," the woman let out a gasp and an unusual word Aiden had never heard before.

She unknowingly held the gem close to Amber's hair, which caused strands of it to glow like firelight.

Aiden's eyes widened when he saw the glowing strands. "What on earth?" he asked as he stared at it.

The woman's eyes widened as well, and she moved the gem away. Amber's hair stopped glowing when the gem was removed. Seraphina moved the gem back, and the strands glowed again.

"Is this hair a recent development in your life, my dear?" the woman asked as she moved the gem back and forth from Amber's hair to see the strands glow.

"I suppose. My hair has always been longer, but last night when we camped out, I found the gem in Aiden's bag. Something about it was drawing me to it. It felt strange in my hands."

"Did anything happen while you were holding it?" the woman asked as she touched parts of the thick braid, completely fascinated by the seemingly magic hair like a small child discovering a new thing.

"I felt a small spark or something at one point while I was holding it," Amber replied as she pulled the braid over her shoulder and stroked some of the strands.

"Mm-hmm. Mm-hmm. Anything else?"

"I started singing a song that I hadn't remembered until I held the gem. It came back to me like a foggy or forgotten memory," Amber replied.

"How interesting," the woman replied as she came to stand in front of Amber again. "What was the song?" she asked.

Amber bit her lip as she tried to remember the song she had sung the night before. She played with a couple of loose strands of hair from her braid and started to sing:

> *The Phoenix takes flight to meet an old friend,*
> *For he knows his journey is nearing an end.*
> *He leaves a precious treasure behind,*
> *A gift that will forever remind.*

*He flies high over painted sands
To a place where his healing tear forever will last.
He cries one last tear, and takes to the sky,
And watches the world go flying by.*

*His journey ends and he builds his nest,
filling it with spices and twigs for a final rest
He gives himself willingly, and says goodbye to the earth,
And bursts forth again in a fiery rebirth.*

The woman's eyes widened as she heard the song. "*The Phoenix Lullaby,*" she whispered in awe. "Did your mother sing that to you?" she asked as she bustled over to a small shelf of books.

"Yes. I believe she sang it to me all the time when I was little. It was the only thing that would help me go to sleep at night."

The old woman nodded her head. "Your mother was very wise. She left you a message in that," Seraphina replied as she flipped through one of the dusty books.

Aiden watched the old woman and asked, "Do you know what the message is?"

"Hmm?" she asked as she closed the book and looked around like she had forgotten what she was doing. Her eyes landed on the boiling pot still hanging over the fire.

"Oh! My stew is ready," she said as she toddled over to the pot. She took a cloth and used it to pull the rod that held the pot away from the fire and stirred the stew, taking a bite to see if it was ready. She smacked her lips together and smiled. "Perfect."

Aiden stood up. "Do you know what the message means?" he asked as he took Amber's teacup and placed it on the tea tray with his cup.

"Oh, yes, yes. We'll get to that, but first let's enjoy some of my tasty stew. I'm sure you are both famished after your long journey," the old woman replied as she waddled over to the kitchen area to retrieve some bowls and spoons. "Come, come. Sit down here at the table, and I'll dish us some stew." She waved her ladle towards the table and went to dish the stew into the bowls. "Now, young man. If you could grab the bread off the counter and slice some for everyone, that would be a great help," she chimed as she started ladling the stew into the bowls.

Amber smiled. "She has you under her control."

"I wouldn't want to upset an old woman, even if she is crazy," he replied as he held out his hand to her and helped her stand.

Aiden led Amber over to the small table and let her feel where the small bench was that sat on one side. Once she was settled on the bench, Aiden went to the counter where the bread sat on the breadboard. He brought it over to the table with a knife and sliced three slices of bread. Seraphina brought the steaming bowls over to them and set them in front of both of them. Amber reached up and touched the table to find her spoon. Aiden caught her hand just as it was about to land in the hot bowl and guided it to the side of the bowl where the spoon was.

"Thank you," Amber said as her fingers felt the wooden spoon.

Aiden placed the slice of bread beside her bowl. "Your bread is beside your bowl on the other side," he said as he guided her other hand to the other side of the bowl.

Amber nodded and smiled as she felt it.

Seraphina hoisted herself on the other bench and started eating the hearty stew. "Mmm. Nothing like a good thick stew to fill the empty stomach."

Amber took a small bite and smiled. "This is wonderful, Seraphina. There is so much flavor."

The woman beamed. "I have been known to make a mean pot of stew when the occasion called for it," she replied as she took another bite.

Aiden's stomach growled as he looked at the bowl filled with chunks of meat and vegetables of various kinds and sizes. He lifted a large spoonful to his mouth and eagerly ate the hearty stew. The meat tasted gamier than what he was used to. He was curious about what it was, but part of him wasn't sure if he wanted to ask and find out what strange thing the old woman might have put in her stew.

The woman cleaned out her bowl by wiping her bread around the edges of the wooden bowl. After she finished, she got up and went to fill her bowl again.

"Now, about this gem and your quest," she said as she sat down and began to eat.

"I didn't realize we were on a quest," Amber said as she ate more of her stew. "It sounds so official."

"You are looking for the Phoenix tear, I believe?" Seraphina asked.

"Yes, we are," Aiden replied as he took a bite of his stew. "Amber's father mentioned it to me before he slipped into unconsciousness. Do you know anything about the tear?"

"The answer is in the song," the woman replied as she lapped up the rest of her second helping of stew.

"Can you tell us what the song means or why my father would have mentioned it to Aiden?" Amber asked as she finished her first helping.

"The tear of a Phoenix is supposed to have immense healing powers. Perhaps he wanted you to find it to bring you healing," Seraphina replied. "You are also on a quest to find the other half of the gem, are you not?" she asked as she looked at Aiden and Amber.

Aiden choked on his bite of stew before answering, still surprised by the woman's uncanny knowledge of their lives. "My brother has been seeking the other half of the gem, but I don't know how you knew that either," Aiden replied as he took a sip of water.

"Seraphina knows many things," the old woman said with a mischievous glint in her eye. "Why does your brother seek the gem?" she asked.

"Our kingdom, the reigning kingdom of the Fall realm, had possession of the second half of the gem for years until it was stolen a few weeks ago."

"Ah, yes. The Fall realm. You are the prince from Havilah, aren't you?" the woman asked as she took in his features for the first time. "Yes. I should have seen it earlier. Yep, yep," the woman said as she placed an old hand over Aiden's. "Your mother, the queen, was a treasure. It is unfortunate the circumstances of her death. To die of a broken heart is the greatest tragedy in the world," she said as she patted Aiden's hand and looked at him compassionately.

"A broken heart?" Aiden asked as he wiped remnants of the stew from his mouth. "She died from complications in childbirth shortly after I was born."

"That is what they told you, I'm sure," Seraphina said as she waved her spoon at him. "Mark my words. The young autumn queen died of a broken heart. She loved your father very much. When he was killed in battle, it nearly destroyed her. But, she had the promise of you to keep her going."

Aiden choked on the bite of bread he had just put in his mouth.

"Oh dear. There you go again," Seraphina said as she slid off the bench and went to grab the amber heart stone again. She brought it to Aiden and placed it over his chest. Aiden held it there for a moment until his coughing fit subsided. He looked at the old woman who had sat back down on her bench.

"What did you mean when you said my mother had the promise of me to keep her going?" Aiden asked as he took a sip of his water.

The old woman looked at him with surprise. "Why, don't you know? Your mother was pregnant with you before your father was killed and the throne was overthrown by that selfish boar of a man."

Aiden sat stunned and silent for a moment. He couldn't believe what this old woman was telling him. He had always thought that Lord Ragnar was his father. That he was only a half-prince because Ragnar wasn't of royal blood. Did his father– Did that man know Aiden wasn't his true son? Is that why he always treated him so callously and harshly?

Amber felt the sudden tension enter the room at the words of the old woman. Her hand felt on the table for Aiden's hand.

"Aiden?" she asked as she sought his hand.

Aiden stood up. "We should go," he said as he removed himself from his bench.

Amber's head turned side to side trying to figure out where Aiden had gone.

"Oh my. You didn't know. I'm so sorry. I thought for sure you would have known that. I didn't mean to speak out of turn. Please, don't let me scare you off. Stay and rest here for the night," the woman said as she got up and tried to stop Aiden from walking away.

"No," Aiden said sharply. "We need to go now."

Aiden went to the small table where they had left the tea things and picked up the Phoenix gem. He then picked up his bag and placed the gem inside and carried the bag and their cloaks over to the table. He placed Amber's cloak around her shoulders.

Amber flinched at the unexpected feel of the cloak on her back. She felt it to make sure it was on and secured the clasp. "Aiden, why don't we stay here for the night? We could both use the rest."

"No. We should head out while we are under the cloak of darkness before my brother—," Aiden paused as he realized he didn't know if he could actually call him that. "We just need to go," he finished staunchly.

Amber pushed herself up from the table while Seraphina bustled about the small cabin. The old woman came over and placed a bundled cloth in Amber's hands.

"Take this for your journey. It's some cheese and bread and some other things."

Amber nodded and smiled as she took the bundle. "Thank you, Seraphina. You have been so kind to us." Amber bent down to give the older woman a hug.

"Where do we find the Phoenix tear?" Aiden asked as he stood at the door impatiently, waiting to leave.

Seraphina pulled away from Amber and looked at him. "You will find the answer in the song," she said simply.

"Great. Thanks for that helpful information," Aiden muttered under his breath. "I'll go get Saleem. I'll be back in a few moments and then we can go," he said aloud as he stormed out of the cabin.

Seraphina pulled Amber's arm down so she would bend down to her level. "Keep watch on that young man. Here's the amber stone in case he needs it," the old woman whispered as she slipped the stone into Amber's hand and closed her hand around it. "And be careful. You may both discover things you do not wish to on this journey."

"I can't keep watch on him, Seraphina. I can't see," Amber replied as she straightened.

"You will find a way. Now go. The Great Mage be with you." Seraphina squeezed Amber's hands and led her to the door.

Aiden had returned with his horse. He put Amber on the horse, a little more abruptly than he had previously, before he mounted behind her.

"Blessings on your journey, my children. Remember, you will find your answers in the song," the old woman shouted as Aiden urged his horse into action.

CHAPTER 15

Aiden rode with Amber the rest of the day and into the dimming light of the setting sun. She had felt how tense his body was behind her after they had left Seraphina's house, and he still felt pretty tense behind her.

"Aiden?"

"Hmm."

"Can we stop for the night soon? My head is feeling heavy and tired with the new weight of my hair."

"Oh. Of course," Aiden replied without much emotion. He stopped Saleem when they reached a small clearing near a stream and helped Amber down, but didn't say anything to her.

Aiden unsaddled Saleem and led him to the water to drink. Amber wasn't sure where she should go, so she took a step forward, but tripped on a tree root and landed face first in a pile of dried leaves.

Aiden turned around just as she pitched forward.

"Amber!" he said with alarm in his voice. He ran to kneel beside her. "Are you alright?" he asked as he helped her up.

"Yes, I just couldn't see where I was going," she said with a half smile.

"I'm sorry. I shouldn't have left you on your own. I guess I wasn't thinking," he said as he helped her sit back. She winced when he took her hands. "It looks like your hands are scratched. I don't think I have anything that will help them, unfortunately." Aiden stood and walked over to retrieve the saddle bag.

"Do you think what Seraphina said was true? About the Phoenix tear, I mean? That it will bring healing?" Amber asked as she gently touched each of her hands to find out where the scratches were.

"I don't know," Aiden said as he grabbed the water canteen and went to kneel by the stream to fill it. "I suppose if everything else she said was true, then that must be true as well."

"Yes. She said a lot of things about both of our mothers. You didn't know about your father, did you?" Amber asked sympathetically.

Aiden sat silently beside the stream with his back to her for a moment as he filled the canteen. He stood up and brought the water canteen to her and knelt to take her hands.

"I'm going to pour some of the water over the scratches so they're at least clean," Aiden said as he poured the water over her hands.

Amber winced slightly as the cool water stung her scratches. She could tell he didn't feel like discussing what the old woman had said about his father, so she changed subjects. "I wonder what the Phoenix tear is. Is it an actual tear or a potion, or something else altogether? I wonder if it would hurt or sting to feel it. And would it heal just physical hurts, or would it heal emotional wounds as well?"

Aiden grabbed a small cloth and gently wiped her hands with it to dry them off. She sucked in a small breath as he patted around the scratches.

"Sorry," he said as he finished drying them.

"It's alright. Pain can't be avoided sometimes."

Aiden stopped for a moment as his heart and head felt the sudden weight of the emotions he had kept bottled up all day. His head and shoulders drooped as the painful words Seraphina had shared with them seeped into his mind. The king of the harvest that had been brutally killed by the man he had thought to be his father all these years was really his father. And, if his mother did truly die of a broken heart and not complications from his birth, why hadn't she fought to stay alive to love him and care for him? The old woman had said that his mother had the promise of him to keep her going after his father died. If that was true, why had she died and let him grow up with Ragnar and Erick as his family. They never cared for him and always treated him harshly. Hadn't he been enough, even for her?

Amber felt Aiden still in front of her. She reached out a cautious hand to touch him, her hand brushing what felt like his shoulder. Her fingers found their way to his face. She held his face for a moment, trying to read what he was thinking. As she held his face, her fingers began to gently explore it. Her hands traced his pointed jaw up to his forehead where she felt deep, furrowed lines in his forehead that felt like the trenches dug for planting season, telling her he was deep in thought about something or worried about something. Her fingers trailed their way down his nose, which was pointed like his jaw. Her hands brushed his cheeks where she felt something wet. Was that a tear? Was he crying? She quickly pulled her hands away from his face.

"I'm sorry," she whispered as she clasped her hands in her lap.

Aiden looked at her, dumbfounded yet moved that she had touched his face. Her touch had started out as comforting at the emotions she must have sensed he was feeling, but then it turned into free exploration of his face. Until she had felt the tear that had escaped unwillingly from his eye.

Aiden cleared his throat and pulled away slightly, brushing the wayward tear from his face. "You have nothing to apologize for. That's how you see what people look like, isn't it?" he asked.

"Yes. It's normal for me, but I forget that other people are not as accustomed to it. I didn't mean to be so intrusive," she apologized.

"No. It's fine. It was just– unexpected," Aiden replied, trying to push down the other feelings her touch had stirred in him.

Amber sighed, feeling she had made things awkward between them. "Where are we off to now?" she asked as she pulled her long braid over her shoulder. "Do we return to my kingdom and let them know that you didn't kidnap me?"

Aiden stood and walked away to fill the water canteen again.

"I'm not sure. If Lord Amir and the guards think I kidnapped you, I don't know how welcoming they would be if I brought you back. Besides, your father's last words were 'Phoenix tear', so I feel he would have wanted me to know about it for some reason. If what Seraphina said was correct and the Phoenix tear can heal people, perhaps he wanted us to find it so you could be healed and see again and regain control of your kingdom while he is unable to rule."

"Perhaps," she said as she played with a section of her long braid. "Or perhaps he knew he would need it for himself if he was as bad off as you said he was."

Aiden thought back to the weakened state of the king. "That could be true as well." He finished filling the canteen and came back to sit beside her.

Amber lifted her head in the direction of where she heard Aiden settle next to her. "Seraphina said the song is the key. What do you think she meant by that?"

"Maybe the words are a sort of map or something. They could be describing specific places," Aiden said before he tipped the canteen back and took a long drink.

Amber's head lifted, suddenly remembering something that reminded her of the song, but wasn't quite able to grasp the memory. "That must be it. What were the words again?"

Aiden leaned his head back against the tree that sat behind them as he tried to think. "The Phoenix takes flight to meet an old friend, for he knows his journey is nearing an end. He leaves a precious treasure behind, a gift that will forever remind."

"He flies high over painted sands to a place where his healing tear forever will last," she continued.

"Okay. So the Phoenix flies to meet an old friend for he knows his journey is almost at end. That implies the Phoenix visiting an old friend. If his journey is almost at an end, he is probably going to say goodbye or something," Aiden said as he twirled the signet ring on his right hand.

"Or to give something to that friend to take care of. The song said he leaves a precious treasure behind," Amber replied.

"True. What would the Phoenix leave behind if he knew his end was drawing near? And did he leave it to keep it out of someone else's hands or was it a gift for the friend to remember him by?"

"It could be the gem maybe. That's a treasure and something that should be protected. Seraphina mentioned the gem being whole when she last saw it, and she talked about the couple that had been there. Do you think they are the couple from the legend that made the Phoenix gem glow?"

"Could be. I always thought that was just a legend though."

"It has to be real though. We have one half of the gem, and you said your brother was looking for the other half that was stolen from your kingdom. One half has been in the Fall realm, and one half has been in the Summer realm. Do you think that the couple split the gem, and each one kept half to remember each other?"

"That's possible. That would mean one of the lovers was from the Fall realm and the other was from the Summer. I wonder what kept them apart or prevented them from getting married or being together. And how did the two halves end up in each of our palaces?" Aiden asked thoughtfully.

"I don't know. The next part of the song talks about the Phoenix flying over painted sands where he knows his healing tear will forever last. Painted sands." Amber chewed her lip as she tried to think through the meaning of the phrase.

"I don't know of any painted sands in the Fall realm," Aiden said as he watched her. He smiled at the expression of intense thought on her face.

Amber's head lifted suddenly, and she turned in his direction. "Painted sands. There is a region of the Summer realm that is in the far southeast corner that is covered in painted sand. That must be what the song means."

"Painted sand?" Aiden asked, confused at the thought of sand being painted. "How is the sand painted?" he asked, trying to picture sand that had been painted by somebody at some time.

Amber's nose crinkled up as she smiled. "I don't think it is actually painted, but the sand is different colors so it looks painted. It's a desert region that we visited when I was younger. There was an oasis there that we used to stop at during our travels. I remember this crystal clear pond that people used to fill their water canteens before continuing on through the desert. Maybe that is where the Phoenix tear is located." Amber's voice rose with excitement.

"That would make sense. A spring of fresh water in the middle of a desert would bring healing and relief to weary travelers. Do you remember how to get there?" Aiden asked.

Amber's face fell. "No. I was so young the last time we were there. I just remember riding in the caravan for days and then how beautiful it was once we finally arrived."

Aiden thought for a moment. He sprung up and retrieved his saddle bag and came back to sit beside Amber. He pulled out the map he had taken from his father's study as well as the Phoenix gem. Opening the map, he held the gem over it. He frowned. Nothing. That's strange. He let out a small grunt.

"What's wrong?" Amber asked.

"I took a map when I was in the palace today because it lit up when I leaned close to it with the Phoenix gem in my bag, but it isn't lighting up now," he said as he stared at the map, disappointed and confused at what he had seen earlier.

"Was the map on top of something?" she asked.

"Yes, it was on the table."

"And was the gem underneath it?"

Aiden's eyes widened. "Yes, it was! That must be it."

He lifted up a corner of the map and held the gem under it. He smiled when little orange flames dotted the map again.

"You are brilliant, Amber. How did you know?" he asked.

"I'm not sure. I just had a feeling. What does the map show?"

"It looks like it is of the realms. When I run the gem under it, little orange flames make a path from the Fall palace to," Aiden followed the path of the flames with the gem, "somewhere in the Summer realm." As he landed in the Summer realm, he saw the blue tear symbol appear in the corner.

"You said the painted desert region was in the southeast corner of the Summer realm?" he asked.

"Yes. Did you find it?" she asked excitedly.

"I think I may have," he replied as he stared at the blue tear in wonder. "The Phoenix gem is showing a blue tear symbol in that region."

"That must be it. The gem must be showing where it is at because it is connected to it somehow."

"I wonder if the other orange flames that appeared on the map are showing where the other half of the gem is," Aiden surmised. He held the gem under the area where they had stopped for the night and a bright, large flame appeared. "The gem is showing a large bright flame where we are right now, so that must be this gem. How incredible. We can find the tear and the other half of the gem as long as we have this map and one half of the gem," Aiden said excitedly.

"That's amazing," Amber replied. "It shouldn't be too hard to find then. We can go to the oasis and find the tear, and then find the other half of the gem."

"Can you imagine, finding both halves after all these years and putting them back together? Lord Ragnar believed the gem would create endless power when the two halves were reunited. If the tear does have healing properties, that could mean incredible things for both our realms if we had the gem and the tear." Aiden ran a hand through his hair as he thought of the possibilities.

"I can't wait to find the tear," Amber said.

"Me neither," Aiden replied.

A cool breeze swept around them, sending a shiver down Amber's spine. Aiden pulled the cloak tighter around her.

"I better get some wood and start a fire," he said as he carefully folded the map and put the map and gem back in the saddlebag. "Will you be okay by yourself while I gather some wood?" Aiden asked as he stood.

Amber nodded amidst another shiver. She heard leaves crunch beneath Aiden's boots as he walked away. Amber pulled the cloak tighter around her shoulders. It was cooler in the Fall realm than it was in the Summer realm and she wasn't used to the cooler nights. She missed the warmth of the sun and the energy she felt from it.

As she sat there, she heard faint singing again. It was the same sound she had heard the night before. Amber removed the cloak and shifted to her knees. Aiden had been sitting beside her to her left, so his bag should be somewhere nearby. She crawled on the ground, her hands searching in front of her for Aiden's saddlebag. Her hand finally bumped soft material. Amber pulled the leather bag closer to her and felt for the clasp. She opened the bag and took out the gem. She smiled as she took the gem in her hands.

"Hello, my precious ember," she cooed with a desirous tone in her voice. She started humming the song she heard in her mind from the gem. As she did, the gem grew hot in her hands and started to glow. Amber sang the words out loud now. A spark pricked her palm followed by a bright red flash that filled the wooded area.

"Amber, I was thinking that we should–" Aiden stopped short as he entered the area where he had left Amber. Amber wasn't there. He dropped the wood and looked around anxiously, wondering if she had left to try to find him or something.

"Amber," he called out into the increasingly crisp air of the Fall woods.

Aiden ran through the small area of trees and called her name. He stopped when he reached the area he started at. He shook his head.

"She couldn't have gone that far. I was only gone for a few minutes."

He looked towards his bag. It was open. An uncomfortable pit settled in his already knotted stomach. He rushed to the bag and knelt to look inside. He furiously searched the bag, but couldn't find the gem.

"Amber, what happened?" he whispered.

He ran his fingers through his dark auburn hair and sat down on the forest floor. He pulled the map out of his bag and looked at it. Without the gem, he couldn't see any illuminations. He had no idea where she was at. He stared hard at the map, begging it to reveal something to him with his stare. He remembered the general area of where he had seen the other gem flickering. If he could find the other gem, he could use it to find Amber, providing whoever had the other gem wasn't on the move.

Aiden leaned his head back against the tree behind him. "Please help me find her," he whispered.

Chapter 16

Lord Ragnar returned to his study after the meeting with the Summer realm guards. He walked to the table where the maps had been scattered earlier. As he leaned against the table to study them, he noticed that one of the maps was missing. He let out a loud growl and shoved the rest of the papers to the floor.

"Erick!" he yelled out.

One of the young page boys appeared. "My Lord," he said as he bowed. "Do you need me to fetch Sir Erick for you?" the young boy asked as he stood nervously on the other side of the room.

Ragnar looked at him with a sneer. "If I called for him, then I would presume that I would like to see him."

The boy nodded, bowed, and ran from the room.

Ragnar pushed himself from his desk and rubbed his forehead with his hands. "The help in this palace is so egregious."

Erick entered the room a few moments later.

"Where is your brother?" Ragnar asked.

"I thought the page boy said that you sent for me," Erick replied, slightly put out that his father's first question was about his brother when he had asked to see him. "I was about to head out to look for the gem. I have no idea where Aiden drifted off to now. I assumed he was in his room writing a song or a poem or something," Erick replied bitterly.

Ragnar eyed his eldest son with a look of disdain and annoyance. "The map of the realms is missing, and I haven't seen your brother since we left him here to go deal with the questioning guards of the Summer realm."

"Aiden," Erick breathed out angrily with a slight growl.

"If he has the map, we are in trouble, Erick. That map is the key to getting both halves of the gem. Once he figures out how to use it, there is nothing that will keep him from finding the gem for himself and taking back his kingdom."

Ragnar stalked towards Erick. Erick's hand went automatically to the hilt of his sword, ready to defend himself against his father's unpredictable rage. Ragnar was slightly bigger than Erick, with long brown hair that fell past his shoulders and strands of braids and beads woven throughout. His face was hard and worn from many years of battle, and his brown eyes had long grown cold and empty. Erick barely remembered a time when those eyes lit up with the joy and happiness of life. He stood his ground staring back into his father's eyes, all the while tightening his grip on his sword.

"Did he say anything to you about the gem while the two of you were in the Summer realm? Have you two been conspiring together this entire time behind my back? Was it the concocted plan of your two minds to burn down the Summer palace, kidnap the princess, and obtain the two halves of the gem for yourselves?" Ragnar asked as he reached down and placed his hand over Erick's on his sword. He stared into his son's similar brown eyes, trying to strike fear and intimidation into his son and remind him of his authority over him.

Erick matched his father's gaze, stare for stare.

"I would never betray you, Father," Erick ground out between clenched teeth. "You know I have always been faithful to you and to our realm. I would never betray you or our kingdom. If Aiden has planned any of this, he has left me in the dark. I am not my brother's keeper."

Ragnar scrutinized Erick for a long moment. Releasing his grip on Erick's hand, he stepped back and returned to his desk, where he sat in his oversized throne-like chair.

"You now have another mission in addition to the one already tasked to you. Find your brother, and the map, and bring them both back to me," he said as he leaned back in his chair and steepled his fingers.

"And if I don't?" Erick asked.

Ragnar leaned forward and braced his hands on his desk. "You know what lengths I have gone to in order to claim this kingdom and this realm. Don't think that because you are my son, I will spare you from anything I have done to retain the crown."

Erick's tightened jaw slackened slightly, and he felt a small drop in his stomach. He quickly clenched his jaw again and stared past his father.

"I will bring you what you want," he said without emotion.

"Good. I'm glad we understand each other," his father replied as he leaned back again in his chair and relaxed his hands.

Erick's hand tightened around the hilt of his sword again. For a brief moment, he had a strong desire to dispatch his father right there and then. No one was around, and his father was so maddeningly relaxed at this moment, he wouldn't even see it coming.

Ragnar glanced up at him. "What are you waiting for? Go, complete your missions before I question making you a knight and captain of the guard."

Erick's hand rubbed the leather that was wrapped around his sword hilt. After a few moments, he removed his hand and gave his father a slight bow before exiting the room.

Zamina wandered through the stalls of a small village market that bled into the desert region of the Summer realm, breathing in the different spices and herbs that filled the various booths. She touched her neck where the leather strap that held the Phoenix gem laid, ensuring it was still there. Making sure the gem was completely hidden, she pulled her hooded cloak closer around her face before approaching any of the colorful booths. She bought bread and nuts and fruit from a couple of the merchants, as well as some other things she would need to replenish her supplies before heading deeper into the forest.

She spotted a bright red and yellow sheer scarf hanging from one of the stalls that enticed her to take a closer look. Stepping up to the booth, she glanced at the array of exquisite headdresses and scarves that created a rainbow of color before her eyes before reaching for the fiery red and yellow scarf. She removed one of her gloves and ran her fingers down the soft fabric. A wistful smile crossed her face as she looked at the beautiful scarf.

"They say one of the knights from the Fall realm started the fire. Burned a good portion of the palace, it did. Nobody was hurt, but the king is pretty laid up from the smoke."

Zamina leaned out past the decorated stall and saw a man with a wagon full of various pots and pans and other trinkets on display on various shelves. He must be a traveling salesman from the king's market.

The woman he was talking to let out a gasp and put a hand to her face. "A fire? How awful. Why would the knights of the Fall realm start the fire?"

The man leaned closer to the woman as though ready to divulge a juicy secret, prompting Zamina to do the same.

"They say that the rebel ruler of the Fall realm sent word to the king of the Summer realm wanting to join their two kingdoms by marriage. The Fall prince was sent to the Summer realm to wed the princess. But...," he leaned even closer and lowered his voice. "I overheard one of the knights from the Fall realm and the prince talking amongst themselves of a rare gem that they was looking for, and they believed the Summer king had it, and they was plotting to take it off his hands and return it to their kingdom for safe keeping. So perhaps that's a reason why they started the fire. To cover their tracks and steal the gem from the Summer realm."

Zamina's hand slipped, and she knocked over a bowl of gold stamped coins that the stall owner probably used to decorate the headdresses. They tinkled as they fell to the ground. The man and the woman stopped talking and looked up at her. She knelt quickly and began to pick up the decorative coins.

"Hey! What are you doing at my stall?" the woman asked as she stomped over to where Zamina was hunched over on the ground. "Those coins aren't real, dearie, so if you were trying to steal them to put some coin in your purse, then you would have gotten away with what you deserve – nothing."

Zamina pulled her hood further over her face as she stood with the bowl of coins.

"I am so sorry, madam. I didn't mean to disturb your beautiful stall. I was walking by and bumped into the corner where the bowl was sitting. I would love to purchase this beautiful red scarf to make up for it," Zamina said as she placed the bowl in the woman's hands and fished out a couple of gold coins from her pouch. She held them out to the woman.

The woman looked at her suspiciously for a moment before accepting the coins.

"Alright, if that's all you were doing. The scarf is yours. Now be on your way and don't knock anything else over on your way past my stall."

"I apologize again. I promise, I will be more careful as I leave. Thank you for the beautiful scarf. My daughter would love it."

Zamina placed the coins in the woman's hand and took the scarf off the peg where it was hanging. She held it up and admired the gold scrollwork embroidery against the fiery red and yellow background.

"You are a beautiful seamstress," Zamina breathed out in awe as she looked at the scarf. "You could sell these at the king's market and fetch quite a bit of coin."

The woman blushed. "Thank you, miss. That is high praise. I don't know that they are good enough for the king's market though. I'm sure the fancy people there have much finer silk and scarf merchants to choose from."

Zamina shook her head and looked at her. "Believe me. I have seen much of the king's market and the wares they sell there, and none are as fine as this. Many of the ladies of the royal court and the kingdom would be envious of anyone wearing such a beautiful scarf and headdress."

"That is very kind of you. Perhaps some day I will make a journey to the king's market and take a chance."

"You should."

Zamina smiled at the woman and bid her good day. She carefully folded the scarf and placed it in the bag that hung at her side. A man on a slender, yet regal, brown horse talking to one of the merchants drew her eye. He didn't appear to be from the Summer realm. Curious, she stepped towards a booth close to him so she could watch him.

"Have you seen a young woman with long red hair?" he asked as he brushed the mane of his horse and patted the horse's neck. "It's fiery red, much like that jewel. You can't miss it."

The merchant shook his head no but held up the fiery opal necklace he had on display.

"If you are looking for a pretty lady, perhaps one of these fine pieces of jewelry would be a pretty addition to her neck."

The young man smiled. "They are fine, indeed. Perhaps once I find her, I will return and purchase one of your fine pieces of jewelry."

He sat on his horse and looked around the small village. After a few moments, he nudged his horse into a slow walk down the dirt covered street. As he walked past her, Zamina felt the gem warm slightly against her chest, as though it sensed something that connected the man to the gem. She followed him as he dismounted his horse near an apple merchant.

"Have you seen a young woman with fiery red hair?" he asked as he placed a few gold coins in the woman's outstretched hand. The woman shook her head no and handed him a small bag of apples. "Thank you."

He started to lead his sleek horse down the street on his way outside the village, but he stopped and turned back to the apple merchant. He pulled an aged parchment from his bag and unfolded it.

Zamina let out a gasp when she saw what was in his hand.

"Can you tell me how to get to the Oasis of Melchizidai from here?" he asked as he held the map out to the woman. The woman shook her covered head again.

Aiden folded the map and placed it back in his bag. Zamina followed him as he led his horse to the outskirts of the village. Sitting on a step outside a yellow-orange clay building, he gave his horse an apple and pulled another one from the bag for himself. He pulled out the map and gently unfolded it. As he looked at it, a shadowed silhouette filled the parchment.

Aiden stood quickly and drew his sword. A woman in a hooded cloak stood at the other end of his blade.

"What do you want?" he asked as he held the sword at the woman's throat.

The woman held up her hands in defense. "Please. I mean you no harm."

"Then why are you following me?" he asked.

"I heard you asking about a young woman with fiery red hair. I only know of one person who fits that description in all the realms, and I wanted to see if it was the same person you were seeking."

Aiden lowered his sword slightly. "Do you know where she is?" he asked, studying the woman, unsure if he could trust her.

"No. But I would give anything to find her and see her again," the woman replied, a slight tremor in her voice.

"Remove your hood," Aiden said, gesturing to the woman's head covering with his sword.

The woman hesitated at his request, but slowly reached her hands up and pushed back the hood.

Aiden's eyes widened as he looked at a woman who had almost the same color hair as Amber, just slightly darker. Looking at her face, Aiden imagined that's what Amber might look like when she was older, but the woman's eyes were what offset Aiden the most. Her eyes bore a remarkable resemblance to Amber's. How had the old woman described them? Honey cinnamon?

Aiden narrowed his eyes at the woman. "Amber told me her mother died many years ago. How is it that someone bearing such a likeness to her is still alive and well?"

The woman's eyes darted to the ground. "Only by a miracle," she replied quietly. She looked back up at him. "I can explain if you allow me to. You said you were looking for my daughter. Have you seen her? How is she? Where is she?"

Aiden looked around the crowded street. "Let's not talk here."

Zamina nodded. "Come. I'll take you to my hiding spot outside the village."

Aiden nodded and took Saleem's reins and followed the red-haired woman out of the village.

CHAPTER 17

Zamina led Aiden into the forest that sat outside of the small village. She stopped when they reached an area that had material strung up between a few trees and a small stoned area with burned logs and ashes in the middle. She took Saleem's reins from Aiden and tied them to a low branch near the makeshift tent and bent to grab a bucket of water. She placed it beneath Saleem and brushed his nose before he lowered his head to take a drink.

"Are you hungry?" she asked as she bent to put a few pieces of wood on top of the ashes in the fire pit.

Aiden nodded and sat down on a stump on the other side of the fire pit.

Zamina got the fire going, put some kind of meat on the iron spit, and placed it over the flames. She sat back on her haunches as she watched the orange flames flickering in the late afternoon sunlight.

Aiden rubbed his hands on his thighs trying to think of a way to start the conversation between them. He sighed uncomfortably.

"You are wondering what a dead queen is doing in the forest of the Summer realm," she said without looking up at him.

Aiden hesitated before answering. "I am wondering about a lot of things," he replied warily.

A small smile turned up the corner of Zamina's face as she finally looked up at him. "As am I," she replied with a slight hint of mischief dancing in her honey-cinnamon eyes.

"Well, I will start," she continued as she sat cross-legged on the ground near the fire across from him. "You obviously know my daughter, Amber, princess of the Summer realm. Are you her intended?"

Aiden coughed and cleared his throat. "I– uh– in a manner of speaking, I suppose," he replied, suddenly very uncomfortable.

Zamina studied him for a moment and then nodded her head. "Ah, intended by others in the ways of an arranged marriage. That must mean you are the prince from the Fall realm."

Aiden gave her a quizzical look, unsure how she knew that information.

She laughed at his confused expression. "I'm sorry. It does seem absurd that I would know that since I'm supposed to be dead and likely haven't been near the palace in years. I overheard a traveling merchant who must have come to the village we were in from the king's market. He was sharing the royal gossip and was telling someone that the rulers of the Fall and Summer realms were hoping to unite their realms by marriage and that the prince from the Fall realm had come to be wed to my daughter."

"Ah, that makes sense," Aiden nodded with understanding.

"Yes. The biddy gossip also mentioned that much of the Summer palace had burned, and it was believed to have been started by one of the knights or the prince from the Fall realm. Is that true as well?" she asked as she looked at him.

Aiden's face went white.

"I can tell by your expression that it wasn't meant to happen. Were you a part of the accident or was it started by someone else?" she asked.

"I'm honestly not sure. I mean, I personally wasn't responsible for it, but I saw my brother rushing out from where it had started and he had a terrified look on his face like it wasn't supposed to happen. I asked him if he had started it, but he said it wasn't intentional."

Zamina nodded her head slightly in understanding. She cast her eyes to the fire before she asked her next question. "I also heard that the king took in a lot of smoke and fell ill. Is he alright?"

There was a slight tremor in her voice and Aiden saw the tears rimming her eyes. His heart twinged at seeing the guarded hurt in her eyes, wondering if her husband was well or not. He couldn't imagine what it must be like to have been apart from one's spouse for years and then find out they were unwell or had some tragedy befall them.

Aiden formulated his words carefully to prevent the queen from experiencing any unnecessary grief or worry, but also assure her that her husband had survived the fire. "I got him out in time, but he was very weak and had taken in a lot of smoke. He slipped into unconsciousness shortly after we got him out of the palace. The healer was taking care of him the last I knew, but I didn't see him before we left so I couldn't tell you how he is."

Zamina's face was a mix of fear and concern and tears.

"Oh. Poor Azar. He shouldn't have had to go through that again."

Zamina put her hand to her face as she tried to cover the sea of emotions that were coming to the surface. She pinched the bridge of her nose to stop the tears and wiped at her tears and nose with her other gloved hand.

Aiden watched her, still wondering about his unanswered questions.

"Amber mentioned the fire that happened when she was younger. She told me that's how you died. And how she lost her sight."

Zamina's eyes shot up to his. Her look of utter shock and surprise was accompanied by a small intake of breath.

"Amber is— She can't see?" she asked, her hand still covering her mouth.

Aiden continued to look at her, the lines in his already creased forehead deepening. "You didn't know?"

Zamina sniffed and shook her head. "No. I had no idea."

"I suppose it would be hard to know something like that if one was supposed to have died in the same fire," Aiden said as he stared at her with a pointed look.

Zamina looked back up at him. "Oh. Yes. I'm sorry. I suppose I have my own story to explain, don't I?"

She wiped the remaining traces of wet tears from her face and placed her hands in her lap as she figured out where to begin.

"Many years ago, the Fall realm and the Summer realm were greatly divided. They had been feuding for many generations, and we were forbidden to have contact with each other. As fate would have it, a young girl from the Summer realm met a young boy from the Fall realm. She had been searching for a special flower to bring back to her mother and had wandered too close to the line of the Fall realm, where a curious young boy from the Fall realm had been exploring. They became fast friends and started sneaking out to meet each other. As they grew older, their friendship blossomed into love. When they told their families, they were forbidden to ever see each other again."

"The young woman came from a long line of Phoenix guardians that carried the power of the Phoenix within them. She had been told of an ancient place where the original Phoenix had received its power. The original Phoenix had long ago disappeared from the earth because of the animosity that developed between the Summer ruler and the mystical bird. The Phoenix's one desire was always to help and protect the people of the Summer realm, but the ruler felt threatened by the power of the Phoenix. When he made his journey to experience his rebirth, he never returned. Legend said he had left a special treasure behind."

"The Phoenix gem?" Aiden asked as he thought back to the song Amber had remembered.

Zamina looked at him, surprised he would have guessed that. If he was the Fall prince, it made sense that he would know about the gem since half of it had been housed in his realm for many years, but it caught her off guard that he would have connected it to the treasure left behind by the Phoenix. She nodded.

"Yes. The Phoenix gem. The woman believed that if she and her love journeyed to the ancient place and found the gem, they would find a way to bring their people together. They made the difficult journey to the birthing place of the Phoenix and when they reached the birthing place, they were lucky enough to find the gem. They decided that before heading back to face their realms, they wanted to declare their love to each other as the first step to bringing their kingdoms together, regardless of what their families and kingdoms said against it. When they did, the gem they found glowed bright and was filled with the flame of the Phoenix. They returned to their kingdoms and tried to convince their families that, just as they had been united with the flame of love, their kingdoms could also be united. Their families would hear none of it. The couple tried to run away together in secret, but they were found out and the gem was broken in half. The young woman had been pledged to marry the king of the Summer realm, knowing her magic would help bring strength to the land, and she was wed to him shortly after she was brought back to the Summer realm."

"And the man?" Aiden asked.

"He was killed in the uprising of the Fall realm."

"Oh. I am sorry to hear that," Aiden replied sympathetically.

"He was a valiant knight in the king's army. He lived and fought most courageously in all his battles, even though he died much too soon."

Aiden thought about her statement. Since their visit with that woman in the woods, he hadn't allowed himself much time to think about the things she had said. But, the queen's talk of a valiant man who died in the uprising caused his thoughts to drift to another valiant man who died during the uprising. If the old woman had been right, his father – the true king – was also killed by the man currently on the throne. That man had ruthlessly destroyed many lives and the Fall realm itself to ascend the throne. And Aiden had called him father his entire life. His mother's death had been something he could handle throughout his life because she died of somewhat natural causes, whether complications in childbirth or a broken heart. But she hadn't died at the brutal hands of the rebel ruler. To find out so many years later that his true father may have died at the hands of his proclaimed father – that was too much.

He redirected his mind from the unsettling thoughts her statement provoked back to her. "And you. You were also said to have died too soon in a horrible fire."

Zamina looked at him, realizing he wasn't going to let her get away with not sharing that part of her story. He had certainly been smart enough to piece other things together, so she might as well share that part with him as well. She moved some of the fiery logs around with a twig to stoke the flames and turned the iron spit over to cook the other side of the meat. She sighed and continued.

"Both kingdoms continued to live in turmoil and angst against each other. It had become more of a silent feuding between the two realms, but there was still an underlying mistrust and anger towards each other. Both of our lands seemed cursed and barren because of the years of feuding and bad choices made between both realms. Killian and I longed to reunite our lands and bring blessings back to the realms, even if we could not be together. We knew the gem had been filled with the flames of the Phoenix's rebirthing place, and we thought that if the two halves of the gem were united once again, the flames of rebirth would sweep through our nations and bring new life and harmony to our worlds. We met to reunite the two halves of the gem, but when they touched each other, it created a spark that very quickly grew out of control. I was severely burned by the spark and almost lost my life in that fire."

"But you obviously didn't. What happened? Why didn't you ever come back after the fire?" Aiden asked as he sat attentively listening to the woman's tale.

Zamina kept her eyes focused on the dancing flames before her.

"I didn't know or remember much from that time. I had been caught in the fire, and as I said, I truly did nearly die that day. Someone picked me up out of the flames and carried me to a place where I could get healed. I was taken to a small cottage in the woods, and this older woman Killian and I had met when we tried to run off together cared for me. I had been so engulfed in the flames that my mind and memory were greatly affected in addition to a fair amount of burns on my skin. I didn't remember who I was or what had happened. It took many, many months for the woman to heal the burns on my skin and even longer to gain my memory back. It came back in bits and pieces. I remembered I was married and had a small daughter and then I remembered I lived at the palace where the fire had happened. I went back to the palace once when I was finally healed, but it was still so burnt and destroyed in places. I remembered that I had been the cause of it and didn't want to hurt my family further, so— I left." She paused. "I had no idea my daughter lost her sight as a result of it." Zamina shook her head and clenched her eyes shut.

"She didn't lose it completely. Not at first, anyway. She told me that she could see shapes and shadows, and after a while, she regained her sight. But she started to slowly lose it again when she was twelve, and now it's almost completely gone. She can still see bits of light, but nothing else. King Azar mentioned something about a Phoenix tear before he slipped into unconsciousness. Do you know anything about it?" Aiden asked.

Zamina sniffed and nodded. "I've heard of it, but I've never seen it. I used to sing Amber a lullaby about it when she was little."

"I know. She remembered you singing that song when she was holding the Phoenix gem in her hands a couple nights ago," Aiden replied, rubbing his hands together in front of him.

Zamina's eyes widened as she looked up at him. "What? What do you mean she remembered it while she was holding the Phoenix gem a couple nights ago?"

Aiden looked at her, surprised to see the alarm that was flickering in her eyes. "Which part do you want me to explain? The part about her remembering the song or the Phoenix gem?"

Zamina's eyebrow raised. "I'd prefer you to explain all of it. How did she get the Phoenix gem, and how did she remember that song while she was holding it?"

"Uh," Aiden hesitated. "I may have followed a couple of the Summer realm's guards to a hidden treasury that housed the Phoenix gem when I went back to retrieve my belongings from the palace."

Zamina's eyebrows raised even higher. "You found the Summer realm's half of the Phoenix gem?" she asked incredulously. "I had no idea where it had ended up."

"Yes," Aiden said slowly as he studied her. His mind started piecing together some more thoughts as he stared at her. "And I believe you were the one who stole the Fall realm's half of the Phoenix gem, aren't you?" he asked as he pulled out the map and looked at the area where he had last seen the orange flames that showed where the other half had been.

Zamina guiltily pulled the Phoenix gem from where it lay hidden beneath her blouse and held it up. "Guilty as charged."

Aiden's eyes widened as he looked at her, surprised that she admitted it so quickly. "Why did you steal our half of the gem?" he asked.

"I thought that if both halves of the gem were returned to the birthing place, perhaps the curses on our lands would be broken, and no one would ever be harmed by their flames again. Phoenix flames are far more powerful than regular flames, and I of all people know of the dangers associated with a Phoenix flame," she replied as she rubbed her gloved hands together.

"But you didn't know where the Summer realm had hidden your half," he said with an understanding tone in his voice.

"No, I didn't. But I knew where the Fall realm's gem was and I knew I had to obtain it at some point."

Aiden shook his head in disbelief. "My brother will be furious to find out our most precious gem was stolen by a woman. And even angrier to find out that he and his soldiers have been eluded by that same woman for several weeks now." Aiden smiled at the thought.

Zamina smiled too. "I have lived in the forest on my own for quite some time and have learned a few things about staying hidden and out of sight. And how did you come to obtain this map?" she asked as she pushed herself up and came to stand beside him.

"You recognize it?" Aiden asked as he held it up for her to see.

Zamina nodded. "Yes. Killian drew this map himself when we journeyed to the birthing place of the Phoenix."

"Did he imbue it with some sort of tracking magic?" Aiden asked, wondering if that's how they found the gem to start with.

Zamina gave him a confused look. "What do you mean?"

"May I?" Aiden asked as he held his hand out for the gem.

Zamina removed the necklace and handed it to Aiden. Aiden took the gem and held it beneath the map.

"This is our way to find Amber," he said as orange flames began to appear on the map.

Zamina's eyes widened. "Iontas," she whispered an ancient mystical phrase. "I had no idea it did that. I have no idea if Killian imbued it or not. He very well could have. Where did you get this?" she asked as she looked at the strange map.

"I took it from my father—uh, from the royal library. I had the Phoenix gem in my bag when I was in there and saw little flames illuminate when the gem was close to it. It shows the location of the other half of the gem."

"Amazing," she breathed out. "And how is it that you came to lose my daughter and the other half of the gem?" she asked as she looked at Aiden. His crestfallen look at being confronted for losing her daughter brought a small smile to her face. She was concerned for her daughter's safety, but he looked like a little boy who had been caught snitching a sweet before dinner.

"I'm not sure," he replied apologetically. "I was with her last night and went to gather some firewood. I had left the gem in my bag, and when I came back, both her and the gem were gone."

"Interesting. And why did you end up here?"

"I remembered the general area of where the other half of the gem had been when we had looked at the map and figured if I found the other half, I could use it to find Amber, assuming they are together, of course."

"Ah," Zamina replied. "Very smart indeed. And here you found it," she said with a smile.

"Yes. And hopefully we will find Amber as well," Aiden said as he ran the gem beneath the map. "Hmm. That is strange. The trail of flames disappeared from where we were in the Fall realm last night and reappears over here," he said as he held the gem under a particular spot in the Summer realm just north of them. "It flickers in this area and doesn't move much, but then there is no trace of it until it reappears over here." He moved the gem to a spot further east of their location.

Fear gripped Zamina's heart as she looked at the sporadic spots on the map. Her hand gripped Aiden's shoulder. He looked up at her.

"What's wrong?" he asked.

"I have a bad feeling about why she keeps disappearing and reappearing in different places. We need to get to her right away."

Aiden frowned as he looked down at the map. "How? It looks like she is pretty far away from where we are currently."

She chuckled at the prince's question. "The power of the Phoenix can do amazing things that other powers and magic cannot. It has been a long while since I have used the powers of the Phoenix, but I think I can remember what I need to do to get us there quickly. Come on. Eat up, and I will get ready to go."

Zamina pulled the animal off the iron spit with her gloved hands and set it on the stones that encircled the fire pit beside Aiden.

Aiden watched as Queen Zamina walked over to Saleem. She held the Phoenix gem and whispered something to the brown regal and then breathed into his face. Saleem knickered and stomped his feet as though anxious to get moving.

"Are you ready, young prince?" Zamina asked as she steadied his horse.

Aiden stood and put the folded map back in his bag.

"What did you do to him?" he asked as he cautiously approached his horse.

"I breathed into him the breath of the Phoenix. It will give him speed like you have never seen before. You might almost feel like you were flying." She smiled and walked over to her bag and finished packing a few things.

Aiden mounted his horse.

"Are you coming?" he asked as he held out his hand to help her mount.

Zamina smiled. "I'll meet you there. Now, steady on." Her eyes glowed orange as she said a phrase in an ancient language and sent Saleem bolting into the forest.

CHAPTER 18

Amber cried out when she finally felt solid ground beneath her feet. Something strange had happened the night before when she had taken the gem from Aiden's bag. It felt like she had been bouncing all over the forest all night, and she had no idea where she was or what had been happening to her. Whatever was happening, she wanted it to stop–and soon. She tried to drop the gem, but she couldn't let go of it no matter how hard she tried. Weariness and total exhaustion gnawed at Amber's mind and body as she frantically tried to scrape the gem from her palm. She sat on the hard ground, hoping with all her might that her body wouldn't start doing whatever it had been doing all night so she could just rest for a moment.

"Oh, Aiden. Why did I have to take that stupid gem from your bag?" she asked as she broke down and started crying.

She heard a strange sound near her. "Aiden?"

Maybe he had found her and was coming to make all things right. She sat silently, desperately longing to hear his voice, or the sound of his boots on the ground, or even smell his scent on the breeze. Nothing.

"Oh, Aiden. Please come find me," she said through broken tears and sniffs.

Suddenly, her palm started tingling again and the strange sensation she had felt the entire night before swept over her body.

"Oh no!" she exclaimed through her sobs as she shook her hand, trying painfully to get the gem off her hand.

"Please. Not again."

Her mind went blank and Amber felt like she had been lifted from the ground again and carried away to another part of the world.

Saleem came to a halting stop somewhere in another part of the Summer forest. "Whoah. Whoah," Aiden said as he calmed his horse after that impossibly quick ride.

Queen Zamina appeared in a cloud of orange smoke not too far from him.

"I had almost forgotten what it felt like to carry the power of the Phoenix. I haven't done anything that exhilarating in years!" she exclaimed as she set down her bag.

Aiden wasn't sure if he truly wanted to know how she got there or what she meant by using the power of the Phoenix.

"Is Amber close?" she asked.

Aiden dismounted and carried the map over to Zamina. She ran the Phoenix gem beneath the map, looking for the orange flames that had previously glowed in the area they were in. To their surprise, those flames had disappeared. Zamina moved the gem around until another area closer to the desert region illuminated with bright orange flames.

"How is she moving so fast? She's not even leaving a trail for us to follow," Aiden said as he let out a frustrated grunt.

"The same way we got here so quickly. But I'm afraid Amber isn't used to the power and probably has no idea what it is or how to control it."

Zamina sighed and walked away, trying to figure out how to get to Amber before the gem caused her to disappear again.

"Is the power of the Phoenix something she was born with, or is it something that is affecting her now that she has half the gem?"

"I'm not sure. As I told you earlier, I came from a long line of Phoenix guardians that possessed various powers of the Phoenix. Amber never showed signs of possessing the magic, but it may have just been hidden all these years. Now that she has the gem, it could be bringing the powers to the surface. Or, it could simply be a side effect of the gem."

"Can we get to her before she disappears again?" Aiden asked. He was growing more and more concerned over Amber having to deal with something like this on her own, especially since she wasn't able to see anything.

"We have to try, I suppose. My magic is not strong enough anymore to see the next spot she will vanish to," Zamina said as she ran her gloved hand along her chin, trying to think of a way to get to Amber. She stopped pacing and looked at Aiden. "Are you ready to ride again?" she asked as she picked up her bag.

Aiden folded the map and returned it to his bag before mounting Saleem.

"Ready."

He nodded at Zamina and she said the magic word, sending Saleem bolting through the forest again.

"Aaaugh!" Amber screamed as she was released from the strange fiery cocoon again. She fell to her knees on the hard forest ground. "Please, make it stop! Please!" she cried out as she broke down into sobs. Her skin crawled with a thousand pinpricks and it felt like her muscles were constantly being torn apart.

"Amber."

A masculine voice landed on her ears.

Amber took in a shaky breath and lifted her head toward the sound. She heard boots hit the ground not too far from her, and then heard the boots running across the forest floor towards her.

"Aiden?" she asked through a broken sob.

"Amber," he said with a worried, yet relieved breath as he knelt beside her. "Hallows Ghosts. You scared me to death when you disappeared. Are you alright?" he asked as he studied her. He reached out his hands to touch her, but when he did, the heat that radiated from her body burned his skin.

"Ouch!" he exclaimed as he pulled back and looked at his hands.

Amber's head cocked towards his voice. "Aiden? Are you alright? What happened?" she asked, her concern for him overriding her sobs from moments before.

"I don't know," he replied. "I tried to touch you, but my hands got burned a little when I got too close."

Amber pulled away slightly. "Don't come too close then. I don't want you to get hurt."

Aiden felt a pang in his heart at her pulling away from him. He wanted nothing more than to draw her close to him and dispel whatever nightmares she had been facing throughout the night, but he couldn't even get close to her without getting burned. And to make it worse, he knew she would keep her distance as long as she thought she might harm him.

"Amber. Where is the gem?" Aiden asked, holding his hands out to keep the burns on his hands from touching anything.

Amber held out a shaky hand. Aiden's eyes widened as he saw the gem embedded in her skin.

"I tried to get it off but I couldn't," she said with a whimpering cry.

Aiden's heart constricted in his chest as he watched the wearied tears stream down her face. He couldn't even imagine what the gem would have been doing to her, but he could tell she was beyond spent and wanted nothing more than to have the gem removed from her hand. Sparks of frustration ignited within him at the gem and the horrors it must have put her through, and at the fact that he couldn't even do anything to help her. His hands clenched into fists in anger at his helplessness. He winced and sucked in a breath as his clenched fingers pressed against his burns.

A puff of orange smoke appeared beside Saleem. Aiden let out a small sigh of relief. He looked at Amber and got as close as he dared without touching her.

"Amber. Listen. Someone is here with me and I'm hoping she can help you," Aiden said in as calming a voice as he could muster. He didn't realize how hard it was to comfort someone without them being able to see his face or touch them.

Amber's agitation grew slightly at Aiden's words. "No," she said as she scooted back a little further from him. "I don't want to hurt her too."

Zamina came to kneel beside Aiden. She looked from Aiden to her daughter. Aiden gave her a reassuring nod, encouraging her to say something to Amber.

"Amber," she said softly.

Amber's head jerked towards the feminine voice. "Who said that?" she asked, her voice still shaky and frightened.

Zamina scooted closer. "Amber, darling. It's me. It's your mother."

Amber's body stilled.

"What?" she asked in a disbelieving whisper.

Zamina sat back on her knees and was about to reach out to Amber, but she didn't want to startle her, so she kept her hands in her lap. "It's your mother."

Amber shook her head. "No. No, it can't be. My mother died in a fire many years ago."

Zamina felt the gem warm against her chest. "Who is the gem telling you I am? Aiden told me you remembered the lullaby I used to sing to you when you touched it the other night. It will tell you the truth."

Amber paused for a moment and tried to focus. Faded memories played across Amber's mind of her mother talking and laughing and singing to her as a child.

"The Phoenix takes flight to meet an old friend. For he knows his journey is nearing an end. He leaves a precious treasure behind. A gift that will forever remind." Zamina sang the words, hoping the gift she had left her daughter in that song would remind her of who she was.

"Mother? Is that really you?" Amber asked incredulously.

"Yes, darling. It is."

"But how? I don't understand. You died in the fire."

"Everyone thought I had, but I didn't. I will tell you more about it later, but first let's remove that gem from your palm so you can find rest."

Amber nodded and held out her hand to her mother. Zamina reached out to touch Amber's hand. As she did, Amber's skin began to tingle again and her muscles burned within her.

"No," she let out a sob. "Not again."

Aiden watched as a strange, surreal flame danced across Amber's skin. A bright red flash of light surrounded her and she was gone in a puff of red smoke before he or Zamina could stop her.

"No!" Aiden yelled as he reached out for where Amber had just been. He turned to Zamina. "What just happened to her?" he asked, frenzied fear filling his voice.

Zamina sat there, eyes wide with shock at what she had just witnessed. "She's an imperforate," she said in a surprised whisper.

"She's what?" Aiden asked.

Zamina blinked and looked at Aiden. "She's an imperforate. That power hasn't been seen since the first guardian carried on the full power of the original Phoenix."

"What does that mean?" he asked heatedly. "What just happened to Amber?"

Zamina let out a sigh. "The imperforate magic is one of the most powerful forms of magic in all the realms. It's a magic that takes on the full magical powers and essence of another magical object or being. Most things or people that possess magic only carry parts of that magic. Imperforates essentially fully become whatever magic they have come into possession of. It was granted to the original guardian because the Phoenix knew its time in these realms had come to an end, but he still wanted someone to carry on his powers. Since then, the guardians have only carried different forms of the Phoenix's power and it has never been fully exemplified in one person. Until now."

"Which means?" Aiden prodded impatiently.

"It means that Amber can take on the form of a full Phoenix. Every few centuries, the Phoenix returned to its birthing place and basically combusted on his fiery altar so a new Phoenix could be rebirthed. It was the Phoenix's way of regenerating his power so he could use it for the next centuries until the time came to do it again. I believe the gem is causing Amber to continually go through this combusting stage, which is why she keeps disappearing and reappearing in another place."

Aiden's eyes widened and were laced with fear. "Can we stop it from happening?" he asked, tension tightening his already agitated voice.

Zamina shook her head. "I have no idea. Like I said. No one has had that power since the original guardian, Kazeem."

Aiden raked his hand through his hair to try to stave off some of the mounting frustration and anxiety that was coursing through his veins. He pushed himself up to a standing position and started pacing. "We have to do something. I can't bear to have her go through something like that without doing anything to stop it."

"I know." Zamina looked up at him. "You mentioned the Phoenix tear. Did you and Amber figure out where that might be? If anything can help her, I think that would."

"The gem illuminated a blue crystal shape in the eastern desert region. We remembered the words from the lullaby about the painted sands and Amber mentioned an oasis your family would stop at on your way through the desert region when she was younger."

"Of course," Zamina said, her eyes lighting up. "The Oasis of Melchizidai. It was said to be the haven for the Phoenix as it flew through the desert region. It would make sense that if he left his tear anywhere, it would be there. Do you think you can make it to the oasis on your own and get the tear?"

"I think so," Aiden replied.

"Good. I'm going to try to find Amber and stay with her. I'll do what I can to help her control the Phoenix power or at least slow it down."

"How will I know how to find you once I obtain the tear?" Aiden asked as he walked over to his saddlebag to retrieve the map.

Zamina followed him and took the map. She removed the gem from around her neck and held it to a spot near the palace. Speaking an ancient phrase, the gem glowed and seared a burned imprint into the parchment. "Whatever happens, plan to meet me here in three days' time. If you get back to this place, I will find you and take you to wherever I left Amber last."

Aiden nodded. "Three days. Safe travels, Your Majesty. Please find Amber and help her."

Zamina smiled at his depth of concern for her daughter. "And safe travels to you, young prince. Bring back that tear."

Aiden mounted his horse and put the map in his bag.

"Oh, Aiden. I almost forgot. Saleem still has the magic of the Phoenix within him, but you will need to say the words Phoenix flight to enact the power to make him go fast."

"Phoenix flight," Aiden echoed. Saleem reared up and took off in the direction of the painted deserts.

Chapter 19

"Lord Amir." The captain of the red guard approached the throne and bowed.

"Sir Cassias. How goes the search for the princess?" Lord Amir asked.

"We have found no trace of her, my Lord. We journeyed as far as the Fall realm, and the ruler of that land said he had not seen any sign of the princess being in that kingdom. His sons had boh returned, but did not have the princess with them."

"Keep me posted," Lord Amir said as he plucked a grape off the plate the handmaiden held out by the throne.

A triumphant smile filled Amir's face after the captain left. "This is turning out far better than I had hoped," he said as he looked smugly at the grape in his hand before tossing it into his mouth. When Amir had set the fire, he had hoped to cast blame on the visitors from the Fall realm, concocting some story about how the visitors from the west were trying to overthrow the Summer kingdom just as their father had done in the Fall realm. But, when the captain from the Fall realm fled, it made him look guilty as sin. Amir had never expected the Fallen prince to take the princess with him, but that only added fuel to Amir's story making it look like they had kidnapped the princess in addition to destroying the Summer palace, and nearly killing the king.

Amir picked up a date from the outstretched platter and eyed it thoughtfully. He would have preferred it if the king had perished in the fire, but his majesty had not been well since the *accident* and would surely succumb to the complications brought on from the smoke before long. With the king so close to death and the princess unable to rule, he would be on the throne before the setting of the Summer solstice sun. Even if the princess returned to the palace before then, she would be easy enough to get rid of permanently. She was blind after all.

Amir's sinister smile widened as he gazed at the wrinkled fruit before taking a voracious bite of the date.

"Amber!" Zamina called as she reached the next place that had shown up on Aiden's map before they parted ways.

A strange red and orange light filled the area. The flaming light dissipated and Amber appeared in the remaining smoke. Her body was so tired and so weak. She stumbled forward and fell to the ground.

"Oh, Amber!" Zamina exclaimed as she ran to her daughter. She picked her up off the ground and cradled her in her arms.

"I just want it to stop, Mother," Amber whimpered as she melted into her mother's embrace.

"I know, darling. I know. We are trying to figure it out," Zamina soothed as she rocked Amber back and forth. "Now, let me see your hand."

Amber held up her jewel encrusted hand. Zamina started quietly singing an old solstice lullaby as she gently took her daughter's hand. She looked at it and brushed the gem slightly to see how firmly it was attached.

"Ouch!" Amber let out a wearied exclamation.

"I'm sorry, darling," Zamina said before she continued singing. The gem that sat around Zamina's neck started to warm against her chest. Zamina removed the necklace and held the gem near the other half that sat in Amber's hand. The gem in Amber's hand pulled towards the gem in Zamina's hand.

"Now, hold on, darling. Remember when you fell and got that big nasty thorn in your hand when you were little? Mother sang to you and pulled it out. It hurt for a moment but then it was better because it was no longer in your hand causing you pain. Do you remember?" Zamina crooned as she continued to rock Amber.

Amber nodded weakly.

"All right, darling. Mother is going to pull the gem out just like she did with the thorn. It might hurt and sting a little, but it will feel much better once it's out. Okay?"

Amber nodded.

Zamina continued singing and carefully hung her gem over the one in Amber's hand. She closed her eyes for a moment, hoping beyond hope that the two halves wouldn't spark or explode as they had done before when they got too close. Opening her eyes, she watched as the gem in her hand slowly drew out the one in her daughter's until it was just on the surface of Amber's skin. She reached over with her gloved hand and pulled the gem out as carefully and painlessly as she could.

Amber took in a sharp breath but she didn't cry.

"That's my brave girl," Zamina whispered as she finished removing the gem. The gem was finally detached from Amber's skin. Zamina placed her necklace and the other gem on the ground beside them, careful to keep them apart.

Amber let out a small sob and turned, wrapping her tired arms around her mother.

"Oh, my dear girl. It's alright. You can cry. You've had a very trying night. There, there, my darling." Zamina relished holding her only child in her arms again. She squeezed her tight and placed a kiss on Amber's forehead.

"Oh Mother. I'm so glad it's you. How did you escape that fire all those years ago? I don't understand," Amber asked as she cried into Zamina's shoulder.

"That is a story for another time. You are probably beyond worn out after that long night you had," Zamina replied.

Amber melted again at the mention of the night before. "What was happening to me?' she asked as she tightened her grip around her mother's waist.

"I can't say for sure, but I believe the gem sensed the power of the Phoenix within you, and when you touched it, it amplified your power within and brought parts of it to the surface."

"Power? What power?" Amber sniffed.

"You have great power within you, my darling. My family is from a long line of Phoenix guardians that carried the power of the original Phoenix through many generations. I didn't know if you would ever gain the power yourself. You had never shown any signs of it, but after seeing what happened to you last night, I am more than certain that you indeed were born with the power. And not just any power. A great power that hasn't been seen since the time of the original guardian of the Phoenix."

Amber pulled away slightly as she moved her head in the direction of her mother's voice. "What does that mean?" she asked as she sniffed again. She reached up to wipe the tears from her face.

Her mother smiled and reached out a hand to wipe away the remaining tears. "You have the ability to take the full form of the Phoenix. With that, you gain all of its powers and strengths. The power to heal and bring rebirth."

Amber moved her head slightly as she tried to process this. "Will that only happen if I am holding the gem or will it happen all the time now?"

"I'm not sure. I will help you figure it out though. That is a lot of power to try to grasp and understand on your own."

"What if I don't want it?" Amber asked as she gently touched her hand where the gem had been embedded. "I don't want what happened last night to happen again. That experience was one I never want to go through ever again. Especially since I couldn't see anything that was happening. I have never felt so out of control in my entire life."

"I will help you control it. We will learn together. It may be difficult at first, but with practice and dedication, we can figure it out and hone your power and skills into something you can enjoy and feel in control of. This gift is a beautiful thing and who knows what magic and healing it will bring back into our land. Possibly even the other realms."

Amber pulled away from her mother slightly. "I don't know if I am ready for such a great power to be thrust on me. I've spent most of my life in my tower where I've been safe and haven't faced much of the world because of my sight. How can I learn to use such a dangerous power if I can't see anything I'm doing?" she asked, worry creasing her forehead as she thought about all the things that could go wrong wielding magic blindly.

"That is a valid fear and question, but I believe you were given this gift for a specific purpose and reason. You will overcome any obstacles that you need to. You just have to trust the power that is within you and let it shine. Do you trust me to help you get control over it?"

Amber thought for a long moment before responding. "I suppose I can try," she replied meekly.

Zamina smiled. "Good. But first, some rest and some food."

She brushed a loose strand of hair back behind Amber's ear. Her eyes widened as she saw Amber's long braid for the first time.

"Amber. Has your father kept your hair growing this long your entire life?" she asked as she touched the long fiery braid that stretched out behind Amber on the ground.

Amber let out a small laugh and shook her head. "No. Of course not, Mother. Strange as it may seem, it wasn't nearly this long before I left the palace. I got a strange shock when Aiden touched the gem at the same time as me, and the next morning my hair had nearly doubled in length. I feel like it grows longer every time I'm in contact with the gem. I can't imagine how long it must be now after being connected to the gem all night," she replied with a weak smile as she pulled the braid over her shoulder and tried to find the end.

"Incredible," Zamina said as she stared at it. "It will be interesting to find out what other surprises the gem will bring to the surface in you."

"Mama. Where is Aiden?" Amber asked with a yawn as she stroked her silky braid.

Zamina smiled at the name Amber called her as a child. "He went to find the Phoenix tear. He should return in a few days," Zamina replied as she took in her daughter's features.

"Oh," Amber replied, her demeanor a little cast down at him not being there with them. "Is he going to the oasis to find it?" she asked.

"Yes. He said you both thought that was the best place to look for the tear," Zamina replied as she continued to sift through every feature of the daughter who had grown into a young woman while she had been away.

Amber sat silently stroking her braid for a few moments as she thought about the man who had come to her rescue on several occasions over the last few days.

"You have seen Aiden, haven't you? Can you describe him to me?"

Zamina's heart clenched at her daughter's question.

"What's wrong?" Amber asked, sensing the change of mood after her question.

"Nothing, darling. I'm going to look around and see what I can scrounge up for food. You should lie down and rest. By the time you wake up, I'll have a feast for you," Zamina said, trying to make her voice sound light and happy to keep her daughter from asking any further questions. She stood up and started looking around to see which direction would be best to hunt for food.

"Sleep sounds divine," Amber replied sleepily. She could still sense the change in the mood after her question, but her mother didn't want to respond for whatever reason, so she didn't pursue it further.

"You just lie down and rest. I won't be gone long, I promise." Zamina knelt to pick up her necklace and placed it around her neck. She took the other gem and put it in her bag to keep Amber from getting a hold of it again.

Chapter 20

Zamina gently shook Amber awake the next morning. "Rise and shine my little sunflower. It's time to see what powers you possess."

Amber opened her sleepy eyes and stretched before sitting up.

"Good Morning, Mother," she said, still a little groggy and half-asleep. "Did you sleep well?" she asked.

Zamina smiled at the picture of her daughter, who at this moment, still looked like the little girl she used to be. "I did, thank you, darling. And you seemed to sleep well."

Amber yawned. "Yes. I think I was worn out enough," she smiled. She sniffed the air. "What are you cooking?" she asked as she inched closer to the sound of the crackling fire.

"I found some eggs and some mushrooms nearby." Zamina scooped some of the food into a bowl she carried in her bag and brought it over to Amber. "Do you need help feeding yourself?' she asked as she knelt in front of Amber.

"I have been feeding myself just fine since before you left. I just need direction on where the plate and silverware are at," Amber replied curtly.

"I'm sorry. I didn't know. I'm new to this with you." Zamina grabbed Amber's hands and placed the bowl into them. She stood up and went to grab a fork from her bag and brought it back, placing it in Amber's hand.

"I'm sorry too." Amber sighed. "I didn't mean to snap at you. I'm used to the servants bringing my food to my room and leaving it in the same place they always do. I guess I have become too comfortable with my routine at the palace. Some may think it is a sad existence to dwell in a single room for most of one's life, but that room brings familiarity and confidence to me because I know where everything is and I don't have to worry about any unknowns." Amber lightly touched the food in her bowl to see what was where before putting her fork in and scooping up some eggs.

"Perhaps the Phoenix tear will change all of that," Zamina replied quietly as she sat cross-legged by the fire and ate her own breakfast.

"I hope so," Amber replied wistfully. She smiled and rested her hands in her lap with the bowl for a moment. "Aiden read the legend of the Phoenix to me when we first met. I was in the library with that book on my lap, sitting in an apparently very dark room when he came in and found me. He told me he had heard my music when I walked past his door and he followed me to the library. He had no idea I couldn't see at the time. He graciously read to me all night." Amber's cheeks pinkened and her smile widened in a coy, unassuming smile as she thought back to that night.

Zamina smiled at her daughter's sweet innocence and obvious fondness for the young man from the Autumn realm, despite her surprise at her daughter sitting in the library in the dark with a book. "You go to the library? What for? You can't read the books."

"I remember you reading them to me. My sight came back for a few years and I often visited the library. I memorized what the spines of the books felt like and read as many of the books as I could. When I started losing my sight again, I made sure to memorize where my favorites were. I sneak down there at night when no one is around and I feel the engraved spines of the books until I find the one I want to remember. I hold onto it and sit and imagine as much of the story as I can. It was such a treat to have someone read to me," she replied as she scooped up some more eggs from her bowl and brought them to her mouth.

Zamina sat there staring at her daughter in amazement. In spite of everything, her daughter still had the brightest optimism, strength, and bravery. The reminder of the fact that she had been the cause of her daughter's loss of sight laid a heavy blanket of sadness and shame over her daughter's amazing feets. "She wouldn't even have to do these things and find ways to adjust if not for you," Zamina said to herself out loud.

"What was that?" Amber asked as she finished the delicious food her mother had made.

"Hmm. Oh, did I say something out loud? I'm sorry, darling. I suppose I have been on my own for too long. I've started talking to myself without even realizing it. Are you ready to begin?" she asked as she stood up and came over to take Amber's bowl and fork.

Amber felt her mother take the bowl from her hands. Her hands sat empty in her lap and started fidgeting at the mention of getting started on learning her new strange magic. "I don't know," she said nervously.

"There is nothing to be afraid of. I will be right here beside you as we figure this out," Zamina said as she knelt before her daughter with the Summer realm's half of the Phoenix gem in her hand. She didn't want to interfere with her daughter's magic, so she had taken her necklace off and tucked it safely away in her bag.

"Now. Some things you should know before we begin. The Phoenix had various powers, one of the main one's being its control over fire. I want to see what abilities you have from the Phoenix so let's begin with that." Zamina carefully placed the gem in Amber's left hand.

Amber cautiously handled the smooth, cool gem, keenly aware of what had happened the last time she held the gem. "How will I know if I'm doing it right if I can't see it?" she asked, still unsure about this whole thing.

"You will be able to feel it. Magic gives off certain energies and vibrations. Not having sight with your eyes, your other senses have become stronger and more focused. You can sense people's emotions even though you can't see them, can't you? I know you can because I've seen it on several occasions in the last day. This power was born within you, Amber. It is a gift given to you that you can give back to the world. To keep such power hidden just because you feel scared or uncertain would rob the world of the beauty of that gift. You have no idea what good you could do for our kingdom and the realms if you don't learn to use it."

Amber sat quietly thinking about her mother's words for a moment, rolling the gem around in her hand.

Zamina reached out and lifted her daughter's face towards hers. "I know it can seem scary. It is scary. All guardians of the Phoenix have had to learn their various powers at some point. It was so varied, we sometimes didn't truly know what each guardian's gift was until they tried different things. Some had multiple powers, but one power usually shone brighter than the rest. It is a lot of trial and error, and even when you are learning, things happen or you make mistakes, but that is all a part of the learning process. You will get the hang of it and be able to control them the more you practice and work at it. Believe me, I scorched quite a few things as I was learning my powers, and terrified my teacher on more than one occasion. But, I kept working at it and got to a point where I could control and execute my magic with grace and power that could actually be used for good. You can do this, Amber. You just have to be willing to stick through the messy bits to get to the more beautiful form of your powers. Are you willing to do that?" Zamina asked as she looked at her daughter's beautiful sunlit face.

Amber's eyes drifted unknowingly around the area as she thought. She bit her lip and lifted her eyes in the direction of her mother's voice. "Okay," she replied. "I'll try."

"Wonderful!" Her mother smiled and leaned forward to kiss her daughter's forehead. "Let's begin.

Chapter 21

Aiden arrived at the oasis late the next day. He dismounted and led Saleem to drink at the large fresh spring of water that sat in the midst of a cover of trees. Looking around at the beautiful oasis, it was hard to believe that such a spring of life existed amidst the barren sands of the desert. Aiden was beyond grateful to be at this place of reprieve after his journey through the unrelenting heat of the painted desert. Something he was far from accustomed to living in the Fall realm. He was especially grateful that the queen had breathed the Phoenix flight into his horse, making his time in the desert sun much shorter than it would have been had they been going a more normal speed. He knelt to fill his canteen in the cool, fresh spring that was so clear it reflected its surroundings like a perfect picture, and took a long drink before allowing his gaze to drift around the rest of the oasis.

The trees at the oasis looked very different from the trees he was used to in the Fall realm. Instead of having branches all the way up, they had just a few branches at the top of the tree with wide green leaves and bunches of what looked like large brown balls of some kind, while others had clusters of dates. The trunks of the trees were striped, kind of like the gold-leafed trees they had at home, but much larger than the thin white striped trees that surrounded his palace.

There was a marketplace on one side of the oasis, similar to the one he had seen in the small village near the forest, with colorful drapes of cloth hanging over and between the booths and some sandstone buildings built up behind it. The buildings were long, connected rows of what appeared to be the homes of those who sold their wares at the market. Quite different from the separate, cottage-like homes in the Fall realm. His eyes shifted to a waterfall set back against some large rocks on the other side of the crystal clear spring.

"If I had been a fabled bird, where would I leave my precious tear?" he asked himself as he continued to look around the oasis. The song had said the tear would last forever wherever he had left it, so Aiden wondered if it could be connected somehow to the spring or the waterfall. He pulled out the map and tried to line it up with the landscape around him to see if he could figure out exactly where the tear could be.

"Welcome to our fair oasis, young traveler. How might I assist you today? Are your supplies in need of replenishment? Do you seek a special gift for a special girl?"

Aiden jumped at the voice behind him. A short, round man stood behind him. His skin had been much exposed to the sun and was very dark and tan. A bushy black mustache that had a sprinkling of gray in it covered his lip and he had a vibrant-colored turban wrapped around his head.

The man glimpsed Aiden's map before he put it down. "Ah, or perhaps you seek something entirely different all together." The man studied Aiden for a moment. "Yes, you don't look like the usual kind of traveler we see here at the oasis. I'd say from the looks of that map, you seek a very special item."

Aiden quickly folded the map and shoved it in his bag. "I was looking for some apples or something for my horse, actually," Aiden replied, trying to make it sound like the man hadn't hit his quest right on the head.

The man eyed him skeptically, but he carried on. "If it is food you seek, Sahir carries some very good apples for a fair price that are sure to please you and your horse. Also, Sahir-that's me-- takes very good care of traveler's horses if you care to leave this magnificent animal with me. My children will brush him down and see that he gets some rest in the cool shade of our stabling pens over there." He nodded towards a small holding area where children of various sizes ran around feeding and tending to the horses that were there.

Aiden smiled at the man. "And how much for such a fine service?"

The man leaned back and patted his rotund belly. "Well, of course for the best service it would cost a pretty coin, but, for you, I'm feeling generous. Shall we say three marah and call it even?" he asked with a gleam in his eye.

Aiden laughed and pulled out two gold coins from his pouch. "Will this do?" he asked as he handed the coins to the man.

The man's eyes widened and he rubbed his hands together eagerly before taking the offered coins. "Ah, most generous to old Sahir. We will take extra special care of our special friend's horse."

"My greatest gratitude, most honorable Sahir." Aiden smiled and handed the reins of his horse to the man.

Before the man walked away, he looked around to make sure no one was near, and pulled Aiden closer by his shirt. "If you seek a special treasure, seek the source of the fresh spring that feeds this oasis." He winked and gestured his head towards the waterfall. Aiden nodded his head in understanding and watched the man walk away with his horse.

Aiden strolled through the small marketplace looking at the many different vendors and items they sold. He stopped at the apple merchant's booth and bought several apples, and then stopped at a booth that sold articles of clothing and bought a scarf to wrap around his head and keep his head and face cool for the journey back. As he left the market, he looked around to see if anyone was watching him before making his way to the waterfall. Everyone was wrapped up in the activity of the busy oasis, so no one noticed as Aiden slipped past the sandstone houses and kept walking around the edge of the spring until he came to the rocks that housed the waterfall. A flash of something caught his eye behind the waterfall. Could it be that easy?

Aiden crept along the edge of the wet rocks, careful not to step into the spring. As he reached the waterfall, he felt a cool breeze coming from behind it. Looking around once more, he squeezed between a protruding rock and the cascading water, only to feel his body lurch backwards as he nearly fell through the hidden opening behind the waterfall. Grasping at anything to hold onto, Aiden flung his arms around a damp rock near his head. Making sure his feet were on sturdy ground, he slowly let go of the rock and looked around, trying to discern his surroundings. Aiden stood in the opening waiting for his eyes to adjust to the dim lighting of the cave he had stumbled into, surprised at how chilly it was inside the cave compared to the overwhelming heat of the outdoors. His eyes landed at last on a small, blue glow coming from the bottom of the cave.

Aiden carefully inched his way into the depths of the dark cavern, using his hands to guide him down the rocky wall since the lighting was too dim for him to see where his feet were stepping. The path down into the cave seemed to take forever, but that was probably because Aiden couldn't see anything and didn't know where he was going. His feet finally reached what seemed to be a flat surface that led to a small pool of water where the blue glow was coming from. Aiden looked around him, but couldn't see anything except the glowing pool. Inching cautiously to the edge, he leaned over and saw something sparkle in the blue light.

"That must be the tear," he said aloud to himself, relieved and excited that he had found it.

Aiden knelt down and took his bag off his shoulder to prevent himself from becoming top heavy and falling into the pool when he leaned over. He leaned out over the clear water and reached as far as he could to grab the crystal. As he reached into the pool, a cool wind swept around him, pulling him back from the edge.

"Who believes himself worthy to take the tear of the Phoenix?" a deep, booming voice sounded behind him.

Aiden turned around and saw a ghostly looking blue man that filled the cavernous space behind him, blocking his exit.

"My humblest apologies for disturbing your rest, good sir. I was not aware of the rules of this cave or what one needed to do to obtain the Phoenix tear." Aiden bowed his head, trying to look humble and hopefully appease the giant blue man.

"I am the guardian of the tear. My name is Kazeem, and it is I that you must go through to obtain it."

Aiden's eyes registered surprise at the name. "Kazeem? You were the original guardian of the Phoenix," he said in amazement.

The blue man looked at Aiden, surprised that the intruder would know his name.

"How do you know who I am?" he asked as he crossed his arms over his large chest.

"Queen Zamina told me of you not two days ago. She said you were the only other guardian to ever be granted the full power of the Phoenix."

Kazeem puffed out his chest. "Yes. I—wait. You said only *other* guardian? To my knowledge, I am the *only*."

Aiden chuckled. "I believe you were, but Princess Amber, daughter of the Summer realm, seems to have attained that power as well."

"Hmph," the man grunted. "Well, the ancient Phoenix must know what he is doing in bestowing such power on a daughter of the Summer realm. You said you spoke with Queen Zamina just two days ago. She was long ago a guardian of our ancient powers, but she died many years ago. How is it that you came to be in conversation with her?" he asked, arms still folded over his chest.

"She was believed to have died in a fire started by the spark of the Phoenix gem she and the noble knight Killian obtained from the birthing place of the Phoenix, but alas, she survived. Much of her memory had been lost to her for many years, but when she slowly regained it, she felt responsible for the tragic fire and did not wish to return to her realm or cause more harm. She remained hidden in the forest of the Summer realm for many years and it was only by a chance meeting that I found her. It is on behalf of her husband, King Azar and her daughter, Princess Amber, that I seek the Phoenix tear. There was another fire at the Summer palace a few days ago and the king urged me to get the princess out of the kingdom. His last words before slipping into unconsciousness were 'Phoenix tear'."

"Hmm. I see," Kazeem said as he floated up and down in his mystical blue smoke. "And who are you to be sent on such a quest?" he asked as he studied Aiden.

Aiden bowed his head. "I am Aiden, prince of the Fall realm."

"Aiden? I do not know that name as the one associated with the Fall realm. The name given to me years ago was Aodhán- the white flame. Are you he?"

Aiden looked at him, confused by the slightly different name. "Not that I am aware of, sir. As far as I know, my mother named me Aiden. Not Aodhán."

"That is not what I was told." Kazeem floated across the pool and pulled out what looked like some sort of scroll from behind the rock. "Ah, here it is. Aodhán—son born of the white flame. Born to King Hallel of the Harvest and Queen Jora of the Autumn Rain. Full-blood prince of the realm of the harvest."

Aiden's eyes widened at the mention of his parents and the confirmation of what Seraphina had told him in the cabin.

"You look surprised. Are these not your parents?"

"No. I mean, yes, they are," Aiden said slowly as he realized he was admitting to his true parentage for the first time since he had learned about it. "I just, why would my name be different from what my mother named me?"

Kazeem kept reading, "Ah, I see here that the false ruler of the realm declared you to be called Aiden and not Aodhán after the death of your mother. Most interesting."

"Well, Master Aodhán, son of the Fall realm. Are you aware of the cost of the Phoenix tear?" he asked as he rolled up the scroll and put it away.

"I'm not, sir. Is the price great?" Aiden asked, hoping he would have enough to purchase it.

"It is very great indeed. The Phoenix was a bird of sacrifice. Every few centuries he would have to sacrifice himself upon the burning altar in order to be reborn and have his powers rejuvenated. That cost did not come cheaply. It was his willingness to lay down his own life so that others might live that gave him his famed power. The tear was said to have fallen from the Phoenix's eye upon his final return to sacrifice himself on his altar one last time. It is meant to bring life and healing to anyone who needs it, but, like the Phoenix, a sacrifice must be made to obtain the tear."

Aiden swallowed hard. "Do I have to sacrifice myself on this altar in order to obtain the tear?"

Kazeem let out a deep, rumbling laugh that reverberated off the cave walls. "Fortunately for you, that is not the required sacrifice. But, you still must be willing to sacrifice something great to obtain it. What are you willing to sacrifice, son of Hallel?"

Aiden looked around the cave as he tried to think of what he had to give. He looked back at Kazeem. "I'm not sure what I have to give."

Kazeem nodded to the pool. "Take a look in the pool. It will show you what you possess that is of great worth."

Aiden tentatively leaned over the pool. Blurry images came to life in the depths of the water, revealing the image of a man with brown hair and a beard holding a silver flute. As Aiden looked at the image, it cleared and he saw the crown that sat on the man's head. A lump formed in Aiden's throat as he realized that the man was his father--his real father. He watched as the music the king was playing on his flute fell to the earth and caused the seeds planted beneath to take root and sprout above the ground. Next, Aiden saw his mother stand beside the king and start to sing. Her song brought rain to the earth and together, they made the seeds grow into tall stalks of grain and wheat and corn. The images changed, revealing someone that looked like Aiden playing his violin. The music he played from his violin caused the wheat and grains to grow, just as his parent's music had. Aiden stared at the image in astonishment.

"Does this mean I have the ability to make the harvest occur with my music?" Aiden asked as he looked up across the pool at Kazeem.

Kazeem nodded and replied, "If that is what you see."

Aiden sat back on his heels contemplating what he had just seen. "Our land has been barren for so long. I had no idea I could have brought the harvest back." He looked back at Kazeem. "Is that what I would be giving up in order to obtain the tear?" he asked.

The man nodded.

"What would Amber gain if I sacrificed my gift and gave her the tear?" Aiden asked.

"She would gain her sight," Kazeem said simply.

Aiden let out a small breath and ran his hand through his hair. He eyed his bag and ran his other hand across the smooth leather that had long protected his violin. He loved to play almost more than anything and it was the one thing that still connected him to his mother. And now that he knew what it could do for his land and for his people, could he really give that up just to help a blind princess see? She had been blind most of her life and seemed to have gotten along fine. But, if he were in her shoes and had lost his sight, wouldn't that be his greatest wish and desire? To see again?

"The hour grows late my friend," Kazeem said in his booming voice. "A decision must be made."

Aiden took in a deep, long breath and looked at Kazeem. "I'm ready."

"I will tell you this, young prince, before you decide. The Queen has not been fully forthcoming with you or the young princess. I know the princess now possesses one half of the Phoenix gem. Her mother caused a great tragedy when she tried to unite the two halves years ago, and she is allowing her fear to rule her decisions. Queen Zamina was not the correct guardian to unite the two halves. It is the princess who must be the one to unite the two halves and bring rebirth to her kingdom. The one half has awakened the power of the Phoenix within her, but without the other half, she will never gain control of the powers that have begun to be unleashed. Regardless of your decision here, you must find a way to get the other half of the gem from the queen and unite it with the other half when it is in the possession of the Princess."

Aiden nodded and stood to give his decision to the ancient guardian.

Chapter 22

Amber had spent a long and wearing day exploring her magic. She had started out by learning how to ignite a flame in her palm. It required a lot of concentration and focus and she had no idea if she was doing things right most of the time. She had eventually gotten a little flame to ignite and stay lit in her palm for a few minutes, but the energy from the magic and the gem felt strange. It wasn't hot like she would have expected a live flame to feel like in her hand, but she could feel the glowing energy like her mother had said she would.

Next, her mother wanted to see if she could transform or shapeshift into the form of the Phoenix. The original Phoenix had the ability to shapeshift into human form to blend in when he needed to, but it was different with a human shapeshifting into the Phoenix form. Zamina believed Amber must have the ability since she had continuously been combusting into the Phoenix flames the day before. Amber held the gem in her hand and focused on becoming the Phoenix. She remembered the pictures of the Phoenix in the book Aiden had read to her, so she pictured that image in her mind's eye and tried to emulate that in her body. The strange burning sensation she had felt the day before ignited in her veins and snaked around her body as she thought of the Phoenix. At some points, she felt like her body was being consumed by flames even though she wasn't burning. At others, things felt generally strange and off like the magic was only half there or coming in spurts. She had no idea what her mother was seeing when she was experiencing these different waves of her magic.

"Good," her mother said as she watched. "You are getting closer."

Zamina then told Amber to try to breathe the spirit of the Phoenix into something and to transfer the ability of super-human speed into the object. "Take a deep breath and focus on the spirit or breath of the Phoenix."

Amber took in a deep breath and focused.

"Now focus your energy into this bowl. As you breathe out, say *Phoenix flight.*"

Amber did as she was told and breathed out as she focused on saying Phoenix flight. When she did, she heard a strange wind-like sound that filled the air around her. A whooshing sound whistled past her ears and something hard and heavy hit a tree somewhere on the other side of the area they had been practicing in. She heard a sharp exhale of breath.

"Mother?" she asked as she reached out to see if her mother was still in front of her.

"Very good, darling. You obviously have that power, though perhaps a bit too much of it for your first time," her mother replied with pinched words as though she had been punched in the stomach or had the wind knocked out of her.

Amber gasped in horror and dropped the gem. "Oh no! I hurt you. What did I do?"

Zamina stood up from where she had been lifted from the ground and thrown across to the other side of the trees and held her stomach. "You did nothing wrong, my darling. Just perhaps a little too much power and focus on one thing. But, that is a part of the learning process. We will try again and see what happens," she said as she walked back over to Amber and knelt to pick up the bowl.

Amber stepped back. "No. I don't want to do that one again. I might hurt you or do something horrible."

"Alright. We will take a break from that one," Zamina replied as she went to set the bowl down by the fire.

"I want to try something else based on what was happening to you yesterday. Do you trust me to try it?" Zamina asked as she stepped towards Amber again.

Amber fidgeted with her hands as she sensed her mother step closer. "I'm not sure. I don't want to go through that excruciating pain again."

"I know, darling. As much as things hurt, most Phoenix guardians have the ability to heal themselves and recover rather quickly. The events of the night before were most excruciating for you, and I wish more than anything you wouldn't have endured it, but let me ask you this. Do you feel like your muscles are in pain or like your body is hurting the way it was yesterday after I removed the gem?"

Amber thought back to the intense muscle-ripping pain she had been experiencing the day before and mentally assessed her body now. The pain had pretty much gone away completely compared to what it had been the day before.

Zamina reached out and grabbed Amber's right hand. "The gem left a mark on your hand yesterday after I removed it. You may or may not have noticed it with all the other pain your body was experiencing, but it is no longer there today," Zamina said as she brushed her fingers gently over Amber's palm where the gem had embedded itself the day before.

Amber moved her other hand to where her mother's fingers had just touched her skin and she felt the smooth, unharmed skin of her hand. Her eyebrows shot up in surprise. "You mean I can heal myself without even realizing it?" she asked as she lifted her head in the direction of her mother's voice,

"You are most resilient, my daughter. Even more so with the power of the Phoenix within you," Zamina replied as she ran her hand lovingly along her daughter's cheek.

Amber smiled. "And to think. Father kept me hidden away in that tower to keep me safe and make sure I didn't get hurt because of what I couldn't see, and I find out I can heal myself."

Zamina's body language changed at Amber's remark. She pulled her hand away and moved away from her.

"What did I say now?" Amber asked as she sensed the change in her mother's mood again.

"Nothing," Zamina replied hesitantly as she turned back to face Amber. "I'm just not sure how your father will feel about you having this power."

Amber's brows knit together in confusion at her mother's remark. "What do you mean? Wouldn't he be excited for me knowing that I don't have to worry about not seeing anymore and being able to take care of myself?"

"I'm not sure, love. Your father was not fond of my magic when we married. He felt it could be a threat and danger to our family and the kingdom."

"He didn't like your power? Then why did he marry you?" Amber asked as she knelt to sit down.

Zamina sighed. "That is another long story, pet. Why don't we continue with your magic?"

"Please tell me. Father doesn't talk about you or the two of you together. Actually, he rarely tells me anything. He just checks in on me once a day to see how I'm doing and if I need anything."

Zamina wiped an unbidden tear from her face and came to sit beside her daughter. She put her arm around Amber and pulled her close. Amber rested her head on her mother's shoulder and closed her eyes so she could focus on every word.

"The royals of the realms are usually born with some kind of magic that will help their kingdom and realm. There are a few faery groups and magical beings that exist outside of the royal families, but they are becoming fewer and farther between. Your father was one of the few royals born without any magic. His cousin, the king of the Spring realm, had been born with sun magic, the magic your father thought he should have been given since he was a royal in the Summer realm. His brother had been born with water magic that helped water the earth. He could control streams and oceans and almost any body of water. His wife had become ill and the healer said the sea air in our southern region might help her. Your uncle abdicated the throne and moved to the seaside, making your father the first king to ascend the Summer throne with no magic."

"I remember visiting the sea when I was little. We never went back, but I never knew why."

Zamina's heart clenched. "Your father's brother and his family were lost at sea after a terrible storm hit that region. Your father always blamed magic for not protecting his brother. He hated magic--partly because he hadn't been born with magic, and partly because he blamed magic for taking his brother away from him. His marriage to me was more of an arrangement by our parents to keep magic in the royal line."

"An arranged marriage. I had no idea. Father was trying to arrange a marriage for me before all this started."

Zamina tilted her head down to look at her daughter. She had already surmised that much from Aiden, but she was curious about what her daughter thought about the arranged marriage. "He did? To whom?"

"Aiden. That's why he invited him and his brother from the Fall realm. To meet me and arrange a union between us." Amber's nose crinkled slightly and she lifted her head from her mother's shoulder. "Although, I'm not entirely sure he was going to have me ever meet or marry Aiden."

"What do you mean?" Zamina asked as she laid Amber's head back against her shoulder.

"Aiden told me that when he first arrived, he was introduced to another young woman who wore heavy veils and hardly spoke. He hadn't met me until he found me in the library that night. I was completely unaware we even had visitors from the Fall realm. My companion had stopped coming to visit that week, and I just assumed she had been ill or something, but Aiden believes Father was using her as a stand-in for me."

"So, your father was trying to marry Aiden off to your companion in disguise?" Zamina asked, shocked at her husband's actions.

"I suppose so. I'm not sure why or if he would have switched us after the marriage. Or even if he was ever going to tell me about it. I think he has always viewed my blindness as a weakness and he didn't want the other realms to know about it," Amber replied, a slight sadness creeping into her voice at the vocalizing of her hidden fears and thoughts that had plagued the back of her mind all these years.

"Oh, darling. I'm sure that's not it," Zamina said as she wrapped her other arm around her daughter and pulled her closer. "Power does strange things to men's minds. They feel they have to be invincible and have no signs of weakness. In their attempts to protect and care for the people that matter to them, they can make certain decisions they view as best. But, the idea of power gets in their heads and often distorts their reasoning and view on things. That's why they need us," Zamina said with a joking smile as she squeezed Amber's shoulder.

Amber smiled, sensing the playful tone in her mother's voice in her last statement. "Aiden doesn't seem to be like that," she said as her thoughts wandered once again to the young prince who had treated her with such kindness and respect in the short time they had known each other.

Zamina rubbed Amber's shoulder. "He may not seem like that now, but power can change people in ways we would never expect. I pray his head doesn't get turned around by that. You like him don't you?"

Amber blushed. "I don't know. I've been isolated for much of my life and never had any suitors or thoughts of marriage after I lost my sight, so I don't know what all these feelings and emotions mean when I'm with him. He is so kind and caring, and doesn't treat my blindness as something to be afraid of or treated differently because of it. He treats me like a normal person, but still helps me and guides me without giving it a second thought." She smiled. "He seems like a genuine prince you read about in stories and everything a girl could dream about." Her smile faltered. "But, it could just be the excitement of being with someone new. I don't know."

"There's your father's logic showing through," Zamina smiled as she kissed the top of Amber's head.

"How will I know if what I feel for Aiden, or anyone for that matter, is love?" Amber asked as she toyed with a loose thread her finger had found on her dress.

"You'll know," Zamina replied with a dreamy tone in her voice as she thought back to her first love.

"Have you ever been in love with someone, outside of Father, of course?" Amber asked.

Zamina sighed and rested her head on top of Amber's. "I have. A long, long time ago. But, that truly is a story for another day. How about we continue with your magic?" Zamina asked as she moved to stand up beside Amber.

Zamina pulled Amber up to a standing position. "Now. Let's try the power from yesterday." She took Amber's hands in her own and took in a deep breath.

"Close your eyes and focus on a place you want to go. Focus all your energy and magic on that place in your mind, and if all goes right, we should be there in a matter of moments."

Amber took in a shaky breath, unsure if she wanted to experience what she had experienced the day before. Her mother gave her hands a reassuring squeeze. "It's all right. I'm right here. You can do it."

Amber bowed her head to focus, then paused and lifted her head towards her mother. "How can I go somewhere if I don't know what it looks like?" she asked. "And, how will I know if I've arrived there?"

Zamina opened one eye and looked at her daughter. "Excellent questions. Perhaps I should do the first one so you know what it feels like. But, you had your sight for a while and saw some things and places. I'm sure you can remember places if you try. Come. Close your eyes and we will see where we end up." Zamina closed her eye again and Amber followed suit.

A flash of red light filled the area and they were gone. The bright flash startled a red guard that had dismounted his horse when he heard voices nearby. He pushed past a few of the trees and vegetation that covered the forest floor and saw the abandoned mound of ashes where a fire had been, a large bag, and a few other things that made it look like someone had just been there.

"That's strange," the man muttered to himself. He could have sworn he had heard voices just a moment ago. As he turned to go back to his horse and continue his search for the princess, another bright red flash of light filled the forest around him. He spun around and his mouth fell open as he saw two women appear seemingly out of nowhere with the remnants of what looked like red flames dissipating into thin air around them.

"We did it!" Amber exclaimed, excited to have accomplished such a high level of magic.

"We did indeed, my darling girl," Zamina replied as she stroked Amber's cheek. "You are going to be a most powerful princess."

The man stumbled back after seeing the incredulous sight before him, his boot snapping a twig and alerting the older woman to his presence.

"Amber. Think of the oasis and Aiden. Now!" Zamina yelled as she let go of Amber's hands.

"Mother!" Amber cried as she felt her mother's hands leave hers.

"Focus, Amber. Hold the gem close to your chest and focus."

Amber did as her mother said and held the gem close to her heart. She focused her mind on the oasis she had visited many times as a child. She imagined the clear spring water that shimmered in the sunlight, the colorful market, and the painted sands of the desert on her way there. And then, she focused on Aiden. She didn't know exactly what he looked like, but the picture that formed in her mind's eye made her feel safe and happy. Amber smiled as she lingered on that thought. The gem warmed in her hand and a fire broke out within her, filling her body with warmth and energy. A flash of light, and she was gone.

Chapter 23

Aiden reclined against a stack of colorful pillows near the fire Sahir had built, smiling as he watched the children run and play. Sahir had convinced him to stay for the night before returning to the spot Queen Zamina had indicated on the map. For the first time since the fire had broken out at the Summer palace, he was able to sit still and relax a little bit. Though his body was more relaxed, his mind was still forever on Amber. Worry that her mother hadn't been able to find her or remove the gem plagued the back of his mind as he sat and subconsciously rubbed the light blue crystal that now hung around his neck. He had felt so helpless when he couldn't reach out and comfort her the way he had been becoming accustomed to doing in the few short days he had known her. He felt such a strong urge deep within him to protect her and keep her from harm no matter the cost, especially since she couldn't see. He couldn't do anything to help her from this far away anyway, so he tried to convince himself that Amber had been found and freed from the gem.

A thought struck Aiden as he continued to rub the blue crystal he had acquired in the cave. If he gave Amber the crystal and it restored her eyesight, she might not need him anymore. That thought pierced his heart in an unexpected way. He hadn't been helping her the past few days to gain anything from her or her kingdom as his brother may have done, but something about being her helper and protector filled him with a sense of purpose and desire he had never experienced in his own home or kingdom. His eyes drifted to the spot behind the oasis waterfall where he had sacrificed his gift so Amber could be healed. What if he had made the wrong decision? What if he should have kept his gift and gone back to his realm to try to heal his land and bring back the harvest? Was the sight of a hidden princess more important than the beauty and prosperity of his own realm being revived?

Sahir came to sit beside him. "You look troubled, my friend. Can an old man help you?" he asked. Sahir's tone had lost its merchant's candor and had mellowed into that of a genuine friend when Aiden returned from the cave.

Aiden removed his hand from the crystal and sat up. "No. I'm fine. Thank you though," he said as he twirled his signet ring on his finger, trying to stave off the wavering thoughts in his mind. "Can I help with any of the dinner preparations, or do anything to help you and repay your kindness?" he asked as he stood, suddenly anxious to be doing something and distract himself from his thoughts.

Sahir patted Aiden's hand and gestured for him to sit again. "Please, sit. My wife hates it when I try to help her when she's cooking and would consider it an offense if a guest tried to help," Sahir replied with a smile. "Sit down, your Highness. Please. Take a load off and rest. You are at the King's Oasis. The place for weary travelers to lay their heavy loads aside for a moment and rejuvenate their souls before continuing their arduous journeys through the desert." Sahir nodded his head to the stack of brightly colored silk embroidered pillows Aiden had been reclining against earlier.

Aiden looked at the short round man in surprise at the mention of his title as he lowered himself down to the stack of pillows.

Sahir grinned. "Yes. I know full well who you are. A man with such a fine horse in this part of the desert with a sack of gold in his saddlebag. And you bear the signet ring of one who is royal. The leaf and grain on the crest indicate you are a ruler in the Fall realm."

Sahir reached out and lifted Aiden's hand and studied the ring that sat on his right middle finger.

Aiden raised his eyebrows in surprise at the man's observance. "That is very astute of you to pick up on all of that."

"It is my job to know things about other people and pick up on their ranking or station. We see many travelers through this oasis and it is good business to know when to address someone with a higher station or know when a family can't afford much. Those with rank feel flattered and instantly ingratiated to me and my family for pointing out their rank, which most often loosens their purse strings a bit more than they would have if I had not so poignantly pointed out their rank and status," Sahir said with a mischievous glint in his eye and a wink.

Aiden shook his head and smiled. "You are a clever merchant," Aiden said, amazed at the man's shrewdness.

Sahir sighed and lowered his head slightly. "It is true I am a clever merchant," he replied with a slight smile towards Aiden. "But, I am also the patriarch of this oasis. It is my duty and privilege to take care of those who live and work here. We see many travelers come through here that can't always afford to buy the merchant's wares, making it difficult for the merchants to provide for their families. Often we take pity on those less fortunate and give them food and shelter and a break from the unyielding desert sun, even when they can't pay. So, if my wit and charm loosens a few purse strings of the rich to make up for provision lost on others, then I take no qualms in that act."

Aiden looked at the man with a new respect. "That is very noble of you, Sahir. You take good care of your people and your village. Most men would do whatever benefited themselves and their own families most, keeping the money for themselves, or not even bother with the less fortunate. You make sure the people of this oasis, both visitor and resident, are cared for. That is quite an admirable quality as a leader. My humblest respect and admiration goes to you." Aiden put a hand to his chest and bowed his head towards Sahir.

Sahir looked at Aiden and let out a surprised laugh. "Oh, Your Highness. Please. No. You have no need to honor Sahir in such a way. You are a son of the crown. I am but a humble servant." Sahir flicked his hands at Aiden as if dismissing Aiden's praise and looked away, embarrassed to be recognized by a prince.

"You are far more than a servant, Sahir. Many rulers should learn from your example in how to lead and care for their people. I hope someday I can be half the ruler you are." Aiden reached out and touched Sahir's dark-skinned hand and squeezed it.

Sahir looked up at Aiden, surprised at the gesture. He smiled and patted Aiden's hand with his other one. "You will make a wonderful ruler some day, Prince Aiden. Your people and your land will be greatly blessed by you." Sahir stood and walked over to the tent where his wife was preparing a feast.

Aiden's cheeks burned slightly at the compliment as he watched Sahir walk away. He had just sacrificed his gift that would have brought blessing and prosperity to his land. He was again questioning his decision and wondered if he should pay another visit to the cave before he left in the morning.

As Aiden pondered this, a bright red light flashed behind him. Aiden stood up and turned around to see what it was. As he looked, he saw what looked like a female figure appear in flickering red flames that dissipated into the night air like a mist on a hot summer morning.

"Amber." Aiden jumped over the mound of pillows that sat around the roaring fire and ran towards her.

CHAPTER 24

Relief soared through Amber's veins as her feet finally touched solid ground. Her head swam from the amount of energy it took to transport herself across the realms, and her muscles felt like rolling waves in the ocean. She just hoped she had reached the oasis and that Aiden was there. The Phoenix gem slipped from her hand as she felt her legs start to buckle beneath her.

Amber suddenly felt something strong reach around her and hold her up before she collapsed to the ground.

"Amber! Are you alright? How did you get here?"

Amber lifted her head in the direction of the masculine voice. "Aiden?" she asked with a weary tone in her voice as she felt her legs melt beneath her again.

"I got you," Aiden said as he swept her jelly-like body up in his arms.

Amber felt her feet leave the ground and her body pressed against Aiden's. The sensation of being carried in his arms was strange and quite different from the weightless flying feeling she had experienced time and time again the last couple days when she had been transported hither and yon across the realm. Where she had felt out of control and unaware of what was happening to her in the grips of her new power, she felt completely safe and secure in his arms. The warmth that spread through her at being held so close to a man's body was also different from the fiery energy of the magic that pulsed through her veins on a regular basis now too. And not just any man's. Aiden's. His arms felt strong and protective as he cradled her close to him. Amber didn't know what this feeling was or if she would feel the same way if any other man had carried her, but she relished the feeling while it lasted.

She felt herself being lowered down and her hand brushed something silky with threaded bumps as Aiden set her down. "Where are we?" she asked as she lifted her other hand to her head, still a little light-headed from her journey, and tried to orient herself with her new and strange surroundings.

Aiden smiled and ran his thumb along her cheek, brushing a smudge of dirt from her face. "You are at the Oasis of Melchizidai. Though how you got here, I have no idea other than you appearing in a burst of flames."

Amber's cheek tingled where Aiden's thumb had just brushed her skin. She tipped her head, feeling her cheeks blush at his touch. The tingling feeling made her remember the gem she had dropped before Aiden had swept her off her feet.

"The gem!" she exclaimed, suddenly worried about not knowing where it was. "I dropped it when I got here. Where is it?" she asked frantically as she attempted to stand.

"Whoah. Whoah," Aiden said as he placed his gentle hands on her shoulders. "Sit down. I will get the gem."

Aiden stood and went to retrieve the gem from where she had dropped it. It was still warm from the energy it must have been exerting to bring her here. He pulled his hand back quickly and looked around for a cloth or something to wrap it in. Spotting his saddlebag, he remembered the scarf he had bought earlier that day. He walked over to it and pulled out the scarf. Returning to where the gem lay on the ground, he knelt and wrapped the scarf around the gem several times before carrying it back over to Amber.

Amber's body was tense as she sat alert and erect, her knees pulled up to her chest and her arms wrapped tightly around them, waiting for Aiden to return. Aiden's heart twinged as he looked at her. He again couldn't imagine how hard it must be not to be able to see one's surroundings and to live life in the dark all the time. Especially with the terrifying sensations of a new power and the numerous unknown environments she had been in over the last few days. He touched the blue teardrop crystal around his neck as he continued to look at Amber and decided then and there that he had made the right decision. He would give Amber the crystal tear and find some other way to regain his kingdom from the man who had brought it to ruin, and bring rebirth and prosperity back to his realm.

He came to sit beside Amber, taking her hand in his.

Amber jumped at his unexpected touch but relaxed when she realized it was him.

"Sorry," he said as he pulled out the gem to hand it back to her. "I should have told you it was me."

Amber squeezed his hand in hers, reassuring herself it was him. "It's alright. I just didn't know who had touched me."

She reached out her other hand to touch him and her fingers bumped into his chest. She moved her hand up slightly to find his face, but drew back her hand at the unexpected roughness she felt along his chin and cheek.

Aiden laughed slightly as he watched her nose crinkle up while she continued to run her hand along the no longer smooth skin.

"Apologies, Princess. I have been without the means to shave the last few days, so your soft hands must endure the growing rough terrain of my face."

Amber smiled as she felt it. "No apologies needed, my good sir. It was just an interesting and unexpected addition to the smooth face I felt a few days ago."

Her hand continued to explore his face, her fingers crossing over the stubble on his cheek and up and over his temple and forehead.

She ran her hand down his nose, and around his eyes, and finally came to rest beside his cheek. A contented smile filled her face as she gently stroked his stubbly cheek with her thumb.

"I'm so glad you're here," she sighed as her hand lingered on his face.

After a few moments, Amber realized what she had been doing and pulled her hand away. Aiden reached up and wrapped his strong hand around hers, pressing it to his cheek.

"I don't mind," he said softly as he held her hand against his face.

A tender softness in his voice reached her ears like the sweet notes of a beloved melody, and she sensed a different intensity as she felt his gaze on her face. She heard something else in his voice too, but she couldn't quite picture what it was. A sudden longing to see what his eyes looked like and what it would be like to see them staring at her the way she felt he was throbbed in her veins. As Amber sat there, she closed her eyes and tuned into the senses around her. Aiden's woodsy masculine scent mixed with the smell of a fire nearby tickled her nose and her ears picked up on the crackle of the fire, as well as various voices nearby. She could hear the rush of water in the distance too.

Amber focused her senses even more on the man before her, aching to know and feel what he was thinking and feeling in that moment. As she focused on Aiden and what she felt beneath her fingertips, something seemed strange or different about him than it had a few nights ago. Her brows knit together as she tried to discern what was wrong or missing. She removed her hand from beneath Aiden's and moved it down to where she could feel his heartbeat in his chest. Her eyes opened and she lifted her head towards Aiden.

"What happened to your gift?" Amber asked as her unseeing eyes looked up in the direction she thought his face would be.

Aiden's body tensed at her question and he suddenly pulled away from her.

"What do you mean what happened to my gift? What gift?" he asked as he readjusted his position beside her.

"Your music. I can feel that it is missing from within you. What happened to it?"

Aiden pulled even further away. "Nothing happened to me. I'm fine. I'm sure you must be starving after your journey. A friend that I met here is making dinner. Let me go see where they are at in the preparations."

Amber felt Aiden shift and stand beside her. Her mind ran around in circles as she tried to figure out what had caused the music to leave Aiden. Sensing the Phoenix gem nearby, she reached out her hands to search for it. Her hands made contact with a cloth bundle that felt slightly warm. She took the bundle in her hands and began to unwrap it. When she finally reached the gem beneath the folds of the wool fabric, she grasped the gem and let her questioning mind settle on the fiery gem. Pieces of a vision played out in her mind's eye as she clutched the gem closer to her heart. She saw a teardrop crystal and a pool of water; different images in the water; the exchange of a beautiful violin; and the crystal around Aiden's neck.

"No!" she gasped as she dropped the gem. She lifted her head and moved her head side to side trying to figure out which way Aiden had gone. She listened intently with her ears to see if she could pick out his voice anywhere near her. Hearing what sounded like the undertones of his voice, she pushed herself up to a standing position. She inched her foot out cautiously in front of her to see if anything was in her way, and was surprised when she hit something soft in front of her. She tried to step sideways to go around the soft object, but her feet kept hitting different objects all around her.

Panic and frustration were starting to rise to the surface within her. She reached out her hands in front of her to feel what was preventing her from walking anywhere, but her hands just waved through empty air.

"What on earth?" she grumbled to herself under her breath. Why couldn't she figure out how to get around whatever her feet were running into? Whatever it was, it was low to the ground, but Amber couldn't figure out what kind of place she would be in that would have low, soft objects and not physical chairs or benches or anything she could reach with her hands.

She tried to move forward with her feet again, but kept bumping into large soft objects with her shins and ankles. Eventually, her feet became tangled up in whatever was surrounding her and she fell face forward into the endless soft objects. An exasperated grunt escaped her lips as she tried to push herself up and figure out what was holding her hostage. She felt around her and felt what must be a multitude of pillows of various shapes and sizes. Amber started pushing the pillows out of the way and wondered how many she had to push through to get free. She put her hand down, thinking she had cleared a spot for her hand to make contact with solid ground, but it fell through a hole between a mound of pillows and she fell face first again into the soft cushions. Her panic was quickly melting into anger as frustration sparked and fanned the flame within her.

"Ugh!" Amber screamed as she felt tiny flames ignite within her.

Aiden left the tent where Sahir and his wife, Hadassah, had been making the meal and saw Amber sprawled out in a mass of pillows.

"Amber. What are you doing?" Aiden asked as he ran to her and knelt to help her up.

Amber lashed out and pulled away from him suddenly.

"Don't touch me," she breathed out with an angry, hot breath.

Aiden withdrew his hand, surprised at the abrupt outburst of anger in her voice. "Amber, what happened? Let me help you up," Aiden said as he reached for her again.

"No! Don't touch me," Amber replied hotly as she tried to push herself up. Her hand slipped on the silky material of the pillow and she fell yet again.

"Amber. You need help. Quit trying to do this on your own,"

Amber felt her body fill with an electric warmth at Aiden's words, making the flames of anger burn even stronger within her.

"Don't tell me what to do. You are not guard and guardian of my life," Amber said vehemently as she sat up and tried to stand.

"Amber. I only want to help. Please, calm down and we will figure this out," Aiden said as he tried to reach out and grab her again.

Amber sensed Aiden's hand reaching towards her and she put her hand up to deflect it. When she did, she felt the tingle of a flame ignite in her hand.

Aiden jerked back, surprised to see an orange flame flickering in Amber's hand.

"Amber. Calm down. I don't want you to hurt yourself."

Amber's head lifted in the direction of Aiden's voice. "Hurt myself?" She let out a curt laugh. "I can't hurt myself. Phoenix's are known for their self-healing powers and nearly indestructible nature. Besides, I'm immune to my own flames. They're only dangerous against other people," Amber said with a strange otherworldly sound in her voice. She lifted her hand as though she could see the flame flickering in her hand while a slow, evil smile spread across her face.

Aiden spotted the glowing gem that sat behind her near the fire. He carefully crawled over to where the gem was while Amber was distracted with enacting her new powers. Amber sensed Aiden move behind her and the gem warned her that he was getting too close. She turned and shot a flame from her hand that went right past Aiden's hand as he reached out to grab the gem.

"It isn't safe to play with fire," she said maniacally as she walked towards the gem. "You could get burned." Amber knelt to pick up the gem and held it in her hand with a greedy smile.

Aiden held his hand where the flame had skimmed it. "Amber. The gem is having an adverse effect on you. We need to get you back to your mother and get the other half of the gem to make the gem whole so you can control your powers."

Amber's face turned towards his. "The other half? I had nearly forgotten I didn't have the whole gem. Imagine what power I would possess if I had the whole gem. Perhaps you have been of some help after all," she said with a malicious laugh. "Thank you for reminding me of the other half," she said as she knelt and ran a flaming finger beneath Aiden's chin.

Aiden winced at the heat of the flame beneath his chin and pushed her hand away. Amber smiled, turned and started to walk away from Aiden.

"And how do you plan to find your mother when you can't see anything?"

Amber stopped, her body half-engulfed in flames that danced across her skin, but didn't seem to burn her. "I don't need to see. This sees what I need to and will get me where I need to go," she replied haughtily as she held up the glowing gem.

Aiden's mind raced as he tried to figure out how to stop her and calm her down. The gem seemed to be feeding the flame inside her instead of extinguishing it. Extinguishing it. Aiden looked down at the teardrop crystal that hung below his neck. He quickly pulled it from his neck and ran over to Amber. Grabbing her, he placed the silver chain around her neck and watched as the crystal glowed when it made contact with her flaming skin. It seemed to bring an instant calm to Amber. The agitated flames disappeared from her skin and her body shuddered as if letting go of something.

Amber put a trembling hand to her head as she let go of the Phoenix gem with her other hand and let it slip to the ground.

Aiden took a cautious step towards her.

"Amber?" He reached out a gentle hand and touched her shoulder. Her skin was still warm, but it didn't burn him as it had a few moments ago.

Amber turned to face Aiden. Strange tears pricked her eyes and filled them with water. She clenched her eyes shut to try to squeeze out the strange moisture. She blinked and continued to close and open her eyes to make the tears go away. At one point, as she opened her eyes, a strange blurr coated her eyes.

"What's happening?" she asked as she leaned her head into her hand and tried to blink away more of the tears.

"You'll have to tell me," Aiden said. "I can't discern what you're feeling or experiencing right now."

Amber lifted her head towards Aiden's voice and blinked again. As she did, an obscured vision of shapes and colors filled her eyes. She let out a small gasp and blinked again, willing her eyes to focus on something.

"Amber?" Aiden asked as he reached up to wipe some of the tears from her face.

Amber forced her eyes to focus on the man before her. An unfocused shape of someone came slowly into focus as the tears left her eyes. She blinked again as the sensation of seeing shapes and light and color hurt slightly, but her desire to see the man before her outweighed the slight ache behind her eyes. She focused her eyes again on the face of the man before her. As her eyes finally adjusted, she saw a face for the first time in ten years.

Amber's eyes saw a man's face that was outlined in a dark auburn color for hair. They saw a forehead that was slightly creased and the dark stubble she had felt when she had touched Aiden's face earlier. They finally came to focus on the intense eyes she had sensed on her many times over the last few days. They were a beautiful cinnamon color that were currently pouring into her with concern and worry. How she relished being able to look into those eyes at long last.

"Aiden." Amber breathed out the word in a soft whisper, half-afraid that this was all a dream and she would be woken up from it if she said anything, and half-afraid that this wasn't truly the man she had been fighting off growing feelings for over the last few days.

"Yes?" he replied with a concerned question in his eyes.

Amber smiled the biggest smile she had ever smiled in her life. "I can see you," Amber said as she reached out her hand to touch his stubbly face.

Aiden's eyes widened and his eyebrows raised in surprise at her words. "You can what?" he asked as he pressed her hand to his face as he had done earlier before she could see him.

Amber's smile lit up her face as she drank in the sight of him. "I can see you," she replied with a felicitous laugh. Tears of joy rimmed her eyes at finally being able to see this dear man.

Aiden's hand left hers and both hands encompassed her face as he drew her closer so he could look into her eyes.

He stared deep into her honey-cinnamon eyes as if trying to see what she could see to prove it to himself. His forehead relaxed as he looked down at her. "You can see me?" he asked as he stared at her in elation and disbelief.

Amber's cheeks blushed at how close he was holding her and how intently he was staring down at her. "Yes," she said sweetly. She didn't care how his closeness made her blush. She was not going to let go of this moment and let her feelings of shyness and uncertainty take her eyes from drinking in every inch of the man she had been longing to see since meeting him a few days ago.

"You mean, you can really, truly see me with your own eyes?" he asked with overwhelming joy and excitement as he brought her face closer.

Amber let out a joyful chuckle at his question. "Yes. I can really, truly see you. You're even more handsome than what I pictured. Especially with a few day's growth on your chin," she said coyly with a twinkle in her eye.

Aiden's face broke into a boyish grin. "I'll be sure to let it grow then so you can enjoy it," he replied with a teasing yet seductive glimmer in his eyes as he lowered his hands from her face to her shoulders.

"I might have to see your face both ways to see what I like best," she said as she reached up and stroked the stubble on his chin.

"I think that can be arranged," he replied with a warmhearted tenderness in his voice as he smiled down at her with a heart-stopping smile.

Amber felt something prick her foot. She looked down and saw that the gem was touching her foot. The tingling warm feeling that was becoming far too familiar filled her veins and started to spread through her body.

"No." Amber let out a half-sob and half-groan as the sensation wound its way up her leg and through her arms. It had happened enough now that she knew when it reached her chest, she would be gone in a flash.

Aiden's eyes darkened with concern as he looked at her. "Amber. What's wrong? Are you losing your sight again?"

A shudder shook her body involuntarily as she looked at him. She shook her head as a flame ignited in her hand. "Promise you'll find again," she said as tears began to roll down her face.

The Phoenix flames broke out across her skin again and Aiden stepped back to keep himself from getting burned. Aiden looked down and saw the Phoenix gem touching her foot. He looked back up at Amber, his eyes locking on hers.

Amber's gaze held Aiden in her sight, taking in every last look at him that she could. She felt the flame ignite within her chest and closed her eyes as the red Phoenix flame whisked her away to another part of the realms.

"Amber!" Aiden called as he stepped forward to reach out for her. A bright red light filled the air, and she was gone. The momentum sent Aiden falling to the ground face first. He pounded his fist on the ground and let out an angry growl, followed by an anguished moan. His eye caught sight of the gem that still glowed orange not too far from him.

"This cursed stone," Aiden exclaimed with a furious tremor in his voice as he picked up the gem and threw it towards the spring.

Sahir emerged from his tent and looked towards Aiden. "What has been happening out here?" he asked as he came to kneel beside Aiden. "The children are all worried and talking of bright flashing lights and a girl who bursts into flames."

Aiden's chest heaved with anger at having lost Amber once again to the whims of that flaming stone. "I can't keep traipsing across the Summer realm trying to find her every time that thing makes her disappear. How am I supposed to keep her safe if every time she touches that blasted thing, something bad happens. No wonder her father kept her locked in that tower all these years and kept that infernal gem locked up in a hidden treasury. It is far too dangerous."

Aiden raked his fingers through his hair in frustration and stood up and started pacing.

Sahir raised a quizzical eyebrow as he watched his new friend. "Ok." Sashir drew out the word, completely confused by Aiden's outburst.

Aiden stopped and looked at Sahir. "I have to get back to the palace and find the queen. She will have the other half of the gem, and we can figure out how to make Amber quit disappearing. That has to work." Aiden looked around for his saddlebag. He spotted it and went to grab it. "Sahir. Where is my horse? I need to leave immediately."

Sahir still looked at him completely confused. "It is over by the outdoor pens. Did I miss something?" he asked as Aiden rushed past him towards the pens.

Aiden turned to look at him, "I'm sorry friend. I don't have time to explain. I have to get back to the Summer palace."

"Tonight? You can't travel through the desert at night by yourself. There are wild dogs that roam those deserts always looking for their next meal, not to mention any number of thieves and bandits."

Aiden stopped short and turned back towards Sahir. Sahir raised his hands in relief. "Ah, good. You listen well to Sahir. Stay here for the night and you can leave first thing in the morning."

Aiden walked past him and walked towards the Spring. He knelt and started digging around in the sand.

"And he's not listening to Sahir," Sahir muttered to himself as he lowered his hands in defeat. "My friend. Come and dine with us and I guarantee you will feel much better in the morning," Sahir raised his voice so Aiden would hear him.

Aiden saw the glowing orange of the gem. He knelt to grab it but it was still warm from the energy it had exerted sending Amber into the wilderness. He pulled back his hand and looked around. Spying his scarf by Sahir's feet, he stood up and walked over to him to grab it. He then went back to where he had thrown the gem and carefully picked up the gem with his scarf, wrapping it in the dark material.

"My friend. Sahir thinks you have been out in the heat too long. Perhaps the sun is not what you are used to in your realm. Come inside and rest. Please."

Aiden stopped by Sahir on his way past him and placed a hand on his friend's shoulder. "I will explain all of this to you someday, dear friend. I promise. For now, I must go, as crazy as I look and sound. Please, take care of your family and thank you for your generosity and hospitality you have shown me today. Goodbye, Sahir." Aiden bent and gave the short, round man a hug before heading once again towards his horse.

Sahir looked after the young man and sighed. "The Great Mage be with you on your journey, young prince."

Chapter 25

"My Lord. Mathias found this woman in the forest. He said he saw the princess with her, but she disappeared."

The captain threw the woman to the ground and grabbed her hair, pulling her head back for Lord Amir to see.

Amir's eyes widened with surprise when he saw the woman's face. "Well, well, well. This is quite the surprise indeed." Amir nodded to the guards to leave them. Sir Cassias threw Zamina's head down and walked out with the rest of the guards.

Amir stood up from the throne and walked over to Zamina. He walked around her once before kneeling in front of her. Placing his gloved hand beneath her chin, he lifted her face towards him so he could look at her.

"How is it that you are here in this kingdom? You were declared dead nearly twenty years ago."

Zamina glared at Amir. "And how is it that you are sitting on my husband's throne? You are not king of this realm, nor will you ever be."

Amir's hand tightened on Zamina's face as looked at her. "Your husband, if you can call him that, is not well. Or perhaps you hadn't heard the sad news."

"I saw exactly what you have done to this palace. You probably thought you could get away with starting a seemingly accidental fire that would hopefully trap the king and his heir and kill them both, clearing the way to the throne. *If* you had succeeded. Pity for you the king still draws breath and his daughter is far away from here and out of your clutches. Azar was wise to send her away from the palace under the protection of the Fall prince."

Anger sparked in Amir's eyes at Zamina's words. "Your magic was exactly why I believe that royals with magic should no longer be on the throne. As I recall, it was because of you that the first fire started and caused your daughter's blindness. Tell me, Zamina. What is more dangerous? A ruler with dangerous magic that should be purged from the land, or one that seeks the safety of the land by having no magic and no means of endangering the people?"

"I have paid for that mistake many times over the last seventeen years. The royals and ancient fae families and beings have magic and gifts to keep their lands safe and bring the life needed to make them thrive. A man that sees only his own selfish gain behind the crown is far more dangerous than any person possessing magic, royal or not," Zamina replied with steely anger.

Amir squeezed her face tighter, causing her to wince. Sir Cassias walked back into the room.

"What is it?" Amir asked, his voice infused with a mix of anger and frustration.

"Some of the scouts just spotted a strange red flame not too far from here. We thought you would be interested in investigating it," the captain replied warily as he glanced between the lord and the woman.

Amir glowered at the bothersome soldier, annoyed at the seemingly insignificant interruption. "And why would I want to investigate it? That is what you are here for," he growled out.

The guard was unsure if he should intervene, or just leave the vizier to his business with the woman they found in the woods. "Because, my Lord. The flame is similar to the one Mathias saw the princess in earlier when he apprehended this woman."

Amir's eyes narrowed at the infuriating soldier. "Then gather our forces and ride out to investigate at once. If it is the princess, merely capture her and bring her back here."

"Uh, Yes. Of course, my Lord. We will take care of the situation right away." Sir Cassias turned and ran quickly from the room.

Amir turned his attention back to Zamina. "What do you know of this supernatural flame your daughter seems to be tied to? Is she a filthy witch like her mother?"

Zamina held his gaze but didn't respond.

"Where is the princess?" Amir raged as he squeezed her face even tighter.

"I don't know," Zamina replied, holding Amir's ominous gaze stare for stare.

He stared at her for a long moment trying to decipher if she was telling the truth. "Fine. I hope you enjoy your time in solitude. You may end up wishing you had died all those years ago." Amir called for one of the guards and released Zamina's face.

Zamina reached up and touched her face where it felt like Amir had branded his fingerprints into her skin.

"Take her to one of the rooms in the east wing and lock the door." The guard nodded as he took Zamina's arm and began pushing her out of the room.

"Oh, Zamina," Amir called after her. The guard stopped and jerked her around to face Amir. "Tell me. Does iron still have an adverse effect on children of the Phoenix?" he asked with a sinister smile.

Zamina's eyes widened as Amir laughed and gestured for the guard to take her from the room.

Amber took in a deep breath as her feet made contact with the ground and the last of the flames disappeared from her skin. Opening her eyes slowly, she looked around her. It was certainly strange being able to see after so many years of darkness, but it was wonderful.

Her eyes drank in the lush green leaves on the trees around her and caught the flying image of a wood thrush that landed on a branch not too far from her. She watched as the cinnamon speckled bird called to his mate. The sing-songy sound the thrush made landed on Amber's ears like the melody of a magical flute, making her smile in amazement that she was able to see the charming creature that made that beautiful sound. A female thrush sang her response back to him before flitting to join him on his branch.

A sweet scent reached Amber's nose, drawing her eyes to the colorful foliage that carpeted the forest floor with ferns and wildflowers and innumerable green plants. She stepped towards a bouquet of colorful flowers that splayed out beneath one of the trees, marveling at the various shapes and colors her eyes saw. Colors she hadn't seen in so many years—yellows, purples, oranges and red. So beautiful.

A sound caught her ear behind her. She whirled around and saw a brown fawn with white spots on its back through the trees. Her eyes drifted to the surrounding area, wondering if she would see the mother deer as well. She waited, holding her breath and hoping the mother would make an appearance. After a few moments, she saw the mother deer trail behind her baby, ears perked up and constantly listening for any threats nearby. Amber watched silently as the mother and her baby meandered further into the forest.

She let out a contented sigh. There were so many things for her eyes to take in. It was wonderful. Amber's heart suddenly filled with a discontented longing as she looked at the picturesque world around her. Now that she could see, she wished more than anything to be back at the palace and see her home once again. Let her eyes feast on the words of her favorite books. See her father's face again. And her mother's. Amber wondered what had happened to her mother after she had told her to find Aiden and the oasis.

Amber's heart sank even further when she thought about the oasis. The place where she had seen Aiden with her own eyes. That was a sight she would forever hold dear in her memory, and she couldn't wait until her eyes could behold him again. If only that cursed Phoenix gem hadn't whisked her away from him so soon. The gem. Amber closed her eyes and put a hand to her head. She couldn't get back to Aiden without the gem.

Amber sat down on the forest floor, unsure of what to do next. She had no idea where she was or how to get anywhere from here. Was there a village nearby where she could ask for help? Was she close to the palace? Now she could see, but she still couldn't take care of herself or find her way home.

The teardrop crystal Aiden had put around her neck felt cool against her skin. She picked it up and looked at it. Remembering what she had seen in the Phoenix gem the night before weighed on her heart even more. Aiden had given up his gift of music to retrieve this tear for her. A gift, that, if the vision was correct, would have been the magic he needed to make the harvest grow in his realm.

"Oh, Aiden," Amber whispered into the still forest air.

Her body felt worn out from the events of the last few days. The transportation from one place to another seemed to take a lot out of her, as did using any of her new powers. Amber looked at her hand and wondered if she could still do any of her magic without the gem. She concentrated on igniting a small flame in her hand. After focusing hard on her empty palm for what seemed like an eternity, a small orange flame tickled her palm at last. She smiled. Maybe she wouldn't need that stone after all. Learning her magic without the gem would be preferable since the fiery gem seemed to cause far more problems than she'd rather keep dealing with. She yawned. She would figure that out later. Right now she needed some rest. Amber curled up on the forest floor and was soon sound asleep.

CHAPTER 26

Amber woke suddenly to the sound of leaves rustling near her. She sat up quickly and looked around her. It was still strange to open her eyes and see a flood of color and light. Her newly restored sight revealed some flashes of red material moving through the trees not too far from where she sat accompanied by men's voices. Amber's eyes darted to the forest behind her, searching for any place she could hide and be out of sight. She could feel her heart starting to race a little bit as fear filtered into her veins. Staying low to the ground, she tried to sink back into the trees behind her without alerting the guards to her presence.

As she put her foot behind her, she heard a twig snap. Her eyes darted to where the guards were quickly filtering into the surrounding forest. They didn't seem to hear it, thank goodness. She pushed herself further back, hoping to find something to cover her enough until they passed by. Spotting some brush and bushes behind her, she carefully crawled over to them and tucked herself between the brush and a tall oak tree. The end of her long fiery braid laid on the path and was too long and thick to be mistaken for a patch of wildflowers. She knew her hair had grown since the Phoenix power had been activated inside her, but seeing it with her own eyes surprised her. She heard the footsteps of the guards drawing closer. If they saw her hair, she was sunk.

Amber tugged on her braid to pull it into the brush, but it must have become caught on something, because it wasn't moving. Her breathing started becoming short and ragged as fear and panic blossomed within her. The footsteps came closer. As Amber tugged frantically on her braid, she felt the small familiar flame ignite within her.

"Oh no," she said under her breath.

The energy from the flame warmed her veins and she felt the newly frequest tingle brush across her skin.

"No, no, no," she muttered as she desperately pulled harder on her braid. Her braid finally broke loose from what it had been caught on and snaked into the brush moments before the footsteps passed by. Amber closed her eyes and leaned her head back against the tree behind her, trying to calm her breathing and slow the inward flames that were ready to make their presence known on her skin.

Please calm down. Please calm down, Amber repeated to herself in her mind over and over again. A large twig snapped close behind her, startling her. Amber's eyes snapped open at the sound, filling with a fiery orange glow.

The brush around her burst into flames, causing the soldiers to all turn and look in her direction. They simultaneously drew their swords and stepped towards the unusual flame. Amber's mind immediately switched into flight or fight mode. Taking a few short breaths, she stood and faced the soldiers that surrounded her.

Amber flung her hand out, sending a blazing flame past one of the soldiers that stepped towards her, pushing him back. The captain held out his hands, signaling for his men to stand down for a moment. He nodded at a soldier behind her who threw a whip made of iron strands towards Amber. The iron tip of the whip touched Amber's wrist, causing her to flinch and lash out in anger. Turning her gaze on the soldier with the iron whip, she lit up the brush around him with a glare from her fiery eyes. The man jumped back out of the flames and dropped the whip. A couple other soldiers lunged towards her from the front and tried to capture her wrists with iron shackles. Amber reacted to the burning sensation of the iron on her wrists by sending the soldiers flying backwards with the force of her magic.

Her power was quickly growing out of control, and she didn't know how to stop it. The last thing she wanted was to hurt any of these men. Amber closed her eyes and focused her mind and energy on a place by a stream with beautiful trees and wildflowers. A place of serenity and peace where she could calm down and get her powers under control.

As Amber focused, she felt the energy shifting inside her. She took in a deep, calming breath and smiled as she let the breath out. Focusing even deeper, her mind was transported somewhere else and she was gone in a flash of light and fire.

Queen Zamina walked restlessly through the palace halls. Amir had given her the freedom to roam the east wing of the palace, but he had placed iron bracelets around her gloved wrists to prevent her from using her magic. He knew the iron burned the skin of those who carried the magic of the Phoenix and was gracious enough to allow her to keep her gloves on as a barrier between the iron and her skin. Luckily, she had been able to heal the bruises on her face before Amir had shackled her wrists.

She yearned to see her husband and had been wandering through the halls hoping to come across his room, but she had yet to find him, which worried her. Who knew where Amir was keeping him, or if he was even attending to the king's needs the way he needed. He probably hoped the king would just wither away and die of complications from the fire so he could assume the throne in his stead. She stepped back to keep out of sight when she saw someone come out of one of the rooms down the hall. Zamina breathed out a sigh of relief at seeing the old healer. She had found her husband's room at last.

The guard that had been posted at the door stepped forward to greet the healer.

"Are you finished, Magdala?"

Zamina's shoe scuffed on the wood floor, causing the healer to glance down the hall in her direction. Zamina stepped further back, hoping Magdala hadn't seen her. The healer had always been loyal to the royal family, but Zamina had no idea if loyalties had been swayed in the years of her absence.

Magdala turned back to the soldier. "Yes. I'm finished, Sir Ishan."

She patted her robe and let out a sigh. "I thought I had brought the thyme herb with me to help relieve some of the smoke that seems to be lingering in his lungs. I must have left it in my room. Would you mind fetching it for me?"

The soldier looked at her, unsure if he should leave his post. "I don't believe I'm allowed to leave. Lord Amir has given very strict orders regarding the king's room."

The healer chuckled slightly. "I understand the lord's concern for the king's health and safety, Sir Ishan, but I am an old woman. My bones will not appreciate the long walk to my room and back. I will stay here. I can assure you that as an old healer, I am not a threat to the safety of the king."

The soldier's gaze shifted between the healer and the room. "All right. I will return shortly," he finally agreed.

"Thank you, Sir Ishan. This old woman's bones appreciate your kindness." Magdala placed her hand on his forearm in a thankful gesture, causing the soldier to smile. "You will be looking for a green bottle labeled thyme."

The soldier nodded and walked quickly down the hall. The healer waited until the soldier had disappeared around the corner before glancing down to where Zamina was standing. "I heard rumors that you had returned, Your Majesty. I am glad to see you alive and well."

Zamina let out a small breath and stepped out from her hiding spot. "You were always so observant."

"I may be old, but these old eyes and senses still work pretty efficiently," the old woman smiled as she opened her arms to receive the long missed queen.

Zamina welcomed the embrace and loved the kindness of their dear healer. Magdala had been the healer of the realm for many, many years and had worked with the guardians of the Phoenix closely for several generations, calling on their healing powers when she couldn't heal the patient herself.

"It is good to see you, Magdala," Zamina said as she embraced the healer.

Magdala pulled back and took in the queen she had known as a young girl, and had grown and matured in grace and elegance in the years she had been gone. "We better hurry before that young buck of a soldier returns."

Magdala let Zamina into the king's room and closed the door behind them. Zamina walked over to the king's bed and sat down beside him.

"Oh, Azar," she said sorrowfully as she looked at her husband's pale, sunken face.

Magdala stepped to the large wood-framed bed. "May I undo your shackles, Your Majesty?"

Zamina looked at her with a wrinkled brow. "How?"

Magdala smiled and pulled a key out of her voluminous bell sleeves. Zamina's eyes widened in surprise at the old woman.

"You are full of surprises," Zamina said as she held her wrists out to the healer. The healer inserted the key in the iron bracelets and unlocked them. She took them in her hands and went back to stand watch at the door.

Zamina rubbed her achy wrists for a moment before removing the glove off her right hand. The scars from her burn years ago had never fully gone away leaving her a constant reminder of the mistake that had cost her everything. She closed her eyes and hoped she could bring some healing back to the man she had married. Reaching out a shaky hand, she placed it on the king's wrinkled and worn forehead. She took in a deep breath and let it out before she started singing the ancient healing song her mother had taught her as a small child. As she sang, she felt a small sliver of energy begin to surge through her veins. She smiled and kept singing. The energy grew stronger and she felt it pulse through her hand and into the king's head. She finished the song and felt the rest of the healing energy filter into him.

Zamina opened her eyes and looked at Azar. A soft glow covered his body and seeped into him. She let out a satisfied breath, hoping the little bit of her healing magic that was left would save him and make him well.

"The guard is coming," Magdala said over her shoulder in an urgent whisper.

Zamina nodded and put her glove back on her hand. She stood and took one last look at her husband. She knelt and placed a tender kiss on his forehead. "Get well, my King."

Magdala gestured for her to come near to the door. Zamina wiped a tear away from her face and ran her gloved hand beneath her nose before going to stand beside the healer.

"I'll step out and meet him and turn him from the door. Can you slip out without being noticed behind me?" Magdala asked as she slipped the iron bracelets back onto the queen's wrists and turned the key.

Zamina nodded. Magdala opened the door and greeted the soldier.

"Thank you so much, Sir Ishan. You have saved an old woman's bones." She turned the man away from the door as she inspected the bottle he had brought her. Zamina slipped out behind them and snuck silently back down the hall, making her way back to her room as Magdala replaced the key on the soldier's belt.

CHAPTER 27

Aiden reached the edge of the forest as an orange summer sunset filled the sky above him. He didn't know how long the Phoenix breath that Queen Zamina had breathed into Saleem would last, but his horse seemed to be losing some of the supernatural speed he had been riding with the last few days. Pulling out the map and the covered Phoenix gem, he carefully unwrapped the gem and held it with the scarf beneath the map. The other orange flame had not left the Summer palace in a few days. He hoped Queen Zamina still had the gem and that it hadn't been taken by the untrustworthy vizier he had overheard the day he stole the Summer realm's gem. He worried that Zamina might not have been welcomed back after so many years' absence and wondered if she was there under her choosing or if she was being kept prisoner. Unfortunately, he couldn't think too much on that right now. Amber was his main concern and he had to find her before anything worse happened to her.

He moved the warm gem beneath the map until he spotted the blue teardrop. He was about to put the map away and kick Saleem into a run when the teardrop faded and disappeared. Moving the gem beneath the map again, he tried to find the spot where the tear would pop up next. Nothing appeared. Aiden watched and waited for a few moments, hoping that if she was transporting herself somewhere, she would land soon, and he could pinpoint her new location. He continued to stare hard at the map, willing the blue teardrop to appear. Still nothing.

Worry filled Aiden's mind at not seeing the teardrop on the map. Any number of things could have happened. The crystal could have shattered, which for all he knew would take Amber's sight with it, leaving her in the dark and alone in a dangerous situation. She could have been captured and the crystal lost or taken. Or, she could have transported herself somewhere he couldn't even see on the map, leaving him with no idea of where to search for her. Aiden's eyes darted back to the palace where the other flame still hovered. Maybe Queen Zamina would have an idea of where to find Amber. She possessed some of the same magic and might have different abilities that Aiden did not. And, if Amber had been captured and was at the palace, he wouldn't have to worry about searching for her elsewhere.

Aiden wrapped up the gem and put it and the map back in his bag. As he did, a horrible thought crossed his mind. What if his brother or his father's armies had found her and taken her back to the Fall realm? Who knew what Lord Ragnar would do with her when he discovered what powers she possessed. Aiden closed his eyes and whispered a desperate plea for her safety into the diminishing light of the summer sun. He bent low and whispered the phrase Queen Zamina had given him into Saleem's ear. Saleem reared up and took off like a bolt into the forest.

Aiden rode most of the night and reached the area he and Amber had stayed the night of the fire. The sun was still a few hours away from rising, and Aiden knew no one would be up and about at this hour in the palace. Not to mention, he was getting sleepy from his long ride, and Saleem could likely use a rest as well.

Aiden pulled back on his reins, prompting Saleem to slow down and come to a stop. Aiden dismounted and led Saleem to the small stream that ran through this part of the forest before tying the reins to a low branch nearby. Saleem bent his brown head, eager for a rest, and drank from the stream while Aiden pulled his canteen from his saddle and knelt to fill it in the stream. The cool, refreshing water poured over Aiden's throat and skin like a long awaited rain in a drought. How desperately he needed the reviving water after traveling through the desert for a day and a half.

Aiden wiped his wet face with the sleeve of his shirt and stood up. Pulling one of the cloaks from his bag, he found a spot that seemed pretty well covered with low plants not too far from Saleem and laid down, rolling the cloak up as a pillow and placing it beneath his head. He wasn't even going to build a fire. It was too dark to see much of anything outside of the small beams of moonlight here and there, and the Summer air was far warmer than the Fall realm, so he was sure he would be fine for the few hours he would be asleep.

Aiden closed his eyes and drifted off, falling asleep almost immediately, only to be rudely awakened by a large hand covering his mouth and startling him awake seemingly moments later. Aiden's body tensed as he reached up to remove the hand from his face.

"Don't move and don't make a sound," a gruff voice said above him.

Aiden took in a couple of short breaths as his half-asleep brain tried to process whose voice it was. It was Erick. Aiden relaxed slightly and nodded his head to convey to Erick that he wasn't going to make a sound. Erick slowly removed his rough hand from Aiden's face.

Aiden sat up slowly and wiped his mouth where his brother's hand had been.

"Where have you been?" Erick hissed into the early morning air.

"I have been in more places than you can imagine," Aiden whispered back. "How did you find me lying here in the dark?"

"I have been waiting near the palace for days for you. When the Summer soldiers told us you had kidnapped the princess, Father was angry and sent me to find you and the gem."

Aiden knew all too well the temper of the man who had usurped the throne in the Fall realm. Many had died or gone missing at his hand when things weren't done the way he expected them to be done. Aiden wondered if he should tell Erick that Lord Ragnar was not truly his father, but decided another time would be better. There were other pressing matters at present that were far more important, and he didn't need his brother's— or whoever he was to Aiden now— ire risen even more against him.

"Erick," Aiden said softly into the dim darkness. "I didn't kidnap the princess. Her father wanted me to get her away from the fire, so I brought her out here for the night."

"So why didn't you take her back the next morning?" Erick asked. Aiden could tell by the direction and tension in Erick's voice that he was alert and keeping watch.

"I was going to but, things got complicated very quickly." Aiden paused as he tried to sort through what all he should tell his brother. He wasn't sure how much he could trust him, but he was at a disadvantage with his brother's overpowering strength, and knew his brother could beat him to a pulp if he wanted to and get whatever information Lord Ragnar had sent him to find. Aiden also had a feeling much of Erick's actions were guided by the endless threats from his father.

"You should have at least gone back to find the gem. Pull some of your own weight for once."

"The gem isn't at the palace anymore," Aiden said pragmatically.

"At least not the one that was originally in the Summer palace," he finished under his breath.

Aiden felt Erick shift in front of him. If he could see him, he would imagine Erick was glaring down at him like he usually did.

"Do you know where it is?" Erick asked in an anxious whisper.

"I do," Aiden finally responded. He looked up as the sky began to lighten slightly. He must have been asleep longer than he thought he was if the sun was starting to make an appearance. He needed to get into the palace and find Queen Zamina so they could figure out how to find Amber.

"Erick. There are some things you need to know about the gem," Aiden said as he shifted slightly and pulled his saddlebag closer in case he needed to run from his brother.

"The princess of the Summer realm had the gem and it activated some ancient Phoenix powers within her. One of the powers causes her to disappear from one place and reappear in another. The map that was in Lord Rag–uh, Father's study the day I returned illuminates the location of the other half of the gem when it is near one of the halves. I have been trying to find the princess so I can return her to the palace with the gem."

Aiden could see Erick's large body move towards him in the growing light of morning. "If you have been using the map to track the Princess, that must mean you have the gem. You had it that day in Father's study and saw it light up so you took the map, didn't you?" Erick asked as reached out and gripped Aiden's shirt in his large hands, bringing Aiden face to face with him. "You've had it this entire time and you didn't bring it back to our realm?" Erick's face was so close to Aiden's he could see the glint of anger in Erick's eyes as he stared at him.

"Like I told you. Princess Amber came into possession of the gem and it activated the Phoenix powers within her. I've only recently retrieved it from her. The other half that was stolen from our realm is with someone here in the Summer palace. I was going to sneak in and find the person who has the other half so I could locate the princess and bring her back."

Erick's grip slackened as he processed the information Aiden had just shared with him. "Where is the gem and the map?" Erick asked as he pulled Aiden close again.

Aiden glanced to where his saddlebag was and Erick saw him looking towards it. He threw Aiden to the ground and went to pick it up. Opening Aiden's bag, Erick pulled out the map and the scarf that held the gem. He was about to set the scarf aside when he felt the unusual warmth radiating through the material. He set the map down and unwrapped the scarf. His eyes lit up when he saw the glowing orange gem.

"Erick. Listen to me. I know your father wants the gem but we can't give it to him. Amber needs both halves of the gem to control her powers. If she doesn't, she will become a danger to herself and her realm. She could even become a danger to all the realms, including ours. We have to find her and give her both halves of the gem."

Erick smiled at the gem and weighed it in his hand as if evaluating its worth and the weight of its power. "Sorry, little brother. My life is worth more than that of a little princess. I'm taking this back to Father." Erick turned and towered over Aiden. "You better get the other half from whoever you know has it in the palace and bring it back. I'm not leaving here until you bring it to me, and you'll have no chance of getting away to find your precious princess if you don't."

Aiden stood up and tried to stop his brother. "Erick. No. Please. We have to use the gems to find Amber and bring her back safely. Your father has ruled the Fall realm with ruthless abandon and has destroyed so many lives to keep a crown that isn't even his. Wouldn't you rather stop living in fear of what he'll do to you— or anyone else— and start making the right decisions? He can only have control over you if you let him. What if we make this right and do it together? Then we can figure out how to handle your father and gain control of the Fall realm again, making the realm good and abundant again."

"Why do you keep calling him my father? He's your father too, and if we're in anything together, it's enduring his wrath when we don't follow through with his commands."

"He's not actually my father," Aiden said through short stilted breaths. "King Hallel was my father. My mother was already pregnant with me before your father overthrew the crown and married her."

Sunlight was filtering into the trees surrounding them, some of the light falling on Erick's face. Aiden watched as Erick's face registered what Aiden had just said. He couldn't tell if Erick felt angry or stunned at the admission, but he was sure he had just lanced him with yet another arrow of separation between them.

They heard some rustling in the trees and brush not too far from them. Aiden's eyes darted from tree to tree trying to pick out what was out there while Erick stood tense and unmoving.

Red guards broke out from the trees surrounding them, swords drawn and ready to attack. Aiden looked frantically around them, counting how many soldiers there were and calculating their chances of getting away. Erick wrapped the gem in the scarf and slipped it into Aiden's bag, then turned to face the guards.

"Here is the traitor who stole your princess. Take him to Amir and let him know that I will be back with the princess within a few days," Erick said, his voice devoid of emotion as he folded the map and put it back in the bag.

Two of the guards sheathed their swords, stepped towards Aiden and grabbed his arms. Aiden's eyes flashed with hurt and anger as he looked at the man he had called brother his entire life.

"You set this all up. You betrayed me," Aiden seethed through clenched teeth as he struggled to break free from the grip of the guards.

Erick looked at him fully for the first time since he had woken him up that morning. "You're the one who has been betraying everybody. Don't be expecting any favors from me, *Your Highness*. It's time for a new reign." Erick slipped the strap of Aiden's saddlebag over his head and walked into the forest.

"Erick. No! Wait!" Aiden cried out after him as the soldiers pulled him back and turned to take him to the palace.

"Erick! Please! If you don't help me, at least help Amber. Find her and make sure she gets the gem. She needs it."

One of the guards threw a burlap sack over Aiden's head, muffling his words, while the other one hit the back of his head with the hilt of his sword. Aiden's body went limp and the soldiers dragged him from the forest to the palace.

CHAPTER 28

Amber's feet touched down and she opened her eyes. This part of the forest looked even more different than the other places she had been in the last few hours. After she had escaped the guards, she kept trying to focus her mind on Aiden, or the palace, or anywhere that was familiar to her, but she couldn't seem to find any place close to familiarity. Amber's body was tired and worn out from exuding so much energy. She put a weary hand to her head and felt her knees buckle beneath her. She allowed herself to melt to the ground and started to cry.

This new found magic had started feeling different since she had been torn away from Aiden at the oasis. She hadn't been holding the gem at the time, and it hadn't come with her, which was probably why it felt different. It felt disconnected and stranger than it had before, and she wasn't sure how much more she had left in her or what would start happening to it without the gem. Amber pulled her knees up to her chest and rested her elbows on them, pressing the palms of her hands to her eyes as she let the tears pour down her face.

Why couldn't she find Aiden? Where had her mother ended up? Why was all this happening to her? It was so much to bear and learn in such a short time. She had spent most of her life in her tower. How was she supposed to deal with all of this on her own?

"I can't do this," she cried as she pressed her head into her hands. Amber felt a strange heat radiate from beneath her legs. She pulled her hands away from her face and looked down to see flames flickering around her.

She gasped and stood quickly. As she did, a trail of flames snaked down her body and into the ground.

"Oh no!" she exclaimed. Amber took a few steps back and was alarmed to see a line of fire follow her feet.

She stumbled backwards and bumped into a tree, sending a burst of flames from her hands that started the tree on fire.

Amber felt the unwelcome spark in her veins that meant she was about to disappear in a flash of light again.

"No. Please. Not again," she whimpered as the flames skirted through her body and over her skin. Amber closed her eyes as the flames once again engulfed her and transported her to another place.

Amber's body continued to reignite and transport herself to other places for most of the day. She was growing so tired and weary and her emotions were raw and out of control, which only made the kindling flames even worse. She would land in one place for a few moments and then a new emotion of frustration or anger would spark, causing the change to happen again. She left sparks and flames in some places without being there long enough to see what damage she was doing, and had no idea how many fires she had been leaving behind. When her feet touched down somewhere else, Amber clenched her fists to her head.

"You have got to gain control of yourself, Amber. This has to stop," she said to herself. Amber opened her eyes and looked around her, focusing her eyes on her surroundings. She took a shaky breath and fixed her mind on the lush trees that stood before her, forcing herself to look at the detail in the rough brown bark. Her mind still felt agitated, so she trailed her eyes down to the patch of wildflowers that were growing at the base of the trees.

"All right," she said as she took in another deeper breath and tried to calm herself. "Focus on the flowers. What colors are they?" Amber focused her eyes on the flowers and took another breath. "There are small yellow flowers and strange purple flowers that look like little grapes. There are delicate white ones—" Amber's words were cut off as she felt a small spark ignite within her. She took in a few short breaths and tried to regulate her breathing again.

"No. No, no, no. We are not doing this again. Control. Focus."

Her mind started to spin again, and she was afraid she would start the process all over again. Amber closed her eyes and tried to think of something that would calm her. She tried to think of her favorite stories, but the words and thoughts just kept getting jumbled in her head. Her mind finally landed on the night she and Aiden had been in the forest when he had played his violin while she sang. Singing. Maybe that would help.

Amber took a deep breath and tried to think of some of her favorite songs. She started humming something, searching for the right song that would calm her mind and body. A song her mother used to sing to her finally came to the surface of her mind. It talked about the beautiful meadows that are blanketed with wildflowers in the summer and the warm summer evenings spent under the glowing colors of the sun's setting light. A calming presence poured over her and filled her mind and body with a peace she hadn't felt in many days outside of the times she had been with Aiden.

Amber smiled and let out a sigh of relief at the peace and calm she was starting to feel and continued singing for a while, afraid her body would start to ignite again if she stopped. When she finally felt she was calm enough, she stopped singing and opened her eyes. The exertion from the last few days hit her with a sudden force, reminding her how tired her body was. She hoped she could rest some and that nothing would ignite the powers within her, at least for a little while. Amber laid down and tucked her arm beneath her head, continuing to focus her mind on her mother's lullabies until she finally drifted off to sleep.

Chapter 29

Aiden awoke to the strange sound of dripping water. As his eyes opened, he saw that he was in a dark room of some kind. His eyes slowly adjusted to the dim light, allowing him to see what appeared to be a high window with bars over it above him. *Amber.* Aiden sat up quickly at the thought of her, but he immediately regretted it. The back of his head throbbed and the sudden movement caused his head to spin slightly. Leaning over his knees, he let his mind and stomach settle from the sudden movement before gingerly touching the spot that seemed to be the source of his pain. He flinched as his fingers brushed over the tender lump he felt at the back of his head.

"Are you alright?" a voice asked in the darkness.

Aiden looked up but couldn't see much in the dim light that came through the barred window. Just shadows of stone and darkness.

"I'll be fine," Aiden replied as he lightly touched his head again.

"Are you sure about that?" the voice asked again.

Aiden lifted his head and tried to focus on where the voice was coming from. He wondered if this was what Amber felt like, always hearing sounds, but never being able to fully see anything.

"Can I help you?" A man asked as he stepped into the dim light that reached through the bars above them.

Aiden's eyes focused on a man with dark hair. He caught a glimpse of a white streak in the man's hair near his forehead. He couldn't see much of the man's face, but the little he could see, he didn't appear to be old enough to have white in his hair.

"Do you have a way to get out of this prison cell?" Aiden asked with a sardonic laugh as he looked around at the dark and dank cell.

The man gave a soft laugh in response. "I've been known to free people from their prisons in the past."

Aiden turned his head back towards the man and gave him a curious look. "Well, if you have a way out, I would sure take it," he replied.

"Why are you so anxious to get out?" the man asked.

"I would think any man would want out of prison if he could find a way."

"You would be surprised at how many remain of their own free will," the man said. "What brought you to be in this cell?" the man asked.

Aiden looked down at his hands as he answered. "The vizier has accused me of kidnapping the princess of this realm and endangering the king and the kingdom."

"And did you do these things?"

Aiden laughed and shook his head. "No. But it's their word against mine. I think the vizier is up to something and is trying to get me out of the way. The king warned me to get his daughter away from the kingdom and not to trust someone. I'm pretty sure he meant the vizier."

The man came and sat beside Aiden on the worn cot. "I was accused of things that the rulers of the land did not like many years ago as well."

Aiden looked at him. "How did it turn out for you?"

"Not how you would expect," the man replied with a sad smile. "But, the end result was worth it." He turned to look at Aiden. "What would you hope to accomplish if you were able to get out of your prison?"

Aiden let out a long breath before he answered. "I would want to find Amber and bring her back to her palace and family and set things right in this realm."

"Anything else?" the man asked.

Aiden twisted the signet ring on his middle finger. "I would love to bring the harvest back to my realm, but unfortunately I bargained away the only means I had to do it." Aiden let out a scornful laugh and leaned back against the wall beside the cot. He winced as his head made contact with the wall. He readjusted his head and found a spot far enough away from the painful lump on the back of his head that it didn't hurt to touch it. "The ironic thing is I didn't even know I had a gift until I was asked to give it away."

"You gave all you had to save the life of another," the man replied with a humble agreement.

"What good will that do me now? Amber is who knows where. The king is dying. My realm is under the brutal hand of a man I thought was my father. And my brother, or the man I called brother, is looking for Amber with the other half of the Phoenix gem. Even if I could get out of here, I would have no way of finding her. I'm useless."

The man smiled. "You are far from useless, young prince. You have a good heart and mind and desire only good for your land and the people of the Summer and Fall realms. You will bring much growth and rebirth to both of the realms."

"How?" Aiden asked as he ran his hands through his hair and looked around the dim prison.

"Do you want to be free?" the man asked.

Aiden looked at him and raised an eyebrow. "Of course."

"Do you believe you can be free? From everything? All your doubts. All your hurts. All your betrayals. All your fears?"

Aiden's eyebrows creased together at the man's questions. He sat and thought for a long moment before responding. "That seems like a lot to be free from in just this cell," he answered quietly.

"Men are often imprisoned by far less," the man replied. "I know your life has not been what you planned or expected. You have learned things on this journey that might cloud your judgment at times or decisions on how to take back your land and deal with the man you have called father your entire life. You have to be aware of those things and willing to give those things up to become a good ruler. If you don't, those things will hold you prisoner for the rest of your life and you will not become the great and mighty ruler you were destined to be. Do you understand that?" the man asked.

Aiden sat and thought about the man's words. "How do you know so much about me and my past?" he asked as he leaned forward and rubbed his hands together.

"I know many, many things," the man replied with a smile. "You have the heart to become a mighty ruler, Aodhán."

Aiden's eyes widened in surprise at being called by the name the guardian had called him in the cave.

The man smiled and laughed. "Yes. I know your true name. White fire. One who burns bright and pure. Are you ready to step out of your prison and into your destiny, son of the harvest?"

Aiden smiled sincerely for the first time since he had last seen Amber's beautiful eyes gazing at him and actually seeing him. He nodded his head. "Yes. I'm ready," he replied. Something about this man made him believe that the words he was saying were true and he had no doubt that the man would somehow lead him from his prison cell.

"Then, go forth, Aodhán."

The prison door swung open and Aiden stared at it with surprise, although he wasn't sure why he was surprised. He looked at the man. "Thank you. How can I repay you for your kindness?" he asked.

"Just live your life in the light of the purifying fire," the man replied.

Aiden nodded his agreement to do so. He stood up and stepped towards the open door. He turned back and looked at the man. "What is your name?" Aiden asked.

"I have been called many names. One you might know me by is Melchizidai."

"Like the king of the oasis," Aiden said, somehow not surprised by this.

"The very same," the man replied with a gentle smile.

Aiden tipped his head and smiled. He looked back up to ask the man something else, but he was gone.

"Melchizidai?" Aiden asked into the darkness. He looked around trying to focus his eyes in the dim light. He didn't see the man. He shook his head and let out a small laugh. He turned back to the open prison door and took a deep breath.

"Live my life in the light of the purifying fire."

Aiden stepped out of the prison cell into the freedom granted him by the mysterious king.

Aiden searched the palace for Zamina and found her wandering the halls in the east wing.

"Queen Zamina," Aiden whispered down the hall from her.

Zamina turned and saw Aiden standing at the end of the hall. Her eyes widened. She gestured for him to come down the hall. Aiden snuck down the hall, following the queen into the room she had entered.

"Aiden. How did you get out of that prison cell?" Queen Zamina asked as she looked at him.

Aiden smiled at the motherly way she was looking him over, making sure he wasn't bruised or scraped or harmed in any way. "You wouldn't believe me if I told you. Do you have the other half of the gem?"

Zamina hesitated for a moment before answering. "I do. Luckily Amir has not been able to find it or take it from me. But why?" she asked protectively.

"Kazeem told me that Amber needs both halves in order to control her powers."

"Kazeem? How did you–?" she began to ask with a questioning look.

"He was the guardian of the tear at the oasis," Aiden responded. "Amber needs the other half of the gem to control her powers. If you give it to me, I will find a way to get to her and reunite the two halves.

Zamina stood silently in front for a few moments before she responded. "The last time the two halves were almost united, it ended very badly for everyone."

Aiden placed a gentle hand on Zamina's gloved hand. "I know. Kazeem told me you would be hesitant to give Amber both halves because of that. But, if we don't get both halves to her, things could become even worse."

"They already are," Zamina whispered into the still air. "Amir received reports of random fires breaking out in the southern part of the realm. They seem to be starting for no reason and spreading at alarming speeds."

"And you think Amber is the one starting them,"

Zamina let out a small breath and replied,. "Yes."

"Then we have to get the gems to Amber, and fast."

Zamina finally nodded and pulled it from her blouse. "Have you seen Amber?" she asked. "Is she alright?"

Aiden met her eyes fully for the first time since meeting her in the hall. He smiled and nodded. "She found her way to the oasis while I was still there. I gave the Phoenix tear to her. She can see," he said with a bewildered smile.

Zamina's gloved hands went to her mouth and tears filled her eyes. "She can see? The tear worked? It healed her?"

Aiden nodded. "Yes. She's healed."

"Where is she?" Zamina asked as she wiped a grateful tear from her face.

Aiden's face fell and his eyes darted to the floor. "I don't know. She was still touching the gem after I gave her the tear and it made her vanish again. I tried following her but I lost sight of the tear on the map. I was headed here to find you and get the other half of the gem and any insight you might have that would help me find her. But, then my ogre of a brother intercepted me outside the palace and took the map and the other half of the gem. I'm afraid he's going to find Amber and take the tear to his father. Who knows what he or Lord Ragnar will do to her."

Zamina put a hand on Aiden's cheek. He looked up at her. "You will find her. I have every confidence in that. Take the gem and let it guide you. It has led lost hearts back to each other before." She placed the gem in his hand and closed his fingers over it.

Aiden squeezed the gem in his hand. "Thank you, Your Majesty. I will bring her home. I promise." He leaned down and kissed her on the cheek.

"Go. May the Great Mage be with you."

Aiden ducked out of the room and made his way out of the palace.

CHAPTER 30

Erick followed the map to the place where the blue teardrop glowed. It had taken him a while to figure out that the blue teardrop was where the princess must be since it kept moving around. Aiden had mentioned that she kept disappearing and reappearing and that was the only thing that kept moving with the Phoenix gem beneath the map. Folding the map, he put it in the bag that was slung over his saddle and dropped the gem into the pouch that hung from his belt. He knelt by the stream and cupped his hands to take a drink of water, alert and waiting for the princess to appear.

Amber's feet touched the ground and she felt the waning energy of the flames as they receded back into the place of their birth within her. She felt dizzy and allowed herself to sink to the ground. She had been transported throughout the realm quite a number of times already today and hadn't slept much the night before either out of fear of the Phoenix flame bursting forth again and setting blaze to the surrounding area, or being found by the guards. She wished she knew how to control this power. It was becoming far too much to bear on her own, not to mention the amount of fires she had been starting without meaning to. She pressed a hand to her forehead and sat languidly in the summer heat for a few moments. As she sat, a strange music reached her ears.

Amber opened her eyes and looked around her. The last time she had heard that entrancing music, she had found the gem in Aiden's bag. She heard the soft whinny of a horse not too far from her. Amber pushed herself up and walked towards the sound. Stepping quietly through the flourishing green trees, she stopped behind a large tree. She peered out from behind it and saw a horse near a small stream, but no rider.

"Aiden?" she called cautiously.

No response. Amber stepped out from behind the tree to take a closer look. No one seemed to be near the horse. Amber continued to look around as she stepped towards the horse. This horse was a darker brown than Aiden's and had a white diamond shaped patch between its eyes and white patches around its hairy ankles. It was quite a bit bigger than Aiden's horse too. She wondered where its rider could be. The large horse squealed slightly and stomped its feet.

"Whoah, whoah," Amber cooed softly as she reached out her hand to touch the horse. The horse snorted and turned away from her hand, but couldn't go far since the reins were wrapped around a low hanging branch.

"Easy. It's alright. I'm a friend. I'm not going to hurt you," she whispered as she stepped closer and held her hand up to let the horse know she meant him no harm. The horse sniffed her hand and finally let her touch his nose. Amber smiled. "That's a good boy," she said as she rubbed his face. "I wish I had a treat for you."

Amber stopped as the strange music landed on her ears again. Sensing it was behind her, Amber spun around and was surprised to see a large man standing a few feet behind her. He had a broad, brute-like frame with short dark, brown hair. His face was covered with a dark beard, but Amber could see a few scar lines on his face.

"Who are you?" she asked, stepping as close to the horse as she could, hoping to find protection beside the large animal.

"I could ask you the same thing," the man said as he took a step towards her. "Surely you are not the same princess my brother and I were introduced to upon our arrival in your kingdom. Of course, that princess wore heavy veils to cover her face, but hair as long and vibrant as that would be hard to miss." He stepped closer and reached a large hand around her face, pulling her long braid over her shoulder.

Amber felt immediately at unease with the large man. She was trapped between him and his equally large horse and wasn't sure what to do. She tried to pull away and walk past him, but he kept hold of her braid, preventing her from going too far.

"Brother. You must be Aiden's brother," she said as she pulled her hair from his hand and stepped around him.

The man snorted. "Well, apparently we aren't even half brothers anymore, but old habits die hard."

"Oh. Yes. I was there when the old woman told him that. It must be strange believing one thing your entire life only to find out it isn't true. I know Aiden was shocked," Amber said as she stepped backwards to widen the gap between her and the large man.

"He always seemed to think he had the upper hand in our family, even before he found out he was fully royal. Father never treated him the way he treated me. Aiden was always the golden child. The half-royal who could never be harmed or forced to do Father's bidding. Do you know how hard it is to grow up in the shadow of a perfect child under the hand of a ruthless father?" Erick asked as he took a menacing step towards Amber.

Amber's heel caught on something as she stepped back, but she steadied herself and kept stepping further and further away. "I- I- don't know exactly how that feels, but my father locked me in a tower for most of my life to keep me hidden and protected from the world," she said as she tried to keep the growing nervousness out of her voice.

"Why would your father do that?" Erick asked as he took another step towards her. "Is something wrong with you? You sick or have some kind of disease or something?"

"N-no," Amber stuttered as she bumped into a tree behind her. She glanced back and stepped to the side of the tree. "I lost my sight after a fire that broke out in the palace many years ago. My father didn't want me to get hurt." Amber saw her fiery braid laid out on the ground in front her. It went past Aiden's brother's feet. She wondered how quickly she could run with her braid that long. He could easily step on it, or it could catch on something and make her easy prey for the man bent on catching her.

Erick stopped and stared at the princess. "You lost your sight? You seem able to see perfectly fine now," he said with an aggressive tone that increased the sense of fear that was building inside Amber.

"Aiden found the Phoenix tear and gave it to me. It healed my eyes."

Erick's eyes went to the crystal around her neck. "That's what was showing up on the map," he said as he started to put the bits of information together in his mind.

Amber heard the strange music again and looked at Erick. "You have the Phoenix gem, don't you?"

"Our gem was stolen from our realm. I came to take it back. Unfortunately, I made a deal with your vizier to return you to him so he would give me the other half. It seemed like an easy enough mission. Return the girl. Get the gem. Bring both halves back to my father so he could make them whole. Then his reign would be endless, and Aiden would have no place in the kingdom my father took from his father. But now, I think I have an even easier way of taking care of all of this."

Amber saw a dark coldness in this man's eyes that she had never seen in anyone else's. She turned to run but he caught hold of her braid and pulled her back.

"Ouch!" Amber screamed as he yanked on her hair.

She saw his large hand reach for her neck and she knew exactly what he was going to do. She felt the energy from the Phoenix gem calling to her from his pouch. She reached for the gem just as he ripped the teardrop necklace from her throat and her world went black–again.

Chapter 31

Aiden found Saleem where he had left him when the soldiers had dragged him off. He quickly mounted and rode Saleem hard for most of the day. He didn't know where exactly he was going without the map, but he clutched the gem her mother had given him close to his heart, trusting it would lead him where he needed to go, and that he would find Amber and Erick before it was too late.

Queen Zamina had said that Amir was receiving reports from the south about the outbreaks of fires, so he set off towards the southern part of the region. After a few hours, he came across an area that looked strangely blackened. A small burnt patch of grass led into a line of blackened grass and back to a burnt tree. She must have been here. Aiden knelt to feel if it still carried any warmth. The sooty dirt felt cold to the touch meaning it had to have been a couple of days since she had been there. Aiden mounted his horse and pushed further south.

As midday approached, Aiden slowed Saleem to a stop and dismounted near a stream. He let Saleem drink and looked around to see if he could see any more signs of Amber's flaming presence. Not seeing any ashy remains in the vicinity, Aiden knelt to drink from the stream. As he did, a bright red flash filled the air. The flash spooked Saleem, sending him galloping off in the opposite direction.

Aiden looked up and knew that a flash like that could have only come from Amber. He stood up and splashed across the stream in the direction of the red light.

Amber felt the spark of energy from the gem course through her veins with a power she hadn't felt before now. The flame ignited within her once again, only this time she didn't feel herself begin to be transported to another place. She stood in the forest, her sight gone just as quickly as it had been restored to her. She turned her head to the right and left to see if she could hear anything or pick up on anything that would tell her what was happening. She felt something large and rough grab her wrist. She flinched and felt a flame snake across her skin, causing the thing that had grabbed her to pull away.

"You are coming with me, Princess. There is too much at stake to leave you here and let you burn down the entire forest."

Amber felt the roar of frustration fill her ears once again as she tried to figure out where the sound had come from. She had to get the crystal back so she could see.

"Give me back the tear and I'll try not to hurt you," Amber said as she reached out her free hand.

"I'm not giving this back to you," Erick said in a taunting voice. "If Aiden so heroically got it for you the first time, he will have to get it for you again. And it won't be so easy going through me to get it." He laughed as he walked around her, enjoying her discomfort at not being able to see him.

A flame of indignation and anger sparked within her at his words. Aiden had sacrificed a precious gift to obtain the tear for her and she was not about to let that sacrifice be for nothing. "You don't deserve any of it. The gem. The tear. The crown. Nothing."

"You don't have to deserve anything when you've taken it for yourself. My father was handed nothing as a boy. He had to fight for everything and take what he wanted. If he hadn't, he'd still be a worthless streetrat scrounging around and living in fear of those that intimidated him. My father took the crown because the king was a weak, sniveling worm who had everything handed to him on a golden platter. He never had to work or fight to get what he had. If my father taught me anything, it's that you have to take what you want in this life. You get nowhere by waiting around for it to fall in your lap. That's exactly what Aiden expects to happen and that's why he'll never be a true king."

Another flame ignited within Amber as she listened to Erick's cruel words. "Aiden is a hundred times the man you will ever be," she said angrily as she felt flames come to life and begin to dance across her skin. She was liking this new power. It felt so strong and mighty within her. She focused her attention on Erick and pictured where he was standing not too far from her. Smiling, she opened her hand to aim a red flame at the fiendish man. She heard a gruff cry not too far from her.

"Have you gone mad? You're going to set the whole forest on fire," Erick yelped as he patted his sleeve where the flame had grazed his arm.

Amber's smile gave an evil turn as she pinpointed where Erick was at. She imagined which hand the tear must be in and focused on it with her mind. As she did, a flame shot from her palm and knocked the teardrop necklace from Erick's hand.

He howled as he shook his hand where the fire had made contact. This seemed to encourage Amber as she heard it make contact with his skin. She stepped towards Erick, her hands and arms a full blaze of unintimidated fire.

Aiden saw small animals and birds scurrying away from the direction of the bright light and he thought he saw what looked like fiery red flames coming from that direction. "Oh no. Amber. Get control over yourself before you set fire to your entire realm," Aiden whispered to himself as he kept running towards the flames.

He reached the place where the flames were coming from and saw a glowing Amber walking towards someone, limbs ablaze and a fiery glow emanating from her eyes. Her power had grown even greater since he had seen her at the oasis, so much so that her hair had even begun to glow. She looked intent on the man like a hungry tiger honing in on its prey. Aiden looked at the man and recognized the broad frame of Erick.

He watched as a flame shot past Erick and set a tree on fire behind him. "Erick. Get out of there!" Aiden called to his brother.

Erick glanced back at Aiden's voice with sheer terror in his eyes. He looked back at Amber for a split second and turned to run the opposite direction. Amber turned her head in the direction of the running footsteps and proceeded to lift her hand to shoot another flame towards Erick.

"Amber!"

Her head turned towards Aiden but her eyes didn't make contact with his. He glanced at her neck. "The tear," he whispered to himself. He felt the gem around his neck start to warm against his chest as if sensing the energy of the other half of the gem. He looked towards Amber, whose behavior was growing eerie and evil like it had at the oasis when she had just the one half of the gem. Kazeem had said she needed both halves of the gem to gain control of her powers. Aiden had no idea what it would take to unite the two halves, but he knew he had to do something quick before she got too far out of control.

Aiden took a breath and stepped towards Amber. He saw the gem in her hand and hoped he could unite the two halves without too much harm to himself or her. He reached for the gem in her hand, but she sensed him reaching for it and pulled away.

"Don't try to take my power again, young prince, or you will regret the day you were born," Amber snapped at Aiden with an evil jeer in her voice.

"I'm not trying to take your powers from you, Amber. I'm merely trying to make the two halves whole. Think of the power you could have with both halves united as one," Aiden reasoned, trying to appeal to her apparent thirst for power when she possessed that half of the gem.

Amber cocked her head slightly and looked at him with her unseeing glowing eyes. "You have the other half?" she asked in her otherworldly voice.

"I do, and I would willingly give it to you if you let me," he replied soothingly.

Amber smiled and reached out her hand for the other gem, but pulled back. "How do I know this is not a trick?" she asked as she set a fiery gaze in his direction.

"You'll just have to believe that I would never trick you or harm you," Aiden said calmly.

Amber thought about it for a moment and must have decided he could be trusted, because she reached out her hand to him again. Aiden reached out and put the gem he had been wearing around his neck around hers, careful not to touch the dancing flames that ebbed and flowed around her skin like a fiery sea. He led her hand that held the other gem up to her throat and let her half of the gem touch the other half that sat wrapped in the leather strand around her neck. The flames within the two gems reached out to touch one another and created a bright spark between them. Aiden watched with wide eyes as the two gems seemed to stitch themselves back together. Amber's hand grew hot beneath his as the gems reunited, causing Aiden to pull his hand away from hers. When he did, a bright flash filled the air followed by a loud crack, causing a large fire to break out in the forest around them.

CHAPTER 32

Amber felt a strange surge of energy pass through her as Aiden's hand left hers. Something reversed course within her and the selfish, power-hungry side of her dissipated. She felt immense heat all around her but she still couldn't see anything.

"Aiden," she called out, trying to make her voice heard over the roar of the fire that seemed to be standing on all sides of her.

She tried to take a few steps here and there, but she felt like she hit a wall of fire everywhere she turned. Her heart started pounding and her veins throbbed as panic built up within her. Aiden had been her only safe place since they had left the palace. He had been able to calm her at the oasis and other times. He had been her eyes when she could not see and he had taken care of her and kept her from harm. Now, she was all alone with no way of seeing where she was or how to escape the fire that encircled her.

"Aiden," she called again. Where was he? What had happened to him after the gems reunited? The gems.

Amber's hands flew up to the gem that hung around her neck. She felt the gem with both hands. It felt much larger than it had before. The two halves must have completely melded back together. She wondered if that had unleashed this full force of the Phoenix flames around her.

"Aiden!" Amber cried again. She stumbled around yelling for him until her voice was hoarse and she could barely get out a whisper. Amber brought her hands to her face and sunk to the ground. She was distraught beyond consolation. She was scared. She was alone. She couldn't see.

"Somebody please help me," she cried out in a hoarse, despondent whisper as tears poured into her hands and down her face.

"Amber," a gentle voice said behind her.

Amber's head jerked up. The voice didn't sound like Aiden's, but she didn't know who else it could be. "Aiden?" she croaked out through her endless tears.

"No. It's not Aiden. But I am here to help you," the gentle voice answered.

"Who are you?" Amber sniffed as she held out her hand to try to find the gentle stranger.

A warm, strong hand encompassed hers. She felt an unfamiliar calm fill her at his touch. The feeling was so different from the constant turmoil and duress she had been experiencing the last few days, she wasn't quite sure what to do with it. She took in a shaky breath and tried to process the strangely peaceful feeling.

"Amber," the voice said again.

She lifted her head towards the voice. "Yes," she answered quietly.

"You cried out for help and I am here. How can I help you?"

Amber's brows creased at the strange question. "I–I don't know."

The man squeezed her hand, "You can tell me, Amber. Why did you cry out for help?"

"I don't know. I'm lost. I'm confused. Everything has been going wrong ever since this gem activated an ancient power within me. I'm setting everything on fire without meaning to or even trying to most of the time. I keep combusting and falling apart and this power keeps changing and taking me different places and it's wearing me down and pulling me apart. I don't know how to control this or make this stop. I can't do this. I don't want this power. I am not cut out for this." The words tumbled out of Amber's mouth like a bubbling stream over rocks. She had kept so many of these thoughts and emotions bottled up inside her the last few days. She didn't know why she was sharing these thoughts so freely, but something about the stranger's presence made her feel safer and freer than she had ever felt in her entire life.

"Why are you so afraid of this power that is within you?" he asked.

"I- I- don't know what to do with it. It's so much to learn and figure out and–," Amber stopped, weary from the overwhelming surge of thoughts and emotions coursing through her.

The stranger gently prodded her to continue. "And?"

Amber took a deep breath and let it out before she responded. "And, I can't see," she said, tipping her head down so he couldn't see her blind eyes.

"Amber. Not having the use of your eyes does not make you any less capable of accomplishing great things."

"But how can I do anything if I can't see what I'm doing? How will I know when my power is in control or being used for good? I saw the destruction I brought in the short time I had my sight. How irresponsible can I be to keep using my power blindly?"

"Being blind does not mean your power would be used blindly," the man replied. "The power comes from within you. You can feel its strength and energy. You know when it is growing out of control and when it is a small flame within your control. This power was given to you as a gift, Amber. You were destined to carry this power within you and use it to bring rebirth to your land."

"It's grown so far out of control. I don't know how to bring it back to where it's supposed to be. I'm bringing destruction to my land. Not rebirth."

"Sometimes things need to die and go through the heat of the fire in order to be reborn," the man said as he took both of her hands in his. "Do you believe you can bring beauty from ashes?"

Amber sat and thought about the question for a moment before responding. "I don't know how."

"I didn't ask if you knew how. I asked if you believed it could happen."

"I don't know," she replied softly.

"Do you believe that I could bring beauty from ashes?"

Amber lifted her head towards his voice. "I don't know you. How would I know if you could bring beauty from ashes."

The man let out a soft chuckle. "You do know me. You just don't remember who I am. Let me show you."

The man spit in the dirt below them and created a muddy plaster. Amber felt a cool wet substance touch her eyelids. The man gently rubbed the mixture over her eyelids and then wiped it from her eyes.

"Open your eyes, Amber."

Amber opened her eyes slowly, not fully trusting that whatever he had put on her eyes would restore her sight. A bright yellow light filled her blurry eyes. Amber blinked and let her eyes slowly adjust to the light. A blurred figure appeared before her eyes as she continued to blink, tears filling her eyes as they adjusted to the light and tried to focus on the man before her. Her eyes finally focused and she saw a man with brown hair and brown beard clothed in white. She blinked again and her eyes focused even more on the man. Her eyes finally focused enough to see his face in greater detail. His face shown with compassion and a brilliant smile as he gazed at her. She looked up at his hair and saw a strange white patch of hair that stood out against his dark brown hair. She smiled at being able to see such a thing.

"If I can restore your sight with dust from the earth, do you believe that beauty can be reborn within this land through you?" he asked.

A strange sense of peace and hope sparked within her at his question. A different warmth started to seep into her heart that was different from the burning fire of the Phoenix flame within her. She looked at him and studied his gentle face for a moment. As she looked at him, a gentle assurance filled her heart and spilled out into the depths of her soul.

"Do you believe beauty can come from ashes?" the man asked again as he looked at her. "Do you believe you can be reborn?"

Amber looked at him and smiled. "Yes," she said with a half-laugh, half-cry. "I do believe."

"Then you shall be reborn and bring beauty from these ashes." The man pulled Amber close to him and gave her an embrace that was filled with the warmth and love of a brother or an old familiar friend. Amber melted into his embrace and cried tears of happiness and joy. All the years of hiding and fearing the world around her because of her blindness melted away in his grip. The fears and worries about this new unknown gift that had restricted her were replaced with a hope and peace that beauty would truly be reborn from the ashes.

The man pulled away and looked at her. "Are you ready to walk through the fire and see what life waits on the other side?" he asked as he stood and held out a hand to her.

Amber looked up at him and nodded. She placed her hand confidently in his and let him lead her through the fire.

CHAPTER 33

The force of the spark they had created when the gems united flung Aiden back, thrusting him into a tree before his body made contact with the hard ground. Groaning, he pushed himself up and turned to see where Amber was. Terror laced his dark eyes at the explosion of flames that surrounded him. Zamina had been right to be afraid. The same thing was happening now that had happened when the queen and the soldier had tried to reunite the gems years before. Why had he given Amber both halves of the gems?

Aiden scrambled to his feet and tried to see into the hot flames that were quickly engulfing the forest. He couldn't see Amber anywhere. Fear gripped his heart at the thought that something worse may have happened to Amber since she was in direct contact with the gems when they were rejoined.

"Amber!" Aiden yelled into the roar of the fire as he ran towards the blazing fire.

"Amber!" Aiden shouted again, frantic to find her before it was too late. He couldn't lose her now. Not after he had tried so hard to find her over and over and over again.

"Amber!"

"Aiden."

A low gruff voice called his name from somewhere in the fiery trees. "Erick?" Aiden mumbled to himself.

"Aiden," Erick said again when he reached Aiden. He was holding his arm from where Amber had burned him earlier.

"Erick. What are you doing here?" Aiden asked as he waved his hands at the black smoke starting to fill the air above his head.

"A lifetime of protecting someone is a hard habit to break. Besides, I don't know how to get out of here. I couldn't see a thing through the smoke and fire."

Aiden shook his head at Erick's inability to actually admit he might care for Aiden. "I was worried about you too," Aiden said with a slight smile as he placed a caring hand on Erick's shoulder. He coughed and looked around him.

"Did you see Amber anywhere?" Aiden asked.

Erick coughed and looked around, "No. That bright light pretty much blinded me for a few moments. Ironic isn't it?"

Aiden glared at him for his underhanded remark about Amber's sight. Erick looked back at him and saw Aiden's withering look. His face flushed, "Sorry."

"We need to find a way out of here and fast."

Erick nodded. He felt in his pocket and pulled out the Phoenix tear. "If this gave the princess her sight back, could it help us see a way out?" he asked as he held it up to Aiden.

Aiden stared at it in disbelief. "You took the tear from Amber? No wonder she was so out of control. Just because Father is spineless and ruthless doesn't mean that you have to be. You are a better man than that, Erick."

Erick gave him a sheepish look. "Actually she was defending you and your honor because I was putting you down. That's what sent her power spiraling out of control."

A branch that had been burning snapped and fell to the ground behind them. "We have a lot to discuss but we need to find a way out before we become like that branch," Aiden yelled as he took the tear from Erick.

Aiden held up the tear. "Please, show us the way out of the fire."

When he said the words, he sensed a strange energy behind him. He turned and saw a glow that was different from the blazing orange fire that surrounded them.

"Come this way," he said to Erick. Aiden followed the glow that revealed the safe path from the flames.

Amir and his men pushed south to find the source of the fires and capture the princess. They stopped short as a bright light filled the forest in front of them. A few of the horses reared back at the sudden flash.

"Whoah," Amir said as he pulled on the reins of his horse, trying to gain control of it. He watched as flames erupted from the source of the light.

"That's where she is. Stop her before she burns down the realm," he commanded.

The soldiers that surrounded him urged their horses towards the flames but stopped when they saw two figures emerge from the flames.

"If it isn't the young nobles from the Fall realm. You are quite the magician, young prince. You somehow managed to escape one of my cells, with some help from the queen, I have no doubt. And you, young knight. You've managed to elude my guards all together after starting the fire in the palace."

Erick's shoulders stiffened and Aiden saw the familiar look of stoked ire in his eyes. Aiden put out a hand to stop Erick and stepped in front of him to address the vizier. "Lord Amir. I give you my word that the fire was not started by my brother. It was an accident, and we are greatly grieved at the misfortune the Summer realm has experienced once again."

Amir sneered at the oversweet apology. "And I suppose the princess just happened to follow you out of the palace on her own. Which is quite funny really, if you think about it, because she's blind. Or were you not aware that the king was trying to deceive you by having her companion stand in for her so you wouldn't find out?"

A vein twitched in Aiden's clenched jaw at Amir's remark. "Princess Amber was in danger and I saved her and King Azar. Somehow, I failed to see you racing to save them from the flames."

Aiden looked at Amir's hands and noticed that they were covered with gloves, much like Queen Zamina's. They hadn't been covered when they had first been introduced to him.

"May I be so bold as to ask why your hands are covered, Lord Amir? Did you get too close to your own fire?"

Amir's lip twitched slightly at Aiden's remark. Aiden bit back a smile at having caught the vizier in his own lies and held Amir's gaze.

A sudden explosion behind them startled all of them. Many of the horses whinnied and stamped their feet, sensing the imminent danger of the fire. Chaos ensued as men tried to gain control of their animals.

Amir struggled to gain control of his own horse, who had reared up and nearly unseated him. He looked toward the captain of the guard. "Bring the princess back to the palace with whatever means necessary." He glanced towards Aiden and Erick. "And make sure they are taken care of."

The captain nodded and charged his horse towards Aiden and Erick. Drawing his sword, he directed his blade at Aiden. The steel blade glinted in the firelight and caught Erick's eye. He pushed Aiden out of the way as the captain rode past. Aiden's body lurched forward and tumbled to the ground from the force of Erick's shove. He turned to see why Erick would have done that just as Erick's body went stiff and slumped to the ground. The captain smirked and continued on into the flaming forest to do his master's bidding and find Amber.

"Erick!" Aiden yelled. He crawled over to Erick and heaved his large body over.

Erick gripped his chest where the sword had pierced him. Aiden swallowed past a lump that had formed in his throat as he placed his hand over Erick's. He looked around, frantic to find some way to get Erick to safety and to help.

"Save yourself," Erick said through a grimace, drawing Aiden's attention to him.

Aiden looked down at the man he had called brother. He hadn't always appreciated how Erick had treated him, but he had been the closest thing to family Aiden ever had, and Aiden wasn't ready to lose him. Not like this.

"We're going to get you out of here. Just don't go and do anything like dying on me," Aiden said with a tight smile, trying to deflect the seriousness of Erick's injury. Even if he didn't admit it, he still cared a great deal for this man, brother or no.

Erick gripped Aiden's hand with his other hand and tried to speak. "I–I'm sorry for how I treated you all these years. My jealousy al–al–always got the best of me and b-blinded me to the man you are becoming," Erick said through gasping breaths as he held onto Aiden's hand.

Aiden looked down at him and shook his head, trying to fight back the tears that were forming in his eyes. "You don't need to be getting sentimental on me now. I wouldn't want you to say anything you'll regret when we get out of this."

Erick let out a half-laugh that was cut short as the searing pain shot through his chest. "I don't think we are meant to be getting out of this," he said as he gripped his chest tighter, trying to alleviate the pain. He took as deep of a breath as he could before he continued. "Tell Princess Amber I'm–I'm sorry for the things I said to her." Erick paused as he started to cough. Aiden tried to steady him, but Erick waved Aiden's concern away as his coughing eased. "I'm especially sorry for t-taking her sight away from her. She didn't deserve that."

Erick gasped for breath as the pain deepened in his chest. He gripped Aiden's arm and made sure he was looking at him. "Tell Father that I tried."

Aiden gave Erick a grim look. "You'll have to tell him that yourself. I'm not letting you get out of facing him that easy," Aiden said with a small smile.

Erick smiled back before another grimace filled his face. Erick closed his eyes and Aiden watched as Erick's breathing became more labored and shallow.

"Hold on, Erick. Please. Hold on, Brother," Aiden said, squeezing Erick's hand and willing him to hold on long enough to get help.

Another bright light filled the area, only this time, the light was more of an ethereal white light. Aiden stared in amazement as two figures appeared in the midst of the light. He recognized the fiery red hair of Amber immediately, but he had no idea who the man was that was with her. Amber stepped out into the clearing, her hand gripped in the hand of the man. An unexpected pang of jealousy shot through Aiden's heart seeing her with another man.

She looked at the man and he nodded, encouraging her to step forward. Amber stepped forward, took hold of the Phoenix gem, and closed her eyes. She focused her energy on the stone and called the flames back from the trees and surrounding forest into the gem. The flames slowly receded from the blackened trees behind them and were drawn to Amber like water into a sponge. The last of the flames disappeared and what was left behind was a smoky, dismal sight. Many of the trees had burned beyond the point of saving and the ground was scorched with black burn scars.

Amber smiled as she felt the final flames recede into the gem. She looked around and saw Aiden holding Erick not too far from them. Her smile quickly faded and she ran to them. Kneeling on the other side of Erick, she placed a hand over Aiden's.

"What happened?" she asked, sparks of concern lighting her honey-brown eyes.

"One of Amir's guards pierced him," Aiden said as he studied her, assuring himself that she was okay and truly before him again. "You got your sight back," he commented as he watched the alertness in her eyes. "How? Erick took the Phoenix tear from you."

Amber blushed and glanced back at the man that had stepped out of the flames with her. "I received a more permanent healing from a master physician."

Aiden lifted his eyes towards the man. "Master physician? Can he help Erick?" he asked.

Amber looked back at the man and he nodded. He knelt beside Amber and placed a hand on her shoulder and his other hand on top of hers and Aiden's. Aiden glanced up and recognized the man from the prison. He nodded at the man, reassured that if anyone could help his brother, he could.

Amber looked to the man, unsure of how to actually heal Aiden's brother. "Will you heal him?" she asked as she looked into the eyes that seemed to overflow with compassion.

He looked at her. "You have the power to heal him within you. You need only believe in that power."

She looked between the man and Erick, nervous to try her powers again. The man gave her a reassuring nod. Taking a breath, she turned her attention back to Erick and touched the Phoenix gem with her other hand. As she focused on the gem, a song she had never heard before filled her mind and she sang it over Erick. A soft glow radiated around Amber as she sang, and Aiden watched as the glow trickled down her arm and seemed to absorb into Erick's chest. Amber finished singing and opened her eyes, hoping to see that her song had healed Aiden's brother.

Aiden looked at Erick's face. Nothing seemed to have changed. His eyes darted to Amber and he saw uncertainty and fear cloud her eyes. Suddenly, Erick gasped for breath, taking in a large amount of air, which startled Aiden and Amber. But, the master physician, as she had called him, seemed unperplexed and unsurprised by the events. He smiled and nodded at Aiden before standing and moving a short distance away.

Amber's eyes lit up as she watched the color return to Erick's face and his breathing become normal. He blinked open his eyes and was surprised to see Amber leaning over him.

"Your Highness," Erick said as he tried to sit up and execute a bow.

Amber placed a gentle hand on his chest, "Rest easy, noble knight. You have been through quite the ordeal."

Erick chanced a look at her and his face burned at her kindness. His eyes darted to the dirt. "I am far from noble, Your Highness. I have made many mistakes in my attempts to gain my father's approval."

Amber looked at him with compassion and smiled. "We all make mistakes, Sir Erick. I have brought much destruction to my land because of a gift I didn't feel ready or worthy to wield. But, I was told very recently that ashes bring new life and I'm holding onto that promise not just for me, but for my realm and my kingdom as well. You have been through a fire of your own today, and perhaps going forward, you will live in the beauty and hope of rebirth as well."

Erick looked at her and nodded. "I can only hope to find such a path," he said as he bowed his head.

She reached out and touched his face. "You will find it. I am sure of it." She smiled an enchanting smile at him, and he couldn't help but return the smile.

She glanced at Aiden and he gave her a nod of gratitude for helping his brother. They held each other's gaze for a moment, both concentrating on so many things they wanted to say to each other. Aiden was about to say something at last when the captain of the guard rode up behind them. He saw Amber kneeling beside the man he had pierced with his sword and realized she had healed him.

"Princess Amber," he said in surprise, seeing her seemingly unscathed and untouched by the fury of flames that had been engulfing the forest.

Amber tore her gaze away from Aiden and stood to face the captain. "Sir Cassias. If I can depend on future loyalty from you, will you please take Lord Amir into custody and take him back to the palace?"

The captain looked between Amber and Amir, who had remained on the outskirts, ready to make a quick get away. He glanced at Erick and knew that his punishment for harming the captain from the Fall realm and being party to Lord Amir's schemes would be great. If he took Amir into custody and pledged his loyalty to the princess, perhaps she would show mercy on him.

He nodded towards Amber. "My loyalty, though assuaged from you for a short time, is yours, my Princess. I pray I will be able to find mercy, though undeserving, from your rule."

Sir Cassias nodded to some of the surrounding guards and urged his horse towards Amir. When Amir saw that he was headed in his direction, he pulled a strange powder from a pouch at his side and dropped it to the ground, creating a trail of fire that followed him as he turned his horse and bolted into the forest. Sir Cassias kicked the flanks of his horse and went after Amir with his men.

Amber looked up in horror as she saw the flames flicker to life at the hand of the man who had been named their trusted vizier for as long as she could remember. Her eyes glowed orange and a different energy coursed through her veins. Before she could think or stop herself, her body took the form of a Phoenix bird. She glanced at Aiden before spreading her new wings and taking to the sky above them.

Aiden and Erick both looked up in wonder and amazement at what they had just witnessed. The master physician stepped up to them. "She will need your help," he said to Aiden.

Aiden looked at him and asked, "How can I possibly help her?"

"I will show you how. Come. We must go if we are to make it to the Summer palace in time."

"My horse took off somewhere. I don't know how to get back," Aiden replied.

The physician held out his hand and one of the soldiers that had remained brought Aiden's and Erick's horses to them. A brilliant white horse seemed to appear out of nowhere behind the physician.

"Shall we go?" he asked as he mounted his horse.

Aiden and Erick nodded and both mounted their horses, taking off after the fiery trail left behind by Amir.

Chapter 34

Amir reached the Summer palace within a few hours. He smiled as he looked behind him and saw the forest aflame. He dismounted and allowed a groom to take his horse as Queen Zamina came out onto the stone steps.

"What happened?" she asked, eyes wide with horror at seeing her beloved realm on fire.

Amir quickly changed his demeanor as he approached the queen. "Your daughter is out of control, Zamina. The entire kingdom is going up in flames because of her magic. This is exactly why I have wanted to purge this realm of all magic for years." He raised his voice so others could hear him.

People who had been gathered in the king's market at the entrance to the palace came closer to hear what was being said.

Zamina looked at him, her eyes narrowed, "I don't believe it," she said in a harsh whisper.

"I witnessed it with my own eyes, my Queen. The princess has dangerous powers that are destroying this land. I tried to control her and bring her home safely, but she grew even more enraged and started throwing flames towards me and the guards. She is a monstrous danger that must be stopped."

People started murmuring amongst themselves.

Zamina stared at Amir with complete contempt. "You really hate magic so much that you would stoop this low to destroy it? You and I both know who started these fires."

Amir leaned closer to her and whispered with a bitter tone, "Magic destroyed my home and my family long ago and I never want anyone to experience that danger ever again. As I recall, your own magic almost destroyed this kingdom years ago."

Zamina raised her hands but was helpless to strike at Amir as her hands were still bound with the iron bracelets that restrained her powers.

Amir smiled. "Good thing your hands are bound, Zamina. You wouldn't want the people to see you use the same magic that is destroying their realm at this very moment." Amir nodded to a guard that was standing in the doorway behind Zamina. The guard stepped forward and grabbed Zamina's arm, pulling her back into the palace. Amir stepped up to address the people.

"Good people of Ashteria. We are faced with a great threat and danger. An ancient magic has been awakened in our land and it seeks to destroy our realm and our kingdom," Amir said in a raised voice to the people.

Various people gasped or huddled in groups trying to figure out what was happening. Amir smiled to himself at their reactions for a slight moment before continuing.

"Even as we stand here, the magic being is setting fire to our forests and is drawing them closer to our kingdom." Amir raised his hand towards the forest that sat outside the kingdom wall. More people gasped and murmured as they saw black smoke fill the air around their kingdom.

"Can anything stop it? What will keep us safe? Who will protect us?" Questions rose up from the growing crowd.

"Iron is the only thing that can stop the magic being. Gather as much iron as you can from your homes and bring it to the square as quickly as you can. We must prepare and defend ourselves against the magic since our king is too weak to save us."

As Amir spoke, a strange flaming bird creature appeared in the middle of the square. Various exclamations sounded from the crowd as people stepped away from the strange creature.

Amber felt her clawed feet make contact with the ground. She had been following Amir in the air after her unexpected transformation into a firebird and hadn't been too far behind him. She took in a deep breath as she felt the power recede back within her. The flaming feathers transformed into a fiery red dress with yellow flames reflected throughout. The feathers that had crowned her head became a fiery red crown of curls with a bright yellow-gold painting the tips of her hair. She felt the fiery glow leave her eyes and focused her attention on Amir.

Amir took a step back, surprised to see the Princess transform from a firebird into her human self. Her power was greater than he had anticipated. He saw the glowing gem beneath her neck dim. The Phoenix gem. If he could get the gem away from her, perhaps he could inhibit her powers, or at least gain control of them.

"Lord Amir. You have endangered my people, my kingdom and my realm," Amber said above the din of the people.

"I am not the threat, Princess Amber. You are," Amir said, trying to instill fear and sense of danger within the people.

"I am no threat, Lord Amir. I want to help my people. You set flame to the forests."

"I?" Amir put a hand to his chest and put on a look of shock at her words. "How could I be the one who started these fires? These good people just saw you appear in a strange flame in the form of a firebird. I saw with my own eyes the large fire you started that consumed and blackened much of the forest in the southern realm."

People gasped and looked at Amber, worry and fear growing in their faces and murmuring voices.

Amber saw parents move their children behind them or place protective arms around them. The evident fear in their faces caused Amber's resolve to stand up to Amir to diminish. She had started that massive fire, and several others with her magic. But surely with both halves of the gem reunited now, she would have better control of her magic. She had completely transformed into a Phoenix and back again while maintaining control of her power the entire time she had been in the sky.

"Did you not start those fires?" Amir asked, giving her a pointed look that she couldn't refute.

Amber took in a few shaky breaths as she regarded the people around her. The people knew nothing of her. She had always been the hidden princess the king kept in a tower. Seeing her for the first time in many years in the form of a firebird would not help resolve any fears they had of her. Amir had the upper hand with them.

"Your silence seems to be the answer," Amir said as his lips curled in an evil smile.

Amber could feel the little spark ready to ignite within her at his words. Her hands shook as she tried to calm the fears that threatened to ignite within her veins.

Amir turned to the crowd. "People of Ashteria. Would you feel safe having such a dangerous being as your future ruler? Previous rulers have had similar powers in our realm that have caused serious damage to the palace and our kingdom. We can no longer entrust the safety of our kingdoms to the magic of royals. They are a threat and a danger to us. They must be purged from this land in order to keep our families and our realm safe."

The crowd raised their hands and voices in agreement. Amber felt her hands shake even more as she tried to stave off the mounting fear within her. Fear that was very clearly reflected in their judgemental eyes. The spark she had been holding back finally erupted, sending flames flick through her veins.

"Capture the monster and bind her in iron," Amir shouted.

Several men stepped towards Amber, gathering iron chains and rings from various merchant's booths before surrounding her. Their threatening stance caused flames to flicker to life in Amber's hands. She took a step back to get away from them, hoping they would leave her alone so she didn't accidentally harm anyone. They stepped closer with burning anger lighting their eyes. She held up her hands, flames glowing, as the men stepped even closer.

"Stay back. I don't want to hurt you," Amber said, her voice quivering like a leaf in the autumn breeze, as she continued to step back. She could feel the flames growing hotter in her veins.

Aiden, Erick and the stranger rode up as the men were closing in on Amber. Aiden jumped off his horse and started towards her. A strong, gentle hand held his shoulder. Aiden turned around and looked at the healer.

"Take this," the man said, holding out a silver and gold violin with his other hand.

Aiden took the intricate violin and gently ran his fingers along the gold-filigree leaves that etched the edges of the violin. He looked at the healer, unsure of what to do with it.

The man smiled. "Play the song she needs to hear."

Aiden held the man's gaze. As he did, an indescribable peace filled him and he knew exactly what he needed to play. Aiden took the bow from the healer and nestled the violin beneath his chin. Placing his fingers on the strings, Aiden took a deep breath and raised his bow. He began to play. He drew forth a sweet, ethereal melody from the strings. He looked at the healer and smiled. The man smiled back and nodded. Aiden turned and started to walk towards Amber. The noise of the crowd drowned out the notes, but that didn't stop Aiden from playing.

Amber could feel her fiery nerves on the breaking point of going out of control and who knew what would happen then. Her worst fear was setting the whole village and king's market on fire and then it growing out of control and destroying the palace, bringing harm to not only her parents, but the villagers as well. Amber clenched her hands to keep the magic at bay and closed her eyes to try to calm herself. Maybe if she imagined another place, she could transport herself away from the situation. Amber focused. What made her calm? Her mind went immediately to Aiden.

Amber focused her mind on Aiden's location, hoping to end up wherever he was at. As she focused, a silvery melody landed on her ears, causing her eyes to open. Her gaze was met by Aiden's brown eyes staring at her. She let out a sigh of relief at seeing him. He was playing a beautiful violin and the melody he was playing reached into the depths of her soul, the notes landing on her veins like the soft welcome touch of rain drops after a drought or famine. As Aiden played, the fire in her veins slowly melted away and was taken over by a sweet elixir of peace. She felt the glow in her eyes dissipate and the flames in her palms extinguish. The crowd around her quieted as Aiden stepped closer, playing stronger and louder than Amber had ever heard any instrument. She had never heard the song before, but somehow her heart and soul knew the melody. She closed her eyes for a moment, allowing the calming melody to wash over her inflamed body. Exhaling slowly, she felt her body relax. All the angst and tension she had been feeling fell away from her as Aiden continued to play.

The melody changed slightly, causing Amber to open her eyes and look at Aiden again. When she did, something leaped within her. Aiden looked at her with a passion and intensity she hadn't seen in his eyes before, and something she was sure she would have felt even if she were still blind. Her heart fluttered, hoping this song was saying something from his heart that was similar to what her heart had been longing to say. He gave her a slight smile as he continued to play. He seemed to be pouring his heart and soul into the song he was playing and it conveyed feelings of strength and safety and protection, and dared she believe it, but possibly love?

Aiden finished the song with a flourish as he stood right in front of her. "Are you alright?" he asked as he studied her with those intense autumn-colored eyes.

"I'm fine now," she whispered as she smiled up at him.

He returned her smile, causing her to blush and look away.

"Your melody does not stop the fires from burning in our realm, Your Highness. Princess Amber is still a dangerous threat and must be taken care of."

"No," Aiden said in a commanding voice as he turned to face Amir. "You are the danger and threat to this realm. I watched you start those fires with my own eyes. You sought to destroy the magic in this realm and blame magic for the destruction that you wrought so you could rule. Amber has never done anything to harm this realm. Her greatest desire is to protect this realm and serve her people. It is you that should be taken care of," Aiden said as he stared pointedly at Amir.

Amir could sense a shift in the people at the prince's words, causing him to grow uneasy. "Why should we believe the words of a half-prince from the Fallen realm who kidnapped the princess and set fire to the palace in the first place. It's probably all a part of his scheme to take over this realm, just as his rebel father did in the Fall realm."

Aiden's hand tightened on his bow.

"Is that how you address a son of a king?"

The crowd turned and looked at the man who had healed Amber and Erick.

Amir scoffed. "Certainly if he was truly a son of a king, he would not be treated in such a way, but everyone knows he's only half royal. Who are you to defend him?"

"I am the son of the Most High King. I know more of you and your character than you would wish revealed to these people. I also know Prince Aiden. His father was King Hallel, King of the Fall Realm and Lord of the harvest. If anyone's honor is to be questioned, it is not this young Prince's honor."

Fear sparked in Amir's eyes at the man's declaration. "Your Majesty. My humblest apologies. I had no idea—"

"Do not grovel to me, vizier. This is Princess Amber's domain and she will decide your fate." The man looked to Amber and nodded his head towards her.

Amber bowed her head to the mighty Prince. "Your Majesty."

She turned to Amir. "I will consult with my mother, the Queen, on what is to be done with you later." She looked at Sir Cassias and nodded her head. Sir Cassias stepped in and put shackles on Amir's wrists and led him away.

The mighty Prince looked at Amber. "Your Highness. The fires." He nodded his head over his shoulder towards the growing black smoke that surrounded the kingdom.

Amber's eyes shot towards the sky. She took a shaky breath. "I don't know how to call them back," she said quietly. "They weren't my flames."

The Prince looked at Aiden. "Perhaps you can help her, young Prince." He nodded at Aiden's violin.

Aiden glanced at his violin before turning his gaze towards Amber. "I'm willing to try if you are."

Amber's eyes rested on the man who had become more than a friend and protector the last few days. Her fears melted away as she looked into his eyes. She nodded. Stepping to the middle of the square, she lifted her hands, palms facing the blackened sky. She nodded to Aiden and he nodded back. He placed his violin beneath his chin and started to play as Amber focused her attention on the flames that were burning her kingdom. She started to sing with Aiden's violin and felt energy prick her palms, drawing the flames from around the realm into a pillar of fire above her. She lowered her hands, allowing the pillar to fall around her. As she stood in the flames, she looked to the healer and smiled. He smiled back. Amber closed her eyes and drew the flames into herself and let the energy feed into her veins. The flames disappeared from around her and she was left unburned and unscathed.

The crowd gasped in awe of what had just happened. The healer stepped towards Aiden and Amber. "I believe there is one more melody you should play, Aiden," he said as he placed a gentle hand on Aiden's shoulder. Aiden was filled with a melody he didn't know, but seemed strangely familiar. He looked to the healer.

"The harvest song?" he asked as he looked down at his violin.

The healer nodded.

Aiden felt suddenly uncomfortable. "But, I gave up my gift so Amber could have her sight. I can't bring a harvest with my music anymore."

"You can. Trust me."

Aiden looked into the gentle eyes of the healer. He couldn't help but try with the encouragement and hope that shone out from the healer's eyes. Aiden took in a deep breath before nestling the violin beneath his chin again. He played the melody his father had played for many years to bring the harvest. As he did, small red flowers began to sprout up from the ground in a circle around Amber where the flames had been. Aiden felt the melody swell within him and could sense other things taking root and sprouting up throughout the kingdom. He played until the song was complete. His eyes brimmed with tears as he looked at the healer.

"I thought I had lost my gift," he said softly, his throat thick with emotion.

The healer smiled and looked at him. "What was lost has been found."

Amber stepped closer to them. "And what once was blind can now see," she said with a grateful smile. "Thank you, Your Majesty." Amber curtseyed and Aiden bowed before the mighty Prince.

"My son and daughter. You have both been granted beautiful gifts. Don't waste them. May you bring rebirth to both of your realms." The Prince bowed his head towards each of them and walked to his horse to leave.

Amber stepped towards him as he mounted. "Can you not stay and help us bring rebirth to our lands?"

The Prince smiled. "I wish that I could, but I am needed in another part of the realms. I will return for the wedding of your cousin and the queen of the Winter realm though."

Amber smiled and nodded as the Prince leaned down and patted his horse's neck before nudging him to move on.

She turned and saw Aiden staring at her with that intense gaze of his again. Her breath caught in her throat at his gaze. She couldn't tell what he was thinking or feeling with how he was looking at her. She stepped towards him, somewhat cautiously, trying to still the racing of her heart.

"Aiden, I–"

Amber's words were cut off as Aiden's hands wrapped around her face and his mouth covered hers. He pressed his lips deeper into hers sending a tingle of little flames running up and down her arms. As Aiden pulled away, Amber was left breathless and pleasantly surprised. She looked up at him, so grateful her eyesight had been restored so she could see his handsome face during this moment.

She blushed as he continued to stare at her. "I wasn't sure how you felt about me, but I think that answered any questions I may have had," she said as she bit her lip.

Aiden's face softened and a sweet, beautiful smile filled his rugged features. "I guess all of the emotions of losing you over and over again bubbled over into that kiss," he said as he brushed a yellow-red curl away from her face. He raised an eyebrow as he realized what color her hair was now. And that it was shorter.

Amber's entranced look changed to one of confusion. He smiled, "That gem made your hair a darker red with yellow lacing the tips like a flame. And it seems to have shortened the lengthy braid."

"Perhaps learning to control it helped manage the hair," Amber said with a smile that crinkled her petite nose.

Aiden's features intensified again as he stared down at her. "Amber. I know I was brought here to enter into an arranged marriage with you but I don't want an arranged marriage with you."

Amber's face fell at his words, confusion and the anticipation of hurt entering her heart. "Oh," she said, trying to stave off the disappointment.

Aiden gently brushed her cheek with his thumb and took her face in his hand again. "I want to marry you, but only if you want to. Not because it was pre-arranged or just to join our kingdoms, but hopefully because you feel the same way about me that I feel about you." He looked down at her with his spiced cinnamon eyes and Amber's skin warmed at his touch.

"And how do you feel about me?" she asked, hope lingering with longing as she stared back up at him.

Aiden took in a short breath before he replied. "I love you. I loved getting to know you those first nights in the library, and finding out which books you loved the most, and being able to read them to you. It killed me every time the Phoenix gem took you away from me. I was so frantic and worried to find you and I didn't want anything to happen to you. I want to be your protector but not the way your father protected you by hiding you away in that tower all those years. You are far too beautiful and brave and strong to be hidden away."

Amber smiled up at him, her honey-cinnamon eyes glistening with tears. "I love you too," she replied. "I wasn't sure if what I felt for you was love since I had never been out of the palace and have had little contact with the outside world, but you have been my safe place and my calm and you didn't treat me like I was incompetent or incapable of doing things just because I was blind. You helped me and cared for me and have been so gentle with me. And you kept coming after me. I'm so overwhelmed that someone would love me like that," she said as a tear rolled down her face.

Aiden's thumb brushed the tear away. "I will always be here for you and I will never stop coming after you." He pulled her face close to his and placed a tender kiss on her forehead.

She pulled back and gazed up at him. "Let's find my parents and make sure they are alright."

Aiden smiled and nodded his agreement. As Amber walked away, Aiden held onto her hand, holding her back. She looked back at him and saw the intense longing in his eyes again. She would never tire of seeing that look. He pulled her close and kissed her lips again. Amber melted into his arms and kissed him back.

When they pulled away from each other, he gazed down at her with such admiration and love, it made Amber's skin tingle with a different kind of energy than what she felt when her powers were getting ready to ignite within her. She liked this feeling.

She smiled back up at him. He wrapped her in his arms and walked beside her as they stepped into the Summer palace.

Chapter 35

People from all of the realms met at the four corners where the realms were joined the eve after the Summer solstice. King Azar was almost fully recovered and was able to attend the wedding with his wife and daughter. Queen Zamina helped her husband to his seat on the side of the Summer realm. Amber stood near the back of the crowd, hoping to see her cousins before the wedding began.

"Amber!"

Amber turned and saw a young woman with long brown hair and a crown of pink roses gracing her head. The woman looked like an older version of her cousin Julianna. Amber smiled.

Julianna came up to Amber and reached out to her. "It has been so long since I saw you last," Julianna said as she squeezed her cousin in an affectionate hug.

Amber returned the warm embrace. "It has been far too long."

Julianna pulled away and looked at her cousin. She smiled. "I remember your hair being fiery red when we were little, but I have never seen it this color," she said as she touched one of the flaming curls that was piled into a braid of curls on top of Amber's head and accented by a bright red and yellow scarf.

Amber smiled at Julianna's remark. "Yes. Things have changed quite a bit since we last saw each other. I discovered I was born with magic after all. The flames of the Phoenix did quite a number on my hair, but I like it."

Julianna's eyes widened. "*See.* Yes. It has been a long time since you've seen us hasn't it? The last time we saw you, you had lost your sight because of a fire in the realm." Julianna looked into Amber's honey-cinnamon eyes that appeared to be looking at her. "Your sight has been restored," Julianna said with an awed whisper.

"Yes. Undeservingly so." Amber caught a glimpse of the man who had healed her eyes. She nodded her head towards him. "He restored my sight in the midst of a fire."

Julianna turned and saw the Mage's Son speaking with Amber's parents. Julianna's eyes widened at the sight of Queen Zamina. "Is that your mother? I thought she had died in the same fire that took your eyesight."

"Yes, it is my mother. That's a long story, and not one for such a joyous occassion as this. But thankfully my sight was not the only thing restored to us," Amber said with a smile.

Julianna returned her attention to Amber and smiled. "Yes. It is quite the occasion isn't it? I'm so excited for Gabriel and Erianna. Have you met Erianna and her sister yet?"

Amber shook her head no. "We just arrived this morning and hadn't had much of a chance to see anyone yet. We held a small Summer solstice celebration last night lighting paper lanterns and releasing them into the night sky as a sign of rebirth to come in our realm."

"That sounds wonderful. I can't wait to return to the Summer realm and see it again. I never knew why we stopped visiting."

"I believe our fathers had something to do with it," Amber said as she nodded her head towards King Azar and King Godric, who were now talking with each other. "My father always felt jilted that your father got the sun magic because he felt he should have had that magic for our realm. He never said as much to me, but I overheard him talking about it on several occasions."

Julianna's face crinkled in an apologetic look. "I'm sorry that is what has kept us apart. I know my father has always felt blessed and honored to have such magic. I didn't realize your father resented him for that all these years."

"It's ok. I'm hoping this new season brings rebirth to many things in our realm and our lives."

"Julianna, you should probably finish getting ready. They are going to start the ceremony soon."

A tall, dark man with ashen skin and longer black hair stepped towards Julianna. He wore a white and gold doublet that made him look very official.

Julianna's pink cheeks brightened and her eyes lit up when she saw the man. "Darien. This is my cousin, Princess Amber from the Summer realm."

Darien turned to Amber and bowed. "Your Highness. It is an honor to meet you at last. Julianna has told me of many happy summers spent in the Summer realm when she was younger." He smiled, causing the seriousness of his face to disappear. Amber could see why Julianna would have fallen for him.

"Amber, this is Darien, Son of Light and most trusted advisor to the king," Julianna said with a playful glint in her eyes. Darien shook his head at her in mock annoyance at her using his full title, but returned her playful grin. She continued, "But most importantly, to me anyway, he is the love of my life and my beloved betrothed."

Amber nodded her head towards Darien. "It is nice to meet you."

"Amber. We should get seated."

Julianna's eyebrows shot up at the ruggedly handsome young man who came to stand behind Amber. She looked at Amber with a quizzical brow.

Amber blushed and introduced Aiden. "Julianna. May I introduce you to Prince Aiden from the Fall realm. Aiden, this is my cousin, Princess Julianna of the Spring realm and her betrothed, Darien. Her brother Gabriel is the one getting married today."

Aiden smiled and bowed his head towards Julianna and held out his hand to Darien. "It is nice to finally meet you, Princess Julianna. And you, Darien. Our realm has been so far removed for so long, I've never actually met the royals from the other realms. I am also in the same ranks as Darien. I am Amber's betrothed. I am looking forward to witnessing this wedding and looking forward to my own hopefully soon." Aiden gave Amber a sidelong glance that made her blush.

"Julianna. What are you still doing out here? They are waiting to start the ceremony." A young girl with almost white skin that seemed to glisten in the sunlight appeared on the other side of Julianna.

"Brinn. I'm so sorry. I saw my cousin and wanted to speak with her before the ceremony started. Brinn, this is my cousin, Princess Amber from the Summer realm, and her betrothed, Prince Aiden from the Fall realm."

The young woman's eyes lit up and sparkled like snowflakes in the sunlight. "Princess Amber, Prince Aiden. It is so good to meet both of you." Brinn hugged Amber and then hugged Aiden, which caught him off guard. Darien bit back a knowing smile at having experienced the unexpected exuberance of the young snow princess before.

"Amber, Aiden. This is Brinn, She is Erianna's sister and princess of the Winter realm."

Brinn's eyes widened and her mouth fell open as she looked around at all of them. "Do you realize what an auspicious occasion this is? This is the first time in our realms history that the children of the royal families have all been introduced and in one place. Isn't that amazing?" she asked with a slight bubble of excitement. She reached out and grabbed Julianna's and Amber's hands. "I hope this is the start of a beautiful friendship and long-lasting relationship for all our realms," she said with a bright smile.

"Which will have an even better start if we get this wedding started," Darien said in a polite but insistent tone.

Brinn gasped. "Oh my goodness. I'm the one who came to get Julianna and here I am standing here going on and on. We should go."

Brinn turned to go, but turned back and gave Amber another quick hug. "It was so nice to meet you. I can't wait to learn more about you. And I especially can't wait to hear about the Summer realm." She smiled and went back to the area where Erianna was waiting.

Julianna looked at Amber one last time. "I'm so happy you got your sight back. We will have to catch up after the ceremony."

Amber nodded her head. "We will."

Darien led Julianna the same direction Brinn had gone.

Aiden turned to Amber and offered her his arm. "Shall we?" he asked as he gazed down at her with a roguish smile.

Amber smiled and took his arm. "We shall."

The large crowd that sat around the four corners tree in each of the realms fell silent as a beautiful melody began to play. There were musicians at the base of the tree in each realm so everyone could hear and see. King Godric and Queen Osanna entered down an aisle that had been set up in front of the tree between the Spring and Winter realms, nodding and acknowledging those in attendance. King Godric wore a bright golden doublet with a big red rose covering a sun emblem on his chest. Queen Osanna wore a long, beautiful lavender and yellow colored dress with little rosettes sewn into the bodice. King Godric led Queen Osanna to a set of chairs set up on the edge of the Spring realm where Osanna's sister, Lady Roxana sat. They bowed to the Mage's Son who stood at the decorated altar before they sat.

Next, Julianna entered on the arm of Darien. She wore an elegant, flowing light pink gown that looked like it had little suns embroidered in gold throughout her skirt and flowing sleeves. Her brown curls cascaded loosely around her shoulders and down her back with a crown of pink roses on top of her head that matched the pink blush in her cheeks. She carried a small bouquet of sunrise colored roses with one white lily in the middle and sprigs of baby's breath sprinkled throughout. They reached the altar and bowed to the Mage's Son. Julianna looked up at Darien and smiled before moving to her side of the altar. He returned the smile and squeezed her hand that rested on his arm before letting her go and moving to his side of the altar.

Last, Brinn entered on the arm of Tharynn. Tharynn wore a white and silver sleeveless tunic that showed his large muscular arms wrapped in leather straps. His long, blonde hair had braids woven throughout and were accented with silver beads. Brinn wore a beautiful light blue gown that flowed like water behind her and sparkled in the sunlight from the crystal snowflakes that had been sewn into the skirt and flowing sleeves. Her white-blonde hair was in an elegant braid and adorned with small snowflakes and roses. She carried a small bouquet of white roses sprinkled with little blue flowers. They reached the altar and bowed to the Mage's Son before splitting and moving to stand beside Julianna and Darien on either side of the altar.

The sound of crystal-like windchimes filled the air followed by a soft and sweet melody. Gabriel stepped out from behind the tree and came to stand beside the Mage's Son. He bowed to the Mage's Son and turned to face the long aisle where two young girls were dropping a mix of white and red rose petals. Gabriel wore a white and gold doublet with a single red rose pinned to his chest. He took a deep breath and watched as the young girls finished filling the aisle with petals, and stepped to either side. The crowd stood and waited with anticipation for Erianna to walk down the aisle.

A vision of white appeared at the other end of the aisle. Gabriel's breath caught in his throat at the beautiful sight of Erianna. She wore a full white gown that bloomed out around her like the petals of a giant white rose. Her bodice looked like a beautiful, sparkling snowflake that reflected the sun. Her sleeves started beneath her shoulders in a band of small white roses that flowed into a sheer opalescent material covered in crystal snowflakes, reminiscent of her dragon wings. Her white blonde hair was braided to the side in a mass of curls and hung over her shoulder with white roses scattered throughout. She wore the most delicate crystalline crown on her head that came to a point in a snowflake in the front with a single light blue crystal hanging from the middle of the snowflake. She had a small bunch of red and white roses pinned to her bodice and carried a full bouquet of white and red roses. The white rose with red edges she and Gabriel had created sat in the middle of her bouquet. The sheer veil peppered with crystal snowflakes and edged with white rosettes flowed like a blanket of snow behind her. Her dress sparkled and glittered in the sunlight like a fresh snow on a still winter's morning. She spotted Archimedes sitting in the front row on the Winter's realm side and winked and gave him a small wave. Archimedes wiped the tears from his face with his giant handkerchief and waved back. Erianna's smile widened as she reached the end of the aisle and stood before Gabriel.

Gabriel beamed and stepped down off the altar to escort her the last few steps. They smiled at each other and turned to face the Mage's Son. Erianna curtseyed before him and he smiled and nodded towards her. He gestured for Erianna and Gabriel to turn and face each other. Erianna handed her bouquet to Brinn and turned to face Gabriel.

The Mage's Son gestured for everyone to be seated. "My friends. We are gathered here today to witness the joining of these two people before you, Prince Gabriel and Queen Erianna. They are joining more than just themselves as individuals, as their kingdoms and realms will also be joined in a bond that cannot easily be destroyed. I hope their union today will spark a sense of unity within all the realms that will reach far into the future. I know the realms of darkness and light will soon be joined in a similar union when Princess Julianna and Sir Darien are wed." He paused and looked at both of them and smiled. Julianna's cheeks blushed a brighter pink at the acknowledgement and she looked at Darien. The Mage's Son continued, "And, I believe the Summer and Fall realms may also be joined in a similar union, though how soon, I am not sure." The Mage's Son looked to where Aiden and Amber sat and gave them a nod.

"The Great Mage created the realms to live in peace and unity. He created beauty within the realms and that beauty is accentuated when it is joined with others and showcased when used for the good of the people and the realms. There are some who seek to see that beauty and unity destroyed and others who, though granted gifts of beauty, use them for ill and to fulfill their own selfish desires. Both Gabriel and Erianna have unique gifts that were gifted to them to help their realms thrive. They have both used their gifts to save their realms in the past, and I know they will continue to use them to help their people and their realms in the future. We gather today to witness the joining of their gifts as well as their hearts, souls, bodies and minds. They invited all of you here on this special day to witness them declare their promises and dedication to each other, knowing this is not a covenant they are entering into lightly." The Mage's Son turned to Gabriel and Erianna.

"Gabriel, you stand here today before me and before this cloud of witnesses to declare your love for Erianna, but also to declare your dedication to her and your people. Do you promise to love Erianna unconditionally, cherish her heart as the treasured gift that has been given to you, and promise to hold her up in times of trials and mourning, and rejoice with her in times of singing and dancing?"

Gabriel's smile widened as he looked at Erianna and heard the words the Mage's Son spoke over him. "I so promise."

The Mage's Son turned to Erianna. "Erianna, you, like Gabriel, stand here today before me and this cloud of witnesses to declare your love for Gabriel, but also to declare your dedication to him and your people. Do you promise to love Gabriel unconditionally, honor him as your guard and protector, and promise to uphold him in times of trials and mourning, and rejoice with him in times of singing and dancing?"

Erianna's pale cheeks pinkened ever so slightly as she stared up at Gabriel. "I so promise," she said as a tear fell down her face. Gabriel reached up and brushed the tear away with his thumb.

The Mage's son nodded to Darien who stepped up and gave Gabriel a delicate silver ring with a small rose crystal nestled on a silver snowflake. Gabriel took the ring and looked into Erianna's crystal blue eyes.

"Repeat after me. With this ring, I give myself wholly to you and promise to love you, protect you, and cherish you for as long as I have life on this earth."

Gabriel repeated the words and slid the delicate ring on Erianna's finger before wrapping his hand around hers.

The Mage's Son nodded towards Brinn who stepped up and handed a larger silver band with golden roses etched into it to Erianna.

"Repeat after me. With this ring, I give myself wholly to you and promise to love you, honor you, and cherish you for as long as I have life on this earth."

Erianna repeated the words and gazed up at Gabriel's dancing green eyes as she slid the silver ring on his finger.

"I now pronounce you man and wife. You may kiss your bride."

Gabriel placed his hand on Erianna's silvery cheek and looked down at her with such love and adoration. He pulled her face towards his and placed a tender kiss on her blush lips. He wrapped his other arm around her and pulled her closer, deepening the kiss. Her arms slipped around Gabriel's waste and rested on his shoulders. As they kissed, a golden glow encircled them with a mix of rose petals and snowflakes that filled the air and danced in the golden glow until it reached the top of their heads. As they pulled away, the petals and snowflakes burst forth from above them. They looked up and smiled as the intermixed petals and snowflakes fell to the ground in a shower of color and sparkle around them.

"I present to you Crown Prince Gabriel and his bride, Queen Erianna. May your kingdoms be infinitely blessed by your union."

Gabriel took Erianna's hand and they walked happily up the aisle.

Chapter 36

The royal heirs all sat around one of the few tables that still had candles burning at it, and talked after many of the guests had left.

"So, tell us about your Phoenix power, Amber," Julianna said as she leaned forward to listen.

Amber blushed and looked around the table. "Oh, I don't even know how to describe it. It's still so new to me."

Brinn leaned forward and put her chin on her hands like an excited young girl eager to hear her favorite bedtime story. "Oh, please, Amber. I'm dying to hear about it. I've only known cold magic my entire life. Tell me about the warmth and fire."

Erianna smiled and leaned forward to pat Brinn's elbows to get them off the table. "You'll have to excuse my sister. She is often overly excited to learn about the other realms. And she is obsessed with the orange color of flames."

"I am not obsessed with it. We just have very limited color choices in our realm and I've always wanted to see that color. And, when you've grown up with blue flames, orange is a very fascinating color," Brinn responded as she sat back in her chair in response to Erianna's mothering.

Gabriel's smile widened. "I remember. You couldn't take your eyes off of the flickering orange flame the first time I started a fire in your realm."

"I believe I started it, thank you very much," Brinn replied with a jokingly superior air.

"Yes. After I showed you how," Gabriel replied with a teasing smile.

Aiden leaned close to Amber and whispered in her ear. "Why don't you show the young princess your magic. I think it would make her day."

Amber smiled. "Fine." Amber held out her palm and focused. Her eyes glowed orange and a small flame appeared in her hand.

Brinn's eyes sparkled with excitement. "Oh. That is so beautiful," she said in awe of the dancing flame. "Does it feel hot on your skin?" she asked as she sat entranced by the flickering orange color in Amber's hand.

Amber shook her head. "Not to me. But, it can be very dangerous to anyone else."

"How fascinating," Brinn said as she continued to watch the flame. "Can you do anything else?" she asked as she looked up at Amber.

"I can do quite a few things. Last known power, I took the full form of a Phoenix bird. It was quite a different experience flying over my realm. I haven't used it much since it first happened, but I'd like to try to keep learning how to use it and get better control over that part of my magic and see how easily I can change back and forth." Amber caused the flame in her hand to disappear and lowered her hand to her lap.

Erianna had a strange look on her face. A mix of nostalgic memories mixed with some pain. "It is strange to be able to fly, although I was doing it for most of my life, so I suppose I was probably more used to it than you may be."

Amber's eyebrows knit together at Erianna's admission. "You can fly too?" she asked, wondering if this snow queen could help her with her own powers.

"Not anymore. I used to transform into a dragon every full cycle of the moon."

"What changed?" Aiden asked from beside Amber.

Erianna lifted her head with a gracious smile. "The Mage's Son. And the love of my dear sister and handsome prince." She held out her hand to Brinn and leaned her head on her new husband's shoulder.

"He seems to have had a lasting effect on everyone," Aiden said as he leaned forward and rested his elbows on the table.

"He certainly has," Julianna said as she looked at her wrist and then at Darien.

"How did he change you, Aiden?" Erianna asked as she looked over at him.

Aiden took in a short breath and sat up a little straighter after being put on the spot. "He gave me something I thought I had lost forever." He looked over at Erianna. "My father, the true king of the harvest, had the gift of music that helped seeds to grow and bring the harvest to our land. My mother used to sing to bring the rain needed to water the seeds. I didn't even know I had such a gift until I had to give it up." He gave Amber a sidelong glance and knew she still felt horrible about him having to give up that part of him for her. He leaned back and put his arm around her and drew her close, placing a tender kiss on her temple.

"Give it up? Why did you have to give it up?" Julianna asked as she leaned back into Darien.

Amber cast her eyes to the table. "He gave it up so I could see," she said quietly.

Everyone at the table sombered at her words.

"That is a noble thing to sacrifice," Darien said as he ran his hand up and down Julianna's arm to keep her warm in the cool night air.

Julianna looked up at him and rubbed the faded mark on his wrist. "You know more about sacrifice than most people, and I know I will forever be grateful for the sacrifice you made for me." She kissed the faded mark on his wrist and intertwined her fingers with his.

"What sacrifice did you make for my cousin?" Amber asked as she leaned into Aiden's embrace.

Darien shifted uncomfortably beside Amber. He still didn't like attention being drawn to him, but had been forced to learn to deal with it since he was often in the eye of the public since becoming advisor to the king. Julianna gave him an encouraging smile and he told them, "My uncle is the Lord of the dark realm. I was trapped in that world for most of my life but I found a way out and made my way to the Spring realm. I met Julianna and knew my life would never be the same, but I doubted that there could be any real future for me in the realm of light, let alone with a daughter of light. My uncle's one desire was to bring Julianna to his realm, and when he succeeded in getting her there, I gave up my freedom outside of the realm so she could go free. I wasn't ever supposed to leave the realm of darkness again, but the Mage's Son granted me passage out of the darkness again."

A cold mist filled the area as Darien finished his story. Julianna shivered and felt a strange tingle in her wrist where her mark of darkness had been. Darien looked at his wrist as he felt it too.

Dark, eerie sand-like smoke swirled around them, filling all of them with an unease that greatly offset the mood of the joyous wedding they had celebrated that day.

"Well. Isn't this a pretty picture," a snake-like voice said behind them. Darien shot up from his chair and immediately pulled Julianna behind him. Gabriel and Tharynn both stood up and reached to their sides for their swords, but forgot they hadn't worn them for the wedding. Erianna stood behind Gabriel, her hands poised and ready to attack the unwelcome visitor if needed, while Brinn followed suit. Aiden stood and pulled Amber close, neither one of them aware of who this man was, but they both sensed the great tension and unease he brought nonetheless.

"What do you want, Luscian?" Gabriel asked in a seething voice. He knew full well what the man had put his sister through, and he was unwilling to let the foul man ruin the happiest day of his life.

"Can't a dark lord give his well wishes to the blushing couple?" Luscian asked with a sneering smile as he looked between Gabriel and Erianna with his seeing eye.

"The only well wishes you could bring would be death and darkness on their happy day," Darien said coldly as he kept a protective arm in front of Julianna.

Luscian shifted his one-eyed gaze to his traitorous nephew. "I would keep my opinions to myself if I were you. Just because you have found a few moments of freedom from my realm, doesn't mean that will be a permanent arrangement. Your soul is very much still tied to that realm and you will never truly find the elusive freedom you so desperately seek," Lusican said with a warning look in his eye as he stared at Darien.

A vein twitched in Darien's jaw and Julianna could tell Luscian was getting to him. She gave the arm she had been holding onto a reassuring squeeze to let him know she was standing by him no matter what.

Luscian's gaze drifted to where Amber and Aiden stood, quietly observing the scene. "Ah. How quaint. The third globe. How is that for irony?" he asked with a sickening smile.

Amber's brows furrowed at his comment. "The third globe? What do you mean?" she asked with an uneasy feeling that rose within her under his scrutinous gaze. She felt something spark in her hand and she wondered if she was somehow connected to the dark man.

"The Great Mage keeps globes in a horribly gaudy room that represent each punitive life on this earth. I had a run in with the three of your globes one day many years ago, and wouldn't you know it, things came to fruition that I saw in those globes that day."

Luscian turned to Erianna. "Your silvery orb had quite the sizeable crack in it when I visited Archimedes in that room that day. Think that could have been cause for your, ah- *destructive* nature?" Luscian asked with a wry smile.

Erianna's hands clenched by her sides. She felt a spark of anger within her that was reminiscent of the days when she had transformed into a dragon. She hadn't changed into that form since the last winter solstice, but she didn't want anything to set that change off in her again. She held her breath and tried to stave off the spark before it blossomed into anything worse.

"And you, my dear, sweet Julianna. You already know what I saw in your sunrise colored orb that day. A spot of darkness that grew into the woman who fought against the two worlds she was trapped between. How sad I was to see you leave my realm, but something that ingrained in your nature, that can't be kept from someone for long." His oily smile grew as he walked past Julianna, pulling a loose curl through his ashen hands that sent a shiver down Julianna's spine.

He stopped at last by Amber and held his staff beneath her chin. "And, the final globe I came in contact with that day. You know, your globe was perfect and whole when I first picked it up, but that louse of an apprentice dropped it, causing a million little splinters to break out within its core. How unfortunate to have such a tragedy happen to an almost perfect princess." He stood eye to eye with her, looking into her eyes with his seeing eye. Amber felt the flame spark in her hand again but held it off, not wanting to start anything. She matched his gaze and didn't take her eyes from him. His brow creased as he stared at her. "Your malady doesn't appear to have come true after all," he said as he studied her eyes that were clearly looking into his. "Unless someone changed your fate," he said as he looked over her shoulder at Aiden. Aiden was about to step up to the man dressed in black from head to toe when the man stepped away from Amber and walked back around to the other side of the table.

"I wish I could say I hope you live long and happy lives, but that's just not in my nature," Luscian said as he turned to face them all. "Take this as a warning, young royals. You may think you have reached your happily ever afters, but believe me when I tell you that this is just the beginning of ever after, and it won't end so happily. Enjoy your lover's bliss now, because the next chapter of this story will make you wish you had never tried to put an end to my reign on this earth. Light and love will never win. I will destroy whatever beauty you sniveling children think you have found in this world and I will make it mine," Luscian said as he held out an empty palm and closed his fingers tight as if squishing all the light and happiness from the world.

"Darkness is coming, and it won't leave so easily this time." Luscian threw back his head and laughed as he struck his staff on the ground, vanishing into a cloud of black smoke.

Gabriel, Tharynn, Darien and Aiden had all stepped forward to grab him, but were too late.

Julianna rubbed her tingling wrist and looked at Darien and Gabriel. "What are we going to do?" she asked.

Gabriel gave her a grim look. "I don't know. But I'm not going to let him ruin my wedding night. We can reconvene in the morning and figure out a plan to protect our realms, but tonight, let's dwell in the happiness and light of the love we still have." He looked at Erianna with the love of a newly wedded husband, causing her to blush before returning his smile.

"My husband is right. Let's not let Luscian ruin this night. We celebrated a joyous union today and still have a greater light to hold onto."

Gabriel took her hands in his and looked around. "Blessed rest, dear friends. We will face the darkness in the morning." He led his bride to the wedding tent that had been set up where the Spring and Winter realms met.

Tharynn wrapped his massive arm around Brinn's slender frame, signaling that they should go as well. They wished everyone a good night as Tharynn turned her to walk her to her tent.

Julianna looked up at Darien. He grabbed her shoulders and gave her an intense yet reassuring look. "We will get through this, just as we have before. Luscian will never dim my radiant light," he said as he looked lovingly down at her.

Julianna's worried face melted into a smile. "I pray you never lose sight of your radiant light," she said as she wrapped her arms around his waist and let him pull her close.

"Never." He leaned down and placed a tender kiss on her lips. Julianna blushed as she pulled away.

"Good night, Amber. Good night, Aiden. I'm so glad to be reunited with you."

"Good night," Amber and Aiden said simultaneously as they watched Darien lead Julianna towards her tent near the side of the Spring realm.

Amber let out a tired sigh. Aiden looked at her and brushed a wayward fiery curl from her face. "Are you alright?" he asked as he studied her face in the dimming candlelight.

"I don't know. So much has happened and I'm so afraid of things going topsy-turvy again. I don't want the peace we have right now to end."

Aiden pulled her into his arms and wrapped his arms around her. She nestled her head beneath his chin. He smiled. "I don't think anything could ever change this," he said as he relished holding her so close.

"I hope not," she sighed.

Aiden pulled one hand from behind her back and lifted her chin towards his. "I will never stop loving you, no matter what happens." He lowered his head and met her lips with his, capturing her in a fiery kiss. Amber allowed herself to melt into Aiden's kiss and delighted in the comfort and protection she felt from it. Aiden pulled away and gazed down at her. "We can get through anything as long as we're together, alright?"

Amber gazed up at him and smiled. "Alright. Together, forever. Promise?" she asked.

"I promise." Aiden lowered his head and kissed her again. Amber felt a flame flick across her skin as Aiden deepened the kiss. A white flame encompassed them as they kissed, wrapping them in the purifying light of their fiery love.

The End